# FURIOUS

# FURIOUS

Jamie Pacton and Rebecca Podos

PAGE STREET YA

PAGE STREET YA

**Jamie:** For my family and for the friends who have become family

**Rebecca:** For the Motorcycle Guy™

# *CHAPTER ONE*

## JoJo

*Some people are born fearless, but most of us think if we keep running fast enough, we'll stay ahead of whatever scares us.*

Maybe that's not really true, but it's what my mom, a professional race car driver, used to tell me whenever I'd ask if she was scared before a race.

Her words echo through my mind as I swipe my forehead with the only clean stretch of my forearm available. It's a boiling Saturday afternoon in early June and I'm standing in front of an ancient rotating fan, which does exactly nothing to cool the swamp in my Grandma Jolene's garage. Sweat soaks my tank top and the upper part of the mechanic's jumpsuit tied around my waist. The syrupy air ambling out of the fan dries my upper lip, but after being in the garage for most of the day, what I need is an ice bath, or a properly working AC unit—even a dip in the local river would do.

Somehow, after all this time away, I'd forgotten how hot North Carolina gets this time of year. It was hot in Charleston, yes, but at least we had breezes off the ocean to cool things down sometimes. Here, in the garage, even with all the doors open, it's at least a million degrees.

More like ninety, the thermometer on the wall beside the fan tells me. But still. Who can work or think in these conditions? I ease the fan up a notch—it rattles angrily at me—and pull a bottle of water from the cooler. Condensation beads on the bottle as I rest it against my forehead. I'm tempted to order an air conditioner from Amazon myself, just so I'm not cooked alive this summer. But it's not like I'm sticking around long. I can survive a little heat. Especially if I'm ever going to make it as an F1 driver, where the cockpit temperature can reach as high as 140 degrees Fahrenheit.

As I gulp down half the bottle of water, I consider the wall beside the thermometer. There's a framed picture of Mom, standing in the middle of a NASCAR winner's podium, clutching a huge bottle of champagne, a ridiculously-pleased-with-herself smile splitting her face. Beside it hang checkered flags, banners from her team, and a few pictures from my early racing days. My favorite picture is of me when I was eight, squished between Mom and Dad, taken moments after my first win, my tiny fists in the air. Mom beams down at me. Dad's smile matches my own.

Mom wouldn't like to know how worry coils in my belly every time I look at this picture. Or think of racing again. Or wonder if I'm even good at it after all these months away from the track . . .

Which is why I have to keep moving. Maybe I'm not fearless, but I *can* keep ahead of whatever scares me. Which is a lot of things these days, not that anyone needs to know that.

Lifting my long hair from my neck, I turn my back to the fan. Warm air caresses my bare shoulders, and I close my eyes, inhaling the smell of grease, dust, and something metal- and car-related that reminds me of my family.

My parents met in this very same garage. Dad was a mechanic, Mom was an up-and-coming NASCAR champion, and they fell in love over a gearshift. Which is about the cheesiest thing ever if you ask me. When they used to tell me the story, Mom would tease me, saying, "Maybe you'll meet your true love at Grandma's garage, too, JoJo."

"No way," I'd say. "I've got no time for that. It's all cars for me."

"We'll see about that when you're seventeen," Mom would say with one of her big laughs. (A laugh like a porch swing on a southern house, Dad says. Meaning it invited you to stay awhile and get comfy.)

Now that I'm seventeen, I'd give anything to hear that laugh again.

But that's silly, of course. I could pull out my phone right now, go to YouTube, and hear Mom's laugh in one of several documentaries about her life. DeeDee Emerson, world-famous race car driver. First woman to, blah blah blah. Died in a fiery crash four months ago. Still can't forget her laugh.

Especially when I'm working on her car.

Ignoring the stomach-wringing grief that grips me at the thought of my mom's death, I leave the fan and pick up a wrench. I hold the tool so tightly I can feel the raised letters on its handle digging into my palm. Slowly, I walk across the garage, each step taking me closer to the electric blue AMC Hornet SC/360 that sits in the center of the room. It's a muscle car and has the curves and racing stripes to prove it, but it's far less famous than something like the 1964 Shelby GT350 Mustang, which has become a collector's item for millionaires. The Hornet is a machine true car geeks adore, and it was Mom's first baby and her greatest love (well, second only to Dad and me, she swore, but it's a close second). Mom named the car Betty and hung a tiny pink plastic cat-shaped toy from the rearview mirror. When I was little, my favorite thing to do was watch that pink plastic cat bob around when we'd take Sunday family drives to the beach.

"I'm going to try real hard not to fuck you up, Betty," I murmur. The Hornet hasn't been run in months, not since the last time Mom visited the garage, and Grandma says it needs some work.

That falls on me, since Dad is now officially done with cars. Not even kidding—he rides a bicycle everywhere, living his life a quarter mile at a time on two wheels. With a helmet on. And fingerless gloves. And all other appropriate bicycle safety gear.

Which, fine. Grieve as you will, but don't take me with you.

I scowl at my own bike, a blue-pink-purple thing—the perfect bi-girl bicycle, my best friend CJ cheerfully told me over the phone when I told them about it—that rests in the corner of the garage. Much as I love to be a bi-on-a-bike, this one has a basket for God's sake, like I'm twelve. Dad wouldn't even get me a racing bike when we moved from Charleston back to teeny tiny Dell's Hollow, North Carolina. Now, I'm stuck with this dorky thing. At least until I get my license.

Which is happening never, since I'm not eighteen for six more months, and Dad won't take me to get my license before then unless I do a bunch of volunteer work for the sake of the college applications I don't even want to fill out—

"JoJo Emerson-Boyd, I swear, I can see the gears in your head turning from here," says a loud voice with a southern accent thick and sweet as raspberry jam.

My Grandma Jolene—don't even ask about the Dolly Parton song, which she most certainly inspired, at least according to her—strides into the garage, her bottle-red hair twisted into a bun and her fleet of wildly impractical gold bangles clacking.

Like me, she wears a bright green mechanic's jumpsuit with a name patch on the chest, but, always glamorous, she's paired hers with red heels.

"I'm just looking at Mom's car," I say, dropping the wrench into a toolbox at my feet. "Promise."

Grandma raises one perfectly tweezed brow. "Uh-huh. You wouldn't dream of taking this thing out for a spin, would you now?" Grandma walks around the car, running a hand lightly over it. "Because your daddy told me you've not got a license yet."

"Grandma. I've been driving race cars since I was seven."

"Go-karts."

"Same difference. I was moving up the junior ranks and you know it. I was winning!"

"Girl, I believe as much as you that you're going to drive for F1 someday, but you're not taking the Hornet out until you get your license."

"But it's not even about the driving!" I let out a frustrated breath.

"Dad knows I'm a good driver! He's just stalling. He's trying to get me to be a part of this local summer volunteer program. Then we're going to maybe—*maybe*—talk about getting me my license."

Grandma's forehead wrinkles as she considers me, and a heaviness crosses her features, as if all her sadness had landed on her shoulders at once. "He just cares about you, JoJo, you know that."

"He's too overprotective."

"He doesn't want to lose you," she says softly. "DeeDee's death cracked him wide open, and he's clinging to all he has left."

The frustration that's been simmering since we moved back to Dell's Hollow two weeks ago, in the middle of May, finally comes spewing out of me. "But I don't have anything left, either! No friends here. No races to compete in. Nothing!" I slap one hand against the side of Mom's car and then immediately regret it.

Grandma eyes the car and hands me a clean rag from a nearby metal table. Apologetically, I rub off the greasy fingerprints I left on the side of the Hornet.

"You have your family," Grandma says. "And this job—which I see you've not been doing too much of today." She looks pointedly at the old Pontiac Fiero someone's brought in for a tune-up.

Because she runs the only garage in a small town at the foothills of the Appalachian Mountains, Grandma and her mechanics work on a lot of cars that have been sitting in mountainside outbuildings for decades. It gives her whole place a retro feel that she plays up with tin racing signs, pinup girl calendars, neon lights, and a continuous soundtrack that's a mix of '50s, '60s, '70s, and '80s music. It's a weirdly wonderful place to work, and, since I grew up helping my dad fix cars, it feels the closest to home since we moved here. Back when Dad worked in this garage, it was also a custom shop where cars were fitted out for the street races near Raleigh, but that's all gone now. Mom's car is the last fast thing in the shop, and it's pretty much not moved in ages.

"Oh please, I was done with that Pontiac an hour ago," I say, waving toward the Fiero. "It's all cleaned up, and ready to go to space."

Grandma snickers at that, sounding far younger than her sixty-eight years. Like me, she's a super fan of the *Fast & Furious* franchise, and neither of us has recovered from that scene in *F9* where a Pontiac Fiero gets launched into space.

"Well, orbit-ready or not, that's not our only car today. And since Willa is out with her sick kids and Mabel Rae isn't in until Tuesday, I need you to look at that Subaru that's parked out front." She tosses me a set of keys on a fluffy rabbit's foot keychain.

I catch them and let a wicked smile curve my lips. "Are you saying you want me to *drive* the Subaru?"

Grandma rolls her eyes affectionately. "I'm saying pull it into the garage and get its hood open, not take it out racing. I don't think that's breaking your daddy's rules. When you're done with it, you can have the rest of the day off. But I'll pay you for a full day."

I grin at that. "You're the best, Grandma. No wonder Dolly wrote a song about you."

She pats me on the shoulder. "Just use some of that time off today to investigate this volunteer program stuff. I want you to fit in here, Jo, and make a good life for yourself. Figuring out how to live by your daddy's rules while still being yourself is a big step in the right direction. Plus, you might actually meet some kids your own age to hang around with."

"Are you saying you're tired of me?" I try not to sound wounded. Dad is between jobs right now and always on his computer looking for work, so since we moved into Grandma Jolene's big farmhouse two weeks ago, I've hung out with her pretty much every night. Which is clearly not her idea of a great time.

"I'm saying I'm a vibrant older woman with a life of her own, who loves watching movies with her granddaughter but who has a vacation coming up soon. Didn't I tell you we're celebrating Florence's seventieth birthday in Florence this year?"

Florence is Grandma's oldest friend and long-term love interest. Flo lives in California where her grandkids are and visits Dell's Hollow every few months. Twenty years ago, after Florence's wife left her and Grandma's second husband died, they'd fallen in love, but neither one of them ever wanted to get married again, so now they just spend as much time as possible seeing the world together. Selfies of them zip-lining in the Amazon, surfing in Australia, and eating cake in Paris cover the walls of Grandma's living room, mixed in among pictures of Mom and Dad's wedding, my early years, me in front of the Karts I've won with, and many other family photos. Family is everything to Grandma, and the evidence of that is all over her house and the garage.

"We leave in a few weeks," Grandma continues. "We'll have a barbecue before we go so you can say hello to Flo. Invite all your friends."

"I have exactly zero friends here."

"Invite the ones from Charleston! Florence will love to meet them. She's always asking about you. Wants to know when you'll start racing again, but I told her that's not her business or mine."

My stomach clenches. How am I ever supposed to race again when the mere thought of it makes me want to hurl my lunch?

I exhale slowly, keeping my voice steady, something only possible after all my years of training. "Are you sure I can't come with you to Italy?"

That sounds better than hanging around Dell's Hollow, friendless and car-less.

"Absolutely not. Who else will run the garage for me these next few weeks?"

"Willa? Mabel Rae? Dad? Literally any adult with more experience than me?"

Grandma waves a hand, making her bangles dance again. "Of course they'll be in charge, technically, but I'm counting on you to make sure all the cars are fixed and drivable. I'm heading out for lunch now, but get that Subaru into the garage, get the tires off, and then you can take off, too."

She winks at me and walks away, leaving me to puzzle out her meaning.

Make sure all the cars are fixed and drivable? As in Mom's Hornet, too? The keys are locked in Grandma's safe, but that wouldn't be the hardest thing to open. It's a hardware-store bought-on-clearance safe, not some top-of-the-line bank vault I'd need a crew to crack.

To be thought on later, once Grandma is safely several time zones away.

Jingling the Subaru's keys, I head out front to pull it into the garage. As I'm getting into the car (which is slime green and looks like a giant rusting booger), my phone beeps with a text from CJ, who lives back in Charleston. They still aren't over me moving, and I miss them dearly. Which is why I haven't been returning their texts this last week. Because I'm afraid if I tell them how lonely it is here, then I won't be able to stand living in Dell's Hollow. Still, though, I click the most recent text open, pointedly ignoring all the videos and messages CJ has sent over the last few days.

> **CJ:** Hello, Sunshine. I know you're probably doing that thing where you pretend you don't have feelings, so you don't have to feel anything, which I'm going to say is cool. Because, *ewww*, feelings

I laugh at that. CJ wants to be a therapist like their mom, and feelings are literally their favorite thing to talk about.

> **CJ:** But, I'm warning you, if you don't text me back, I'm going to show up in that tiny town and do something like take out a billboard and plaster it with your third-grade school picture
> **CJ:** Don't test me JoJo
> **CJ:** You know I'm capable of this
> **CJ:** Seriously. I have so many pictures of us in third grade

They include a picture of me in third grade standing on the beach in the worst two-piece bathing suit ever, holding up a jellyfish on a stick. My hair is cut into this weird permed mullet I somehow thought was cool. I'm gap-toothed and beaming at the camera. My grade school picture from that year is far, far worse than this one.

I can't help but text back.

> **JoJo:** You wouldn't dare
>
> **CJ:** *Ahhhh*, there you are. Hello friend
>
> **JoJo:** Swear I'm not ignoring you. Things are just . . . weird
>
> **CJ:** I get it. It's okay. Just miss your face
>
> **JoJo:** Here's my face

I take a picture of myself inside the old Subaru, overwhelmed suddenly by how much my life has changed in the short time since we moved. I should be spending this summer with CJ, playing at the beach and racing at our local track. Instead I'm here, working in my grandma's garage. I force a smile while trying not to cry.

> **CJ:** Cutie. Why are you in a car? Are you driving? Did your dad finally let you get your license?!!
>
> **JoJo:** Not even a little bit. Call me tonight and I'll tell you all about it?
>
> **CJ:** Done. And seriously, just say the word, and I'll drive up there to come see you
>
> **JoJo:** That's such a long drive. I know how you feel about cars. And highways

CJ's anxiety leaves them unable to drive on highways, forcing them to navigate the wild, twisting southern backroads between Charleston and Dell's Hollow. Which is not a great option.

CJ: For you I'd manage. Or get James to drive me

James is CJ's boyfriend, and we both like him tremendously. Far better than some of the other dirtbags CJ has dated.

JoJo: I'm okay for now, promise. Though Grandma Jolene has a BBQ coming up soon, and she's requested your presence so she can "introduce Florence to all my friends"
CJ: You know I love the Flo-Jo love story. I'll be there

A honk makes me look up. From the driver's seat of her nearly new purple Dodge Charger, Grandma waves at me to get moving. Then she pulls away to go get lunch.

Signing off with CJ, I slip my phone into my pocket and take out the folded picture of Jamie Chadwick—the amazing female British driver who won all three seasons of the W Series (a women's-only circuit that was meant to help women break into F1 racing)—I always keep handy. Jamie Chadwick is my idol, and, although the W Series was shut down because of COVID and the F1 Academy took its place, I put her on the dashboard of any car when I drive, as a reminder of what I hope to accomplish. The F1 Academy is a way to get noticed in the ridiculously competitive and expensive world of F1 driving.

I'm planning on applying to the F1 Academy this year—I even have an application in my bag, all filled out and ready to send by August 1; it's just waiting on my dad's signature—and if I get in, it could change everything. That is, if I can still drive a race car at all. But, of course, that's half a world away and far outside my grasp at the moment. Before I can even think about F1 or the academy, I have to get my license. And

12

before I do that, I have to find a way out of this volunteer program Dad's so smitten with. But even before any of that, I have to get this Subaru into the garage and get working on the tires.

Right, time to get moving.

# *CHAPTER TWO*

## El

Once upon a time, the 2004 Yamaha YZF-R1 was superbike royalty. I've tattooed its stats on my brain the way a football fan memorizes their favorite player's . . . ball speed or whatever (I don't football). A 998cc, liquid-cooled, short-stroke, twenty-valve, in-line four-cylinder engine capable of producing 180 horsepower at an absolutely wild-for-the-times 12,500 rpm. A narrower motor, valve angle, fuel tank, and frame compared to the 2003, and *massively* strong. Fifty-six damn degrees of cornering clearance.

Not that I've ever actually tested the capabilities of this bike. At least, not alone.

Despite the dust motes that speckle the air, the liquid silver side panel in front of me is spotless. It'd better be. I polish the R1 every other week, even though it hasn't seen its owner for three months now, roll it backward and forward to rotate the tires, run the engine, and service the chain—the reason I'm on my knees in a storage shed in North Carolina summer weather, soaked to my elbows in kerosene and sticky with chain spray.

I've just finished wiping the extra lube from the links when my phone bleats repeatedly. That alarm means I've got an hour and fifteen to clean up, change, and clock in at Putt by the Pond. Mopping my forehead sweat with my equally sweaty bicep, I scoop up my supplies and step carefully around the other dirt bike in the shed to put them away. My hand-me-down Husqvarna leans forlornly against its kickstand; probably it feels abandoned. It's been in the dark for just as long as the R1, but I've got too much going on to get to Devil's Paradise, our local motocross track. Between my part-time job at the local mini golf, go-kart, and pinball parks, the two-evenings-a-week volunteer program I cofounded for the sake of my looming college applications—and for, like, the general spirit of humanity—plus the, you know, family stuff, the summer before my senior year has been . . . complicated.

I set my supplies on the makeshift workbench I cobbled together from a row of leftover paint cans with Max's old skateboard propped across the lids. Seems like everything in the shed is my sister's old *something*. There along the back wall: milk crates full of her paperbacks and comic books and old concert T-shirts. Bagged up in a corner: her riding gear. Carefully packed into a box behind the spare gas cans: her motocross trophies and medals, dozens and dozens of them. Everything she's outgrown.

Except the R1.

Stretching my back, I walk out of the shed into sunshine and cicada song. I blink in the light for a long moment, basking in the damp breeze and fresh air, before padlocking the door behind me. Then I walk across the grass, past Dad's vegetable beds, and toward the house, where the shower calls to me.

But when I slip through the screen door, I stop on the mud mat at the sight of Mom. She stands at the kitchen counter in her workout clothes with a pile of mail in hand, her shoulders stiff in that familiar way.

"Anything in there?" I ask, absolutely failing to sound chill.

With a bone-deep sigh—she already knows I know—Mom slides the postcard halfway across the counter to me. "Wash your hands before you touch anything," she warns.

I hold my hands out in front of me like surgeons do in medical dramas, careful not to brush against the furniture on the way to the sink (and fighting the deadly urge to throw my filthy arms around Mom in her cream yoga top). I even elbow the tap on. Toweling my hands on my pink shirt, I make myself walk slowly back to the postcard.

This one's glossy, bright blue, and says *Greetings from Boston* in bold bubble letters. Inside each letter is a picture of a building or a bit of skyline. As much as I want to, I can't flip it over with Mom right there, pretending not to watch me. So I wedge it into my back pocket and announce, "I'm gonna go shower."

"You don't need to run off, El," she says.

"I'm not, I just . . . I have work at three, and I don't want to be late."

"Oh. Well, good. I'm glad you're taking it seriously. I know it's only a summer job, but—"

"Mom, I really gotta get ready," I cut in, keeping (I think) all traces of annoyance out of my tone even though I've heard my parents' *I know it's only a summer job, but* speech a dozen times since vacation started.

She reaches out as I pass, but when she can't find a clean place to touch me, she drops her manicured hand to her side. "Want me to drive you to work? I'll pick you up after," Mom offers.

"Why, do you need the minivan?"

My mom's a science teacher at the middle school, which frees up her summers. Unfortunately, it also frees up her oatmeal-colored Toyota Sienna, which I share because we're down to two cars since Max, and Dell's Hollow has no public transportation unless you count the little bus that carts folks from the senior center to the grocery store once a week. Plus I think my parents like being able to ask where I'm going and exactly when I'll be back, while pretending it's all about the car. As if I'm ever going anyplace I shouldn't.

"No, I don't need it," says Mom, "but I was thinking—maybe we could grab some ice cream, bring it home for Dad?"

"I told Zaynah I'd give her a ride home, though." My best friend, Zaynah Syed, and I applied for our jobs together at our high school's teen employment fair this spring. It was either Putt by the Pond or the town's exciting new Applebee's, and I'm allergic to barbecue sauce.

Mom shifts into tree pose without meaning to, tapping her nails against the counter. "You can invite her over for ice cream, if you like. We hardly see your friends these days."

"Oh. Sure. Okay." I offer a little smile.

"It's a plan, then." She turns back to the mail, sliding a finger beneath the envelope flap of some bill. "And please use one of the beach towels to wash up. If you *have* to mess around in the shed, I've asked more than once that you not get the good towels dirty."

Well then! Mother-daughter moment over, I guess.

I take the stairs two at a time, and though I really do have to get ready, I pause a moment before skipping the second floor with my bedroom and bathroom to head up the spiral staircase to the attic. Which is really more like a loft; this became Max's space when she was too old to share a bedroom with her five-years-younger baby sister. She painted the squat walls and sloped wood a banana pudding yellow, so when I push through the shower curtain that hangs on a circular rail around the entrance, I always feel like a little chick inside a yolk. Even though most of her stuff's been shifted to the shed, the room still smells like her, I swear. Like her candles from the World Market in Fayetteville, and her clothes after riding—hot engine oil, smoldering brake pads, and exhaust—and like the jalapeño popcorn we'd eat while binge-watching our all-time favorite movies.

I'm talking, *obviously*, about the *Fast & Furious* films.

It's been a year and a half since my sister dropped out of college and came home to Dell's Hollow. It was immediately clear how tense things were between Max and our parents, but if I'm honest, I was happy to have her back. Even after she'd moved upstairs, her curtain was never closed to me. Whenever she was having a shitty day or could tell that I was, we'd curl up together in her daybed with her laptop. We'd watch Dominic Toretto and his found family pull off increasingly improbable stunts and heists while Max lamented every custom 1969 Ford Mustang run over by a tank, and every 2008 BMW M5 thrown through a building. We're not Car Girls™, but we share an encyclopedic knowledge of the *F&F* movies and their many trashed classics.

Then there was Letty Ortiz.

The moment Michelle Rodriguez first stomped on-screen in her flame-painted motorcycle boots, camo pants, and resting go-fuck-yourself face, a little lesbian lightbulb clicked on over my head. Or possibly bi lightbulb, or pan—I haven't nailed it down just yet. When Letty slid that black Honda Civic under the cargo truck during the electronics heist, I swear eleven-year-old me had a religious experience like I've never had during Shabbat services at Temple Beth El. Naturally, Max was the first person I came out to (as though she hadn't noticed that whenever I looked at Letty, the tips of my ears turned as deeply red as the Nissan 240SX Letty drove in Race Wars). My sister tucked my hair behind my burning ears, smacked a sloppy kiss on each of my cheeks, and announced, "Okay El, we're putting this marathon on pause to watch another classic: *Blue Crush*. It's gonna change your life."

Flopping back onto the daybed, now permanently in day mode, I finally turn over the postcard. I skim my thumb across Max's chaotic handwriting on the address lines:

Eliana Blum
15 Cider Lane
Dell's Hollow, NC 27010

As always, the message is nearly as short as the address, just a couple of scrawled sentences:

*Miss you EL. I heard that song in a diner last week, the one with the snake for a necktie, and thought about you. Hey, do me a favor and tell Jolene I want my jacket back? I think I left it in the shop.*

No return address. There never is, though the postmark is from Boston, sent June 1—two days ago.

I sit upright as the realization hits me.

Bursting back through the shower curtain, I practically rappel down the spiral staircase and run for my own bedroom. From the color-ordered row of mini notebooks in my desk cubby, I pull out the red one with my postcard collection tucked inside. It's not much of a collection, just five other cards sent over the last three months, postmarked from five different cities:

Pigeon Forge, Tennessee, March 6.

Tupelo, Mississippi, March 17.

Muskogee, Oklahoma, April 2.

Great Bend, Kansas, April 10.

Boston, Massachusetts, May 1.

The cards came so quickly at first, I figured they were sent from the road, slipped into a mailbox as Max passed through town. But twice is a pattern, right? That's what my parents say, as in: *Once is a mistake. Twice is a pattern.* According to the cards, Max has been stationary for over a month now.

Huh. I would've thought she'd land someplace in the south, or anyway, a city with a racing scene.

As the box full of trophies in the shed attest, my sister is fucking extraordinary on a track. From the moment my parents bought a used kid's mountain bike for fifty bucks and strapped a helmet on her so she could ride easy park trails with them on weekends, Max was absolutely fearless. She moved up to a little 70cc mini dirt bike when I was still a toddler, and she qualified to compete at Loretta Lynn's—that's the AMA Amateur National Motocross Championship in Tennessee—a month after her bat mitzvah. Then again when she was fifteen, and sixteen, and seventeen. That last year, she took third place in her category. Some of my earliest memories are of watching Max on her (now my) white-and-yellow Husqvarna, slicing through plumes of mud and gravel I could practically taste from the stands, soaring over the jumps and trusting the track to catch her.

It was Max who got *me* on the track, riding the 70cc we still had in the shed back then. And look, I wasn't bad! I did some junior events at Devil's Paradise in Deerfield, and even won medals of my own. They're still tacked to the corkboard above my desk, alongside my Honor Society medallion, merit medals, and a community award for Zaynah's and my volunteer program.

Still, I could never ride like Max. I wasn't fearless enough to keep it pinned.

Max just *had it*. Her coach said she did, and so did the scouts who watched her race at Loretta Lynn's. Everyone was pretty serious about her career; her coach even suggested homeschooling so that she could compete more often and rack up enough points to apply for her professional license even sooner. She'd been racing with the pros as an A-class amateur for a while and wanted to compete full-time as soon as she graduated high school. Everybody wanted it for her.

Except my parents.

They expected her to go to college. Max fought it—I know because I heard their barely muffled shouting matches drift up through the floor while I did my sixth-grade science homework in my room—but she went in the end. Which is I guess where the trouble started between them. And when she dropped out just before her last semester, it got a lot worse. Max never told me why she left college so close to graduating, except to say, "I just wanted to go off-road, El, you know?"

I didn't know. Even then, I was already planning for college, asking my guidance counselor questions about sports medicine and programs near-ish home. But like I said, I didn't care, because I had my sister back.

My sister's favorite place in the world might be behind the handle-bars, but mine is on the passenger seat. Just me and Max on the R1, the sky above us blue and smooth as sea glass, my hands fisted in her jacket—

I read the nothing-message one more time:

*Miss you EL. I heard that song in a diner last week, the one with the snake for a necktie, and thought about you. Hey, do me a favor and tell Jolene I want my jacket back? I left it in the shop.*

She means Jolene Boyd, Max's boss for the year she lived at home. Kind of a town icon, Jolene clips around the garage she runs in heels as red as her dyed hair. Jolene only works on cars, but she's the one who tipped off Max that a 2004 Yamaha YZF-R1 was sitting in a friend-of-a-friend's shop for a sliver of what it was probably worth. She even loaned my sister the money to buy it (our parents certainly weren't gonna) and let me hang around while Max used the shop tools to fix up the bike in her off-hours. As she worked, Max would recite the superbike's stats to me like a bedtime story, over and over again, and I'd ask her to tell me them just one more time.

The R1 is my sister's greatest treasure. She asked me to take care of it for her while she's gone, but she'd never have left it behind if she planned to stay away for months. I guess we both thought Mom and Dad would let her come home by now.

Funny Jolene never called to tell us she had Max's riding jacket, though. And I don't know how Max plans to get it back from her without a return address, unless . . . Unless Jolene knows something I don't.

I check my phone again to find I'm down to an hour before work. If I want to wash up, I have to get back on track. It says in the employee handbook (which Zaynah and I studied together before starting) that Putt by the Pond's policy is a verbal warning the first time you're late to a shift, and a write-up for the second. Even if I haven't been late yet, I *could* be late again for totally unavoidable circumstances. Then I'd be kicking myself for the warning I could've prevented. And Mom's right—it might only be a summer job, but I'm counting on them to hire me back next summer, so I can save up for my own car before college. UNC–Chapel Hill is over a four-hour drive from Dell's Hollow, and if I get in there, I can't have Mom and Dad dropping me off and picking me up from campus in the Oatmobile. I simply cannot.

And I *really* should wash up, because I must smell like the love child of a gas station and a compost heap.

I stand frozen with indecision in the middle of my bedroom for a long, precious moment before springing to action, peeling off my oil-stained joggers and pulling on a clean pair of jeans. My T-shirt is grease spotted, but I'll be changing into my work shirt anyway. After slapping on an extra layer of deodorant and finger-scrubbing a streak of grime from my short blond hair (with some beachy-smelling dry shampoo on top to try and mask my *odeur*), I grab my backpack and run out my bedroom door.

I do a lap of the first floor to find Mom, now in her chair in the living room, immersed in her latest paperback biography. This one looks like it's about a figure skater from the '80s, judging by the cover.

Already shrugging on my backpack, I say, "Hey Mom? Zaynah just texted, and her dad can't drive her to work anymore, so I told her I'd pick her up." The lie burns in my cheeks, and I hope she'll think I'm still overheated from working in the shed. It's not that I think one little white lie is so terrible, but I know what it would mean to my parents if they found out.

Mom starts to set her book down. "All right, just give me a few minutes, and I can—"

"That's, um, that's okay, 'cause we might get coffee on the way, so . . . maybe I can just take the minivan for the afternoon, and we can do family ice cream tomorrow? Or actually, I have a volunteer shift at the Syed's. Um, so Wednesday?"

"Oh." The way her forehead crinkles sends a fresh wave of guilt all the way down to my toes. But what am I supposed to say? *I know you hate talking about your other daughter, the one you guys kicked out of your lives and mine, while you were at it, but I have this hunch . . . .*

"That's fine, El."

"Okay, cool. But Wednesday, right? We can do ice cream Wednesday?"

"Sure. We'll see how the week goes." Mom returns to her paperback.

By the time I've grabbed the keys from their hook and escaped into the van, I'm sweating worse than I was in the shed. Still, I force myself to start the engine and pull away without glancing back at the house. Who has time for second thoughts? If the two traffic lights between Cider Lane and downtown Dell's Hollow are good to me, I can easily make it to work by three—*after* stopping to talk to Jolene.

See, my sister's boss wasn't just her boss, but like, her mentor. Her Yoda in a bright green mechanic's jumpsuit and spangly chandelier earrings. So if anybody who isn't my parents knows where Max is—knows how and where to send her the prized possession she left behind—it has to be Jolene Boyd.

# CHAPTER THREE

## JoJo

I turn the key in the Subaru's ignition, closing my eyes for a moment as I pretend it's the purr of an F1 car and not the wheeze of an old station wagon that greets me. Despite my anxiety about racing, I have to admit I've missed driving. My hands move slowly over the wheel, my fingertips sliding over the stitching, caressing it as I imagine a whole stretch of track in front of me, waiting to be eaten up by my car. I grip the wheel tighter, pretending to shift into first. Both my hands slide across the wheel as we take the first turn and—

A knock at my window startles me out of my reverie.

My eyes fly open and I see a girl with what looks like handprints of motor oil on her pink T-shirt standing outside my window. She wears jeans and a tremendous scowl. Her blond bob is half pulled back, and she has a pen stuck behind her ear. A small streak of grease marks her neck.

Everything about her sparks my curiosity.

Mortified to be caught feeling up the Subaru, I release the steering wheel and unroll the window. "Uhm, hi?"

"Do you work here?" she asks, looking around the parking lot. It's empty except for a minivan the color of reheated oatmeal and the Subaru. Her dark eyebrows knit together and there's an intensity to her I instantly like. She reminds me of other race car girls I've known—an intoxicating cocktail of grit and determination all contained in the arc of her eyebrows and her slight frown.

I swallow hard as she stares at me. "I do work here, yes."

"Good. I have some questions for you."

She has questions? For me? Lord help me, I might actually melt under that stare. JoJo Emerson-Boyd, now a puddle on the floor of the Subaru.

Instead, I arch an eyebrow, trying to keep my cool. "What are you, a private investigator?"

"No." Her frown deepens. It's adorable.

"An intern at a private investigator's office?"

The girl lets out a huff. "No."

My curiosity rises as does my need to know more about this girl, but rather than asking a decent question, I blurt out: "Are you the assistant to an intern at a private investigator's office?"

The girl looks vaguely murderous. "What? Oh my God. Are you always this annoying?"

I smirk, desperately wishing I was behind the wheel of anything besides this booger-green Subaru. "I think you meant to say charming.

And yes, I'm always this charming."

The girl rolls her eyes so hard, I'm certain she's going to strain her optic nerve or something. "I'm kind of in a rush here. Can you just answer my questions? Please?"

Her voice carries an edge of real pleading and suddenly I want to buy her coffee, not keep teasing her. "I can do that, but first I have to get this car parked. Meet me inside and we can talk?" I offer the words like an olive branch, hoping she sees them for that.

"Fine." The girl storms toward the open garage doors before I can say anything else.

"Real smooth, Jo. Such cool-girl energy," I mutter to myself as I put the Subaru in Drive and pull away. "*This* is why you're single."

Exactly one minute later, I've parked the Subaru inside and grabbed my picture of Jamie Chadwick. The girl in the pink shirt sits in Jolene's office, arms crossed, frowning at a tin sign on the wall.

Because she's cute even though she's grumpy and because I'm trying to think of what to say to her—I've literally not flirted with anyone since we moved to Dell's Hollow, and talking to a cute, oil-streaked girl does strange things to my insides—I sit in the car for a few seconds longer than necessary.

"She's just a customer," I say to myself as I slide the keys out of the ignition. "Probably here about something wrong with the car her parents got her for her Sweet Sixteen. Nothing remarkable or interesting about her. Plus, she probably smells like stale Cheetos and is a terrible kisser, so no need to worry about anything."

Immensely cheered by that thought, I step out of the car. After I untie my mechanic's jumpsuit from my waist and slip my arms back into it, so I look vaguely less sweaty, I stroll toward Grandma Jolene's office.

When I open the door, the first thing that hits me is the smell of coconut with a metallic undercurrent of kerosene and engine oil. The second is the power of the girl's scowl when she turns it toward me.

"Where's Jolene?" she asks, glaring at my chest. For a moment, my heart leaps, hoping she's checking me out, but then I realize she's reading my name tag.

"Uhm, eating a chicken salad sandwich somewhere?" I manage through an outbreak of nerves that nearly knocks me flat. How am I the same girl who has stared down and beaten racers twice my size? I fiddle with the buttons on my jumpsuit.

The girl looks around the office, like I'm hiding Grandma Jolene and her chicken salad in a closet.

"I mean, she's at lunch." To cover my flushed face, I take a seat behind Grandma Jolene's desk.

"When will she be back?"

"That's anyone's guess, but I can help. I'm—"

"JoJo," interrupts the girl.

For a moment I'm flattered she's heard of me, then I remember: name tag. Right.

"Do you know if she'll be back soon?"

I shrug. "Depends how good the chicken salad is, I guess."

"Well . . . what do you do here?"

"Fix cars, make coffee, change tires, you name it." I fidget with a pencil, and the girl's eyes follow my grease-stained fingers. It's unnerving and vaguely embarrassing to be so filthy from work next to her—even with her oil-streaked neck—and for the first time in my life, I wish I'd taken Grandma Jolene up on her offer of a manicure.

"Do you have access to information about former employees, then?"

I shake my head. "I mean, I can tell you a few things, like stories Jolene's told me, but I've only worked here for a few weeks."

"Where were you before that?"

"Do I have the right to talk to a lawyer before answering, Investigator?" I ask.

"No," the girl says dryly, but I swear, she's biting back a smile when she does.

I shrug. Might as well tell her about myself. Maybe it will get her talking, too. Plus, I've not talked to anyone my own age in person for weeks, and I kind of miss it. "I just moved here with my dad from Charleston. Jolene's my grandma."

"That's why she's got a framed picture of you, I guess." The girl nods toward a photo on Grandma Jolene's desk. It's of me and Mom, who wears her racing jumpsuit and stands in front of her car. Number 17. She's grinning, as usual when she was on the track, and she's got an arm around me. The other one holds an enormous trophy.

"That's my mama. It was taken right after she won the Busch Light Clash in Los Angeles this year."

And three weeks before she died. Which I don't tell this girl.

She looks at the picture, then back at me. "Wow, that's impressive. She's pretty."

"She was," I agree. "And she was really, really fast. She taught me to drive. Before moving here, I raced cars as a job. Well, karts. Which is hardly a job, but it was fun and sometimes I made money off it."

"I race, too!" she exclaims, dropping the PI attitude for the first time to fully smile, and the shift is adorable. "Or I did. Not as a job, though, and not cars. But maybe I've heard of your mom; is she famous?"

I shrug. "You might know her—DeeDee Emerson?"

"That sounds familiar."

"She was a NASCAR champion."

Recognition lights up her eyes. "Wait! I know how I know her. We have this plaque dedicated to her at work!"

I could ask more questions about that, but I leave it. Lots of places have plaques about my mom. DeeDee Emerson bought tires here. DeeDee Emerson signed our wall. DeeDee Emerson ate a cheeseburger in this very booth. It's nothing new, and I don't feel like getting into all that mess with this girl. "Do you follow the circuit?" I ask instead.

She shakes her head. "I don't really watch NASCAR."

"What about F1? The F1 Academy, which is the successor to the W Series?"

"What's that?"

A long sigh rushes out of me. Patience. It's not this girl's fault that most people outside of racing don't know about the F1 Academy or how it's changing the sport. "It's a training program for elite female race car drivers. It helps them get into F1 someday, which is my goal in life."

"So what are you doing working here?" the girl asks. "I mean, if you're a race car driver and your mom's famous?"

"I work here because it's our family business." No need to tell her my entire sad backstory. "Hey, what's your name?"

The girl considers me for a long moment. "I'm Eliana—El—Blum. I'm looking for information about my sister, Maxine Blum. She used to work here, until three months ago."

"Where is she now?"

"That's what I want to talk to Jolene about. I'm hoping she has an address for her."

"Why don't you have her address if she's your sister? How does a private investigator lose a sister?"

As soon as the words are out, I regret them. Because, as I know, there are all sorts of ways to lose people. And El's sister is none of my business.

She winces, but answers the question I wish I could take back. "*I* didn't. There was this . . . incident, with the town fountain . . . it wasn't really even Max's fault. She made a mistake. Max is a really good sister," El insists. "And she races, too, you know, but bikes. She's amazing on a track. You'd like her."

"Sure. I like her sister," I say with a boldness I do *not* see coming.

El blushes furiously. "Um, thanks. But um, my parents kicked her out. She had to leave, and she's been moving around ever since."

"Oh. Okay . . . ."

"Anyway." El clears her throat, back to business once more. "I got this postcard from her today." She pulls it out from her bag, holding it up to show me the *Greetings from Boston* printed across the front.

"Looks like she's in Boston?"

"Boston is a huge city. I can't just show up downtown and call her name in the middle of the Common. I'll never find her without an address."

I consider El again, noting the way her hands clench the desk as she looks hopefully at me. Her tough-girl vibe is gone, and she just looks vulnerable and sad and lost.

All feelings I know too well.

Wishing I could give her a hug but not wanting to be that kind of weirdo, I stand up and go to the filing cabinet. "I don't think Grandma Jolene keeps tabs on every employee she's ever had. Especially after they're gone." I rifle through the top drawer—the only one that's unlocked—hoping I find a folder that says "Maxine Blum" on it.

El drums her fingers on Grandma Jolene's desk. "This is different. Jolene liked Max—she helped her out a lot when Max came back to Dell's Hollow. They were closer than just a boss and employee."

I close the filing cabinet drawer. "There's nothing in here and the rest of the drawers are locked. Sorry." And I really am. I would've loved to see a smile on El's face as I handed her a folder with her sister's contact info.

El lets out a sigh. "It's fine. I was just . . . hoping. Well, maybe you've seen a racing jacket around? I have a picture of Max wearing it." She pulls up a picture on her phone of a girl with hair a shade lighter than her own and thick black eyebrows.

"That's Max?" I ask, as El hands me her phone.

El nods.

Max is pretty, in an aggressive way. She stands with her hands on her hips in front of a bike. Her motorcycle jacket immediately brings visions of Letty from *Fast & Furious* to mind.

"I wish I'd seen that jacket lying around," I admit. "I'd probably be wearing it now if I had, summer heat be damned." My eyes linger on the asymmetrical zipper, the curved stitching, and the hood at the back. It's the perfect badass don't-mess-with-me jacket and far cooler than my green coveralls.

"Don't," says El, her voice sharp.

Because I'm an ass when I'm nervous, I laugh at her super-serious tone. "Relax. I promise I'm not going to steal your sister's jacket. I've not even seen it. Do you want to stick around and ask Grandma Jolene about it?"

El glances at the clock above Jolene's desk. "I can't. I'm on my way to work. But maybe you could ask her for me? I can stop back by the shop tomorrow. Or I'll be at Putt by the Pond till my shift ends at seven, if you find out anything."

"I love that place. Maybe I'll stop by for racing sometime." I've been avoiding it since we moved back because Putt was where Mom and I used to race karts when I was a kid, but maybe it's time. Time to see if I can still race a car. Or at least pretend I'm still on the right track. Or at least time to forget myself and my troubles in the roar of an engine and the smell of rubber on the road. Even if it's just hokey go-karts at a local track.

"I never know where I'll be working," El says. "Maybe I'll see you there."

"Maybe you will. And don't worry; I'll ask Grandma Jolene about Max."

El nods, then holds out her hand for her phone. Which I'm still holding after looking at Max's picture. Like the world's biggest dork.

"Right, sorry. Here." I start to hand it back, but then I pause.

"Want me to put my number in there? Just in case we don't bump into each other again?"

El slides a quick glance my way and our eyes meet for a moment. "I never take a girl's number until at least a first date."

I blush redder than Jolene's heels at that. At least I know El's into girls, but that doesn't mean she's into me. Quickly, I shove the phone toward her. "Right, of course. Sorry."

"I'm teasing," she says. "But that's okay. I know where to find you. And thanks for helping me look for Max."

Still embarrassed by nearly giving her my number, I blurt out the first thing that comes to mind, which is, of course, a *Fast & Furious* quote because I'm still thinking of motorcycle jackets and pretty girls and feeling generally overwhelmed by the smell of coconut and motor oil. "No worries. Where you ride, I ride."

El's eyes widen at my words. "*Furious 7*, nice. Love a girl who can quote Letty Ortiz."

"You have no idea," I say, trying for a laugh and ending up with a small, weird cough. "*Furious* superfan here."

"I bet I could beat you at *F&F* trivia." A grin pulls at the sides of El's mouth.

"Not a chance. I'm positive I could beat you at that *and* at go-karts."

"Oh, that's a bet I'll take."

El walks away with a wave, and once she's gone, I collapse into Grandma Jolene's office chair, my heart going faster than Dom Toretto's signature 1970 black Charger.

# CHAPTER FOUR

## El

I know what they say about small towns and the kids who grow up in them. We're supposed to feel trapped, like a goldfish in a glass bowl, just swimming tight little circles in our own crap till we bust out or die trying. But there's a lot I've loved about growing up in Dell's Hollow. Like sure, we've got one hair salon in town; Shelly Fry runs it out of the converted utility room in her mother-in-law's house twice a week, and if you dared to drive into Deerfield and cheat on her with CostClippers, Shelly would hear about it before you made it back home. And okay, I've eaten everything on the menus of both of our town diners, neither of which have changed since before I was eating solid foods. There are no strange and unexplored corners, no uncharted alleyways to lead you someplace you've never been.

But that just means that every place is a memory.

Even Putt by the Pond, where Mom and Dad would take us to celebrate—a perfect test score for me, a track win for Max, an exciting Panthers victory, whatever. Aside from the Cineplex, and unless you count the Walmart parking lot where the "troubled" kids (never me) hang out after dark, it's pretty much the place to be in Dell's Hollow. It has a mini golf course, batting cages, a go-kart track, an arcade, and thirty-two flavors of sno-cone, all of which I've sampled. My paychecks are minimum wage–sized, so my car fund could barely fill a gas tank at the moment. Still, summer jobs demonstrate responsibility—to colleges and to parents. Plus I get free tokens to use every week, so I haven't paid for a round of the *Fast & Furious: SuperCars* arcade game once this summer.

On my way to the employee locker room to change, I pat the Day-Glo orange machine. A tween in the seat races through Shinjuku in the '06 Dodge Viper SRT-10 from *Tokyo Drift*. It's one of the easy tracks, but they plough spectacularly into a train as I pass.

I can't help thinking that I'd love to watch JoJo play; I bet she picks the hard tracks every time.

Zaynah's already in the locker room when I elbow through the door, re-pinning her daisy-print hijab in the mirror. She hasn't been less than fifteen minutes early for a shift all summer. "Sixty-four seconds to spare, Blum," she comments, nose wrinkling, "and please don't take this the wrong way, but you kind of smell like a gas station?"

Lifting my T-shirt hem to my own nose, I groan. That extra layer of deodorant and dry shampoo clearly didn't help. I pull out my flaming-red work polo before stuffing my backpack into my tiny locker. Zaynah shows up for her shift wearing her polo over a long-sleeved shirt so she can dress at home, in privacy, but she doesn't care that I'm shameless (about my body, at least). I wrestle off my contaminated T-shirt as I catch her up. "I skipped a shower to stop at Jolene's garage before work. Did you know she has a granddaughter?"

"Sure. I met her when we were kids, at one of our Hug-a-Horse events while she was in town with her parents."

The first thing to know about Zaynah Syed is that she's a Horse Girl™. Her family runs the Syed Rescue Farm, which is mostly a ranch for unwanted horses, but they've also got pigs, donkeys, chickens, and at the moment an alpaca pair named Bonnie and Clyde. They run on donations and grants and volunteers. Plus they do parties and events to take care of their animals, either until they find homes, or forever if they're sick or old or just too wild to be wanted. It was Zaynah's idea to cofound the Dell's Hollow Volunteer Club with me, inspired by her parents' work.

The second thing to know about Zaynah is she's my best friend, even if we have spent our whole lives competing—in the classroom, in middle-distance events when we ran junior high track, in crushes (we never actually *act* on our crushes, and Zaynah doesn't date; we just like to prove to each other that *our* crush of the moment is the deepest and truest and crushiest). A day doesn't go by without us texting, even if we're sitting in the same room, sending TikToks back and forth.

"Why were you at Jolene's?" Zaynah asks. "Did the Oatmobile break down?"

"If only, but no. I was looking for something Max might've left at the shop. I, um, got another postcard today."

Zaynah shines her big, thoughtful brown eyes at me, and asks carefully, "Oh yeah?"

"I think Max is staying in Boston."

"Well, that's . . . good." She takes a paper towel from the dispenser by the sink just to twist it in her hands.

It's not Zaynah's fault she's turned into an awkward turtle. Nobody really knows what to say about Max, at least not to my face.

My sister has something of a reputation around Dell's Hollow, and not just because of her brilliant amateur track career. She *might* have taken the car out one night—the car my parents meant to let me drive once I had my license, but they loaned it to Max after she moved home—and she *might* have driven straight through the roundabout that circles Dell's Hollow's town green. She then *might* have crashed it into the Founder's Fountain in the middle of the green.

But it wasn't her fault! This was in March, during a rare snow for North Carolina, and she never could help moving just a little faster than the rest of us. She was barely speeding. She made one mistake, but anybody could.

*I* could, as hard as I try not to.

"I think it is good," I tell Zaynah as I finish buttoning my polo.

"Sounds like it. El, just be . . . never mind. Come find me at the cone counter during break? I'll make a kiwi cone for you."

"Z, do not," I say. It's true there's no actual kiwi in the kiwi flavoring, but I don't believe that fruit should be neon green, as Zaynah well knows.

I choose to ignore the part where she clearly meant to say *be careful*. It's nothing I haven't heard before, and it's nothing I need to hear again. I'm always careful. I follow every rule in the employee handbook, including leaving my phone in my locker, which nobody does but me, not even Zaynah. I have a 4.1 GPA going into senior year, and have had my application essays to UNC–Chapel Hill drafted for months, even though I can't apply for early decision to their sports medicine program until October. I floss every day so that when the dentist asks me about my flossing habits, I can say *I floss every day* and snag that sweet nod of dental approval. I'm never late for curfew, I weed the garden beds every Sunday like clockwork, and I don't lie to my parents.

I hardly ever lie to my parents.

After I clock in at the front desk, the shift manager sends me out to the go-karts. We have a jellybean-shaped asphalt track surrounded inside and out by a barricade of stacked tires. I relieve Jericho Brown, who works the opening shift, and take his place on the stool beside the narrow starting lane of empty karts. There's an overhanging roof, so I don't have to sit in the baking sun all afternoon, and it's not a hard job. I lower the chain to let the next group in line onto the concrete loading platform, then help them each choose their karts. We have two speeds: a red 16-mph kart for kids, and a blue 24-mph kart for twelve and up. I list off the rules: no crashing into other drivers or the barricade, keep your hands and feet inside the vehicle, shoulder harness must stay buckled, etcetera. When I move the traffic cones that block the starting lane from the main track and flip the stoplight to green, customers get five minutes to race. I announce the last lap over the loudspeaker, flip the light to red, and put the cones back out in time for folks to pull back into the cart lane. Easy peasy, but since it's technically the most high-stakes attraction in the park, I do have to pay attention.

On a summer day like this, there's hardly ever a lull, and I'm relieved when I get to pull out the BACK IN FIFTEEN sign for my scheduled break. I'm all set to hang it on the chain then head for the cone counter when the small round bronze plaque set in the concrete of the platform catches my eye:

DEEDEE EMERSON DROVE HERE

I don't remember seeing it in the fall, when I was just a customer. They must've had it installed this spring. Now I remember; it was after . . .

Oh my God.

It was after DeeDee Emerson died.

How had that slipped my mind? It's true I don't follow NASCAR, like I told JoJo, but DeeDee Emerson's death made our hometown newspaper, the *Dell's Hollow Daily* (it's actually a monthly paper, but I don't think anybody's ever complained about the false advertising). DeeDee—JoJo's mom—really was a hometown hero. It was a point of pride that a real live racing star had eaten the hush puppies at one of our two diners, and hugged a horse at our local rescue farm, and driven one of our go-karts. I mean, North Carolina is the home of NASCAR. And there I was, bantering with and harassing this nauseatingly cute girl about my sister's jacket, completely forgetting the article that ran in the *Daily* when her mom crashed mid-race . . . .

"Hey, you," says a voice right behind me.

Goosebumps shoot down my back despite the wet summer heat,

and I swivel around so fast, my stool nearly tips. I stumble up onto the platform to keep from spilling over with it. "JoJo!" It comes out in a kind of squeal.

She's swapped out her mechanic's jumpsuit for a pair of denim shortalls over a cropped black tank, her work boots for sneakers, and her long brown hair is pulled back with a claw clip, the pink tips spraying out the top. Shading her green eyes from the sun as she looks out over the track and crinkling her pierced nose (holy guacamole), she says, "God, I remember this place. Is it smaller than it was back then?"

"You might just be taller."

"Not much."

It's true, she's a few inches shorter than me, but skinny-strong. If she competes the way Max did, even if it's on four wheels, then she probably trains the way Max did. Though my sister is soft-strong, like me. "As long as you can reach the pedals, you can ride. So are you, uh, waiting to ride? I was about to go on break."

"Ride alone? No," JoJo scoffs, shoving her hands into her shortalls pockets. "We have a bet, remember?"

"Ah. What exactly are we betting on?"

"Hmmm." JoJo's nose crinkles as she considers this. "How about if you win, I'll help you with your investigation, Detective. I didn't get the chance to ask Grandma Jolene about Max's jacket. I looked around and I haven't found it yet—sorry about that. But I can help with other stuff. Like, you're looking for your sister's address, right? Well, Grandma would never just give it to you, even if she had it. Privacy laws or whatever. She's ethical like that. But I'm in the shop almost every day, and she's headed out of town for a while. More than enough time for me to snoop."

"Snoop how?"

"You know. Through the files in the locked cabinet."

"That's not what I meant when I asked for help. I don't want you to get in trouble. Not to mention, *I* don't want to get in trouble."

"You don't?" JoJo smirks. Smirks!

"Can't you just ask Jolene? Hold on." I pause negotiations to hang my break sign on the chain at the entrance to the loading platform, where a line of customers is building anew. They grumble, but wander off for the moment. By the time I turn back to JoJo, she's looking down, mesmerized by the dull gleam of her mother's plaque.

She glances up at the squeak of my sneakers on the concrete, and damn it, I forget to fix my expression for *just* long enough that her cocky smile falls away. "So, I guess you know," she says accusingly.

"I—"

"It's fine. It doesn't matter." JoJo crosses her arms, staring out at the empty track instead of meeting my eyes. "Let's talk about what I get when I win."

I choke out an anxious laugh. "If you win."

"*If* I win, then you cover for me with this volunteering crap," she says, suddenly more businesslike. "You're the club leader, right? My dad's trying to get me to join up. He's literally holding my license hostage. I looked at the paperwork he gave me, and it lists you as the student contact."

"Well, I'm the co-leader," I correct her, reeling a little. Is this the whole reason she showed up here? And if it is, why should that bother me? It's not like she's personally invested in me or my family.

"Great! So if I win, you put my name down on your attendance sheet or whatever. Then I get to take a nap in a park twice a week while I'm supposed to be doing my civic duty, and I still get my license at the end of the summer."

"You want me to help you scam . . . me?"

"Basically. Is it a bet?"

I weigh my options. Obviously I want to know whether Jolene has Max's address, but breaking into her files, *or* falsifying club attendance? Honestly, this is the kind of thing my sister would agree to, which means it should be an instant pass for me. Max might live her life a quarter mile at a time, but I make all the right choices, and everybody in town knows it, so no one has to worry about me.

"Scared you'll lose, or scared you'll win?" JoJo challenges.

Her words kick up the old flare of competition I used to feel at Devil's Paradise before my nerves inevitably set in: staring out across the natural slopes of the winding red-clay and sand track, determined to hold the inside line on the turns, to stay in attack position, to keep it pinned. To win, and maybe more importantly, to have Max watch me win. "Fine. Let's do this. But like I said, I'm not off until seven."

"You can't sneak in a race on the clock?"

"Absolutely not," I say, aghast.

"Okay, then." The smirk returns. "I can wait."

Five minutes after my shift ends, and after I've let Zaynah know her ride home will be just a little bit late—though I decline to explain exactly why—I'm harnessed into a blue kart of my very own in front of JoJo in line. She said I deserved the advantage because she's just that confident. But I'm not worried. Okay, yes, dirt bikes and go-karts are different beasts, but she's never seen me ride; maybe she'd be worried if she had. I glance back over my shoulder at JoJo, who tosses me a nod that's exceedingly cool and completely annoying. I refocus on the road ahead, determined to win. And when my shift replacement flips the light to green, I only hesitate for a sliver of a second—like always—before I stomp on the gas pedal. I swerve around a kid in a red kart and a burly guy wearing a Tar Heels snapback to take the lead. For half a lap, up the long arc of the bean-shaped track, I keep it.

Then, all of a sudden, it's gone.

It turns out JoJo wasn't bluffing. I get the holeshot, taking the first corner, but by the time I've straightened out, she's pulled up alongside me. She flashes her teeth at me, green eyes shining, and then I'm inhaling her dust as she pulls away. This girl is *fast*.

I stand a chance at overtaking her as we round the corner at the other end of the bean, since I've been sticking like a burr to the inner barricade, but just as I think I've caught her, JoJo muscles past me and I'm forced to let up on the gas. And that's it. I don't catch her again for the rest of the race; in fact, she laps me halfway through. By the time my replacement announces the final lap, I'm still hopelessly behind. She laps me once again right before we pull reluctantly into the lane beside the loading platform, both of us windswept and laughing. I lost, but it turns out, I've missed this in the months since I last took the Husqvarna out of the shed. I missed the rush and the way I think about nothing but the path in front of me for five whole minutes when the sound of my heart is impossibly loud but everything else gets perfectly quiet.

"I almost had you," I quote *F&F* to JoJo as she appears on the platform above me.

"You almost had me?" She follows the script, even as she holds out a hand to help me out of the kart. "You never had me! You never had your car!"

I let her haul me up by the arm with her extra strong grip, but before I've even found my footing again, the consequences of my loss settle in. The race was whatever. She did warn me, so it's not like she's some kind of kart shark. I should've seen this coming. But I let myself get excited at the idea of having an ally, even a cocky-on-the-verge-of-obnoxious one. It was nice, talking about Max with someone who hadn't decided a long time ago who my sister was, and that I—and Dell's Hollow—are somehow better off without her around. Which is just not true, for the record. And now I'm back to square one, unless I can sweet-talk Jolene and her ethics into helping me. Even though I'm just some girl who she let buzz around in the background of her shop for a few months, without ever exchanging more than three sentences . . .

JoJo must notice my good mood fading because she shakes me by the wrist, which she's still holding onto. "So. Grandma leaves for Florence with Florence soon—"

"Huh? With whom for where?"

JoJo laughs. "Grandma Jolene and her soulmate, Florence, are going to Florence, Italy. Anyway, she leaves a bit later this month, and I'm not like, in charge or anything, but I'll be alone in the shop pretty regularly. Seems like that's the perfect time to start."

"To start?"

"Our investigation."

I know I can't just keep repeating JoJo's words back to her, and yet: "*Our* investigation?"

"Why not?" She lets go of me at last to slick the flyaway hairs from her ponytail back out of her face. "I acknowledge that I kicked your ass, but it's not like I'm so busy, I can't help you. Doesn't seem like there's much hope for a social life in Dell's Hollow, and now that I don't have to make time for volunteering . . ." She trails off with a smug little grin.

Even though I should be thanking JoJo, like on-my-knees thanking her, I suddenly want to wipe that smile off her face. I don't like to be pitied (I should know, because everyone looks at me with pity whenever the subject of Max comes up), and I don't like how she's talking about my town. "You know if you showed up to volunteering club, you might have a social life? I get that we're small, and we're like 85 percent farm-land, and we're probably not as cool as whatever cool-people place you came from. But this is my home, and now it's your home, too, so maybe you're not actually any better than me."

I meant to say "us"—you're not better than "us"—but the punch seems to land all the same. JoJo takes a step back, and then another, right across the memorial plaque. Which reminds me of *why* she moved to Dell's Hollow in the first place.

Well, shit.

"Um, I'm gonna head out," JoJo announces. "It's like a twenty-minute bike ride back to Grandma's, and I don't want to get run off the road by a horse cart in the dark." She smiles, but weakly.

"I didn't mean—do you want a ride, at least? I'm driving my friend home, but we've got a bike rack and everything."

"It's okay. I missed my workout today, so. I'll see you around, Detective?"

"See you after your grandma leaves for Italy, right?" I feel like crap taking her up on her offer now, as much as I need her.

"You never know. Maybe sooner." She taps my sneaker with the toe of hers and strolls off, hands in her shortalls pockets, leaving me behind on the loading platform to wallow in my shame and annoyance and gratitude. A whole mess of emotions.

Nothing is going to be simple when it comes to JoJo—I can already tell.

# CHAPTER FIVE

## JoJo

The day after I absolutely trounce El Blum at kart racing—it felt amazing to race again and my anxiety disappeared the moment I hit the gas— I wake early and linger on my air mattress, staring at the ceiling and deciding what to do with my day. Sunlight filters through the lace curtains in the craft room where Grandma Jolene has set up a space for me, and I've been awake for almost an hour already. Just lying here.

Rolling over, I grab my F1 Academy application from my messenger bag and read it for the thousandth time.

*Name, Age, Experience, Short Paragraph About Why You Want to Be Part of the F1 Academy, Awards Won, Career Goals...*

Everything is completed, except for the blank line on page four, which needs my dad's signature since I'm underage. I scowl at the empty space. If Mom were here, she would've signed it the minute I printed the form.

Of course, if Mom were still here, then we'd still be working on our plan for my career and I could've afforded to wait a bit longer. Now that she's gone, though, I have to make my own way in the racing world.

Sighing, I let the application pages drop onto my face in a heap.

I could just forge Dad's signature, but then if I get in and it's discovered I did that, I'll probably be banned from F1 for life, so that's not an option.

I haven't even told Dad about the form yet or my dream of leaving Dell's Hollow later this summer to join the F1 Academy, which is a training program for young elite female drivers. How can I ask him to sign this when he won't even let me get my license?

But how can I not ask him? If I wait until I'm eighteen, six months from now, it might be too late. I might be too slow. Too out of practice. Too distracted. Plus, if I don't apply this summer, I'll have to wait another full year for the next application window.

From underneath the sheets of paper, I can feel my racing future moving further and further away from me.

Shit.

Sitting up, I let the application sheets waterfall off my face and down my torso. I have the day off from Grandma Jolene's, and I wasn't planning on attending El's volunteer club meeting. I really, truly wasn't. After all, I won the go-kart race and our bet, meaning she had to cover for me.

But, let's face it, what else am I going to do? Sit around the farmhouse and watch Grandma pack for Italy? Help her decide whether Florence would like her better in a red sundress or a pink one? Of course, I could just spend the day wandering around Dell's Hollow on my own. Or I could stick to the couch, bingeing HGTV and talking to myself like the friendless shut-in I am. Shudder and no thank you on all fronts.

Plus, I kind of hate the idea of El thinking badly of me. Like a lot. Even now, remembering the frown that scrunched up the place between her eyebrows when I asked her to . . . how did she put it, "help her to scam herself"? It makes me cringe.

She's the cutest girl I've met in ages. Who also happens to be into *Fast & Furious*. And funny. And hurting now that her sister has disappeared.

Oh no.

Am I crushing on El?

That's ridiculous. I've met her like twice—and thought about her all last night after I left Putt by the Pond, and checked out all her social media, but who's counting that? Not. Me.

Really, there's only one way to confirm if I'm solidly in crush territory: see El again. And that means going to the volunteer gig at a place called Syed Rescue Farm, of which I have vague memories from my childhood visits to this town.

Yes, okay, fine. I also looked up all the club's scheduled events, and planned out the quickest bike route between Grandma Jolene's house and the farm. But there's nothing suspicious about gathering information. That's called being prepared.

Right.

I'm so prepared, I can still remember how El's hand felt in mine as

I helped her out of her kart. And how her laugh sounded. And that she smelled like coconut shampoo and motor oil.

Hello, I am officially a creep. Okay. Time to go see this girl for real, rein all this in—ha! horse puns for a day at the horse farm!—and figure out how to get my license without tricking interesting girls into helping me.

After a shower, clean clothes, and—Lord, help me—some actual winged eyeliner and lip gloss, I pound down the stairs. (Not a crush. I just have on a dress and makeup to look nice. To help brush horses and clean out stables. Ooof. I am in trouble, aren't I?)

As I skid into the living room, I see Dad in the kitchen, working on his laptop. He stares intently at the screen, ignoring me as I grab my blue Doc Martens instead of the usual grimy brown ones I wear to work. Boots and backpack on, I'm almost out the front door when Dad hollers at me.

"JoJo, come in here, will ya?"

I freeze. It's his serious tone of voice. His "we-need-to-have-a-talk" tone. Has he somehow figured out I have the F1 Academy form? Or that I'm hoping to leave Dell's Hollow for the world of racing?

Faking confidence I don't feel, I call out, "What's up? I need to get going."

"Come talk to your old dad for a minute."

A long sigh escapes me. Since Dad's been so busy with finding work and keeping up with his fitness (i.e., riding his dorky bike around the local bike trail in a loop for several hours a day), this is the first time he's wanted to talk in a while. There was a time after Mom died when all he did was lie on the couch and cry. Then, he started seeing a therapist who wanted him to talk, and he pulled me into that. For a few weeks this spring, he was constantly asking me what I was feeling and how my grief was shaped.

Seriously. *How my grief was shaped.* Like I could give a coherent structure to the bone-deep ache of never being able to feel Mom's arms around me again or the finality of her just suddenly being gone.

I had no idea what to tell him then and I still don't now. All I know is that if I keep moving fast enough, my grief doesn't have a chance to catch up with me or to take a clear shape. And that's been enough to keep me going these last few months. Well, that and the hope of getting into the F1 Academy.

"Hi, Street Racer," Dad says as I walk in. "Grab a biscuit. Just made them fresh."

Swiping a biscuit off the pan on the stove (Dad's been baking, which is a good sign, since he's not baked anything since Mom died), I turn a chair around backward and straddle it. "How's it going, Dirty?"

For reasons that are beyond both my understanding and my desire to know, everyone in town, including his own mother, calls my dad, whose real name is Brian Boyd, "Dirty." It's an absolutely unsettling nickname, and I cling to the hope that it has to do with his days as a mechanic and head of Mom's pit crew and not something more sordid. But who really knows with southern country boys and their nicknames?

"Dad," he corrects, holding back a grin. "Please, please don't call me 'Dirty.'" He runs a hand through his thick brown hair—my hair, though the rest of me, from my lack of height to my face shape and eye color, is all Mom—and takes a long sip of coffee.

I pull my biscuit apart, letting steam escape and breathing in the sweet scent of butter and flour. "Fine, how's it going, Dad?"

"Better," he says, gesturing to his laptop. "I've found a job selling car parts online. Should bring in enough money to get us our own place."

It's ridiculous to think that my dad, a man who used to stand by the edge of the most famous racetracks in the United States, cheering loudest of all in a stadium of thousands as Mom's car whipped around the curves, would take a job selling auto parts online.

"Don't we have a shit ton of life insurance money from Mom? And all her money from endorsements? Why do you need to work?"

Dad massages his temples. "We do have a lot of money, yes, but I've put most of that aside for your future. Plus, I need to stay busy."

What he doesn't say is that he hasn't been able to set foot on a track in months. And that he's turned down multiple job offers from race teams across the country. But, still, even if he's processing his grief, I can't imagine him hunched over his computer all day.

"We don't need our own place. I like Grandma's house," I say quickly through a mouthful of biscuit.

"Sure you do," he says with a sigh. "I bet you love sleeping in that tiny craft room on a lumpy air mattress."

"It's not that bad."

It really is, and it makes me long for my comfy queen-sized bed, which has been in storage since we moved. But I'm not telling Dad that. The last thing he needs is to be worrying about me while he's dealing with his own pain.

"And what about Dell's Hollow? How are you settling in here?" Dad takes another sip of coffee.

"That's a totally different question, but I'm figuring it out. I'd be able to settle in better if you let me get my license."

Dad shakes his head. "Nice try, but you know the terms. Do the volunteer stuff, and we'll talk about your license."

I finish my biscuit and stand up. "Well, you're on. As it so happens, I'm on my way to my first activity with the volunteering club now."

Surprise crosses Dad's face. "Really? What are you doing with them?"

"Horse stuff? I don't know exactly, but we're working at the Syed Rescue Farm."

"You're wearing that to go work at the stables?" His eyebrows raise at my purple babydoll dress and leggings, and it occurs to me that I've not worn a dress since Mom's funeral.

I push away from the table. "Gotta go, Dad! Tell you all about it later."

Before Dad can ask any more questions, or try to give me an awkward hug, or say he's proud of me for doing the bare minimum, or really dig into why I'm in a dress for a day of stable cleaning, I hurry out of the house.

When I pull up on my bike, El is already at the stables, looking her usual blend of serious and adorable. Today she clutches a clipboard to her chest and wears a gray tank top, jeans, and scuffed-up motorcycle boots. Once again, there's a pen stuck behind her ear, and she's talking earnestly to a pretty girl in a green hijab. Behind them, inside a paddock, stands a brown-and-white horse. It nudges El's shoulder with its nose, and she rubs its cheek affectionately. Three other kids stand a bit farther down the fence, petting a gray horse and feeding it carrots. I tuck my ridiculous bike away beside the barn and head toward El. My heart, of course, gallops along like a merry horse out for a ride.

*Keep it cool, Jo. You're just here to help.*

"Hi!" I say rather too brightly once I'm beside El and her friend.

Both El and the other girl jump about a foot.

"JoJo?" asks El, her eyes widening as if I've materialized from thin air rather than walked up to her. "What are you doing here?"

"Volunteering."

"But our bet . . . you won . . . you don't have to be here." Her eyes flick to me and then back to the clipboard.

Beside El, her friend nudges her in a not-so-subtle way, and they share a look. Right. They've been talking about me. I know that look.

Ignoring El's confusion, because I don't want to blurt out my real reasons for being there, I turn to the girl at El's side. "Hi, I'm JoJo. Race car driver, new to town, and eager Horse Girl in training." I stick out my hand like a businesswoman, which is probably totally weird and good grief, why aren't I better with kids my own age? I would give anything for CJ to be here, ready with one of our inside jokes and something encouraging to say about my chances with El.

The girl laughs at that and shakes my hand before I can overthink my life choices any further. "I'm Zaynah. Certified Horse Girl™, El's best friend, and future neurosurgeon. This is Pickles." She nods toward the brown-and-white horse. "And this is my family's farm. I'm glad to meet you. El told me a lot about you on the way home from work."

This earns Zaynah a fierce glare from El. But I like her instantly.

"Nice to meet you, too. So, what do I need to do to be part of this group?"

El fumbles with her clipboard and then thrusts it in my direction. "Sign up here and we'll get started. First thing we're doing today is mucking out stables. We'll pair up and then get working."

"You two can work together," says Zaynah quickly, with a gleam in her eye. "I'll see who else needs a partner over there."

"Wait, Z, you don't have to go!" protests El.

But Zaynah hurries away and then it's just El and me. We stand there for a second, and I shift from one foot to another, painfully aware of how overdressed I am for today's event.

El narrows her eyes at me. "So, why did you really come today?"

"I've never mucked out a horse's stable in ninety-three-degree heat. I wanted to see what all the fuss was about."

"In that dress? You look like you're going to a Goth prom."

"It's not like there was a dress code on the paperwork. Besides, this is a totally functional outfit and you have no idea if I've got a Goth prom lined up after this."

El snorts, but her face softens just a bit. "You have to take this seriously, you know. Zaynah's parents are counting on us to do a good job. The work we're doing in the volunteer club matters—to the town, and to me."

I mock salute her. "Fear not, brave leader, I'm here to do good work. Though I will need a pen if you want me to sign this in something other than my blood. Which upon consideration might be perfect as a pre-Goth-prom activity."

"Why are you so weird?" deadpans El as she pulls the pen from behind her ear.

"Why are you so cute?" I mutter under my breath as I sign my name with a flourish and put my email and phone number in the appropriate sections on the attendance form. So much for El waiting until a first date to get my number. Check and mate. I chuckle.

"What?" El takes back the clipboard and pen, her voice tense.

"Nothing. Let's go scoop some horse poop."

Once we're inside the stable, I immediately regret my decision to come to today's volunteer activity. It's not that I don't need the workout—as an aspiring F1 driver, fitness is a huge part of my life and I've not been great about running or training lately—and it's not that I really mind shoveling poop or replacing dirty straw with clean stuff. It's just that El is so damn close, I'm barely resisting the urge to pluck out the pieces of straw that have ended up in her hair. She's also shoveling at a truly alarming rate and ignoring all my jokes.

"So, last night I talked to Grandma Jolene about your sister's jacket," I say without preamble after yet another of my jokes flops.

"What?" El spins around. Her shovel clangs onto the concrete floor and she grabs at it, but misses. "Why didn't you say something sooner?"

I shrug—I guess I'm back to that as my default response with El. "You seemed very busy with the clipboard and the horse poop and my upcoming Goth prom."

El looks like she's going to fling a shovel full of poop at me. "Well? What did Jolene say? Does she know where Max is?"

I'd found Grandma Jolene sitting on the back porch of the farmhouse last night, watching the sun sink below the spine of the Appalachian Mountains.

"Hey," I'd said, plopping into the rocking chair next to hers.

"Howdy. Want some sweet tea?" Grandma had gestured to the glass pitcher and the extra glass on the side table. "I figured you might join me."

I poured myself a glass of the sweetest sweet tea (Grandma Jolene's secret recipe, which is famous for making your teeth hurt after the first sip) and we sat there for a long minute while I gathered the courage to ask her about Max without giving away my interest in El. Which would be tricky, since Grandma Jolene knew me better than I knew myself at times.

"So, I have a random question for you," I said, taking a sip of my sweet tea. "Something about an employee you had once."

Grandma Jolene raised her eyebrows. "Yes?"

"It's about Maxine Blum. Max?"

"Now how do you know about Max?" asked Grandma Jolene with an edge to her voice. "You're not hanging out with her old crowd, are you?"

"No ma'am." I took another fortifying sip of tea. "It's just that I bumped into her sister at the garage and she asked me about Max and I didn't know what to tell her and so I said I'd ask you and . . ."

"Ahhhhh." Grandma Jolene slid me a smirk that looked just like my own. "Little Eliana. I've been wondering how she was doing. Is she a friend of yours?"

"Not even a bit. I just met her today, but she was really worried about Max, and I thought I might be able to help."

"Mighty sweet of you, JoJo."

"I hesitate to use the word *hero*, but if it fits . . ."

Grandma Jolene cackled at that reply and swatted me. "Pour me another glass of sweet tea and I'll tell you what I know, though I'm not sure how helpful it'll be."

There was a lot Grandma Jolene told me that I don't think El needs to know, or wants to hear. I wouldn't, if it was about someone I loved.

"Grandma Jolene does remember Max," I say now to El, carefully. "Though she couldn't tell me where Max is and she wouldn't show me any of her files. But Grandma Jolene thinks the jacket might be with some of Max's friends. She mentioned someone named Riley, who stopped by the shop to pick up the stuff your sister left behind. Do you know who that is?"

El shook her head. "Never heard of him."

I paused, not quite sure how to reply. Grandma Jolene had a lot of things to say about Riley. None of them kind.

"I only know what she told me," I say, trying for casual but coming across a bit squeaky. "But, according to her—and these are Grandma

Jolene's words, not mine—'Riley is an asshole and total dirtbag. He was Max's on-again, off-again boyfriend and they used to get into trouble. He loves bikes and races them illegally, but he also is a jerk.'"

El scoffs as my words land. "That can't be right. Max always told me about her boyfriends. And she wouldn't date a guy like that. I know she wouldn't."

"I just know what Grandma Jolene told me." I kick at a clump of hay. "I'm not sure why she would lie, but it might not be true."

"Of course it's not true," snaps El. She scrunches up her face, as if she's holding back tears.

That look tells a different story than El's defensive words. It says that if Max was keeping one secret from her sister, maybe she'd been keeping other bigger secrets. Maybe El didn't really know the person she misses. Shit. These are big feelings and hard ones.

Suddenly, I know in my bones that getting close to El is about a whole lot more than flirting with a cute girl. If Max was the person Grandma Jolene depicted and not the perfect older sister El had in mind, it is going to hurt for El to wrap her brain around that fact. And I'm not sure how much hurt I can take while grappling with my own pain. Maybe the best thing to do is to leave it alone. Get out of there before I get to know El any better and this tiny crush of mine digs in and becomes anything serious.

El interrupts my thoughts. "So, Riley has Max's jacket. Do you think he knows where she is?" She leans against her shovel, all her certainty gone, her shoulders slumped.

"That's what Grandma Jolene thought."

El chews on her bottom lip. "Max didn't exactly ask me to find her. My parents don't even want to find her, and . . . I don't know how to do this alone." Her voice shudders on the last word, the one syllable, her voice carrying months of heartbreak and doubt.

It's her hesitation that makes up my mind. It's sweet, vulnerable, and somehow it feels like she's trusting me with an enormous secret. Besides, I can't do much about Dad's pain, but this is a problem I can help solve.

"Hey." I put my shovel down and rest my hands lightly on El's shoulders. Her eyes widen at my touch, but she doesn't move away. "You're not alone. Where you ride, I ride, remember?"

El shoots me a tentative smile, making my heart leap. Okay. Fine. This is definitely a crush, I like El, and I don't want to see her hurt. CJ would probably tell me this fierce, protective feeling is due to my not having anyone else to talk to besides my dad and Grandma Jolene, but it feels like more than that.

*Two days, JoJo. You've known this girl for two days. Keep. It. Together.*

I drop my arms and pick up my shovel.

"Thank you," El says, picking up her own shovel.

We finish cleaning that first stable and move on to the next one. Conversation flows, and I find out El's favorite ice cream flavor—licorice! unbelievable—her first movie crush—Letty Ortiz, relatable—and that she likes to sing '80s songs under her breath while she works. ("Girls Just Wanna Have Fun." Adorable.)

After we've groomed the horses and ridden a few around the paddock (my first time riding a horse in years, and it's not like a bicycle;

you definitely forget, and I nearly fell off several times), things start to wrap up. I say goodbye to Zaynah and the others, but there's no sign of El. Which is fine. Totally fine.

Except she's waiting for me by my bi-bicycle.

"Nice wheels," she says, holding back a smile.

"Barely street legal," I say as I strap on my helmet.

"So, will we see you at the next volunteer gig?"

"Remind me when it is?"

"Next Saturday, at the Dell's Hollow Nursing Home. We're doing crafts with the seniors and helping them bake cookies."

That's so not my scene, but I can't say no to El. And maybe there's more to this volunteer stuff than I thought. I liked helping today. I liked being useful, being a part of things.

Maybe Dad is onto something with making me do volunteer work. Or maybe it's just the thought of seeing El again. But whatever it is, I know the answer.

"I'll be there."

"Good," she says, holding up her clipboard. She waves it in my direction. "We can make a plan of attack for the asshole street-racer slash secret boyfriend." Her smile is weak, but at least she's making jokes. "Plus I have your number now." She walks away, heading toward Zaynah and the other members of the club.

"I guess that means this was our first date," I say to myself as I get on my bike and ride away.

# CHAPTER SIX

## El

Blum family dinners used to be a strict No Phone Zone. If my parents caught us peeking at our screens, we lost them till after cleanup, and we had to spend the rest of the meal answering trivia questions on any subject of their choice. Pop songs of the '80s, or state capitals, or the bones of the foot—Dad's pet category, as a podiatrist. Very educational and completely obnoxious.

Not anymore. After we ran down the standard dinnertime questions—How was your afternoon? How are your friends? Anyone know what the weather's like tomorrow?—Mom pulled out her tablet to read an article in *The Post and Courier*. Dad's thumbing through a catalog of heirloom vegetable seeds while ignoring the homegrown eggplant stir-fry on his plate. At least I'm trying to be sneaky in case either of them looks at me.

Luckily, they don't.

I scroll through Max's Instagram with my phone just below the tabletop. She didn't post often and hasn't posted at all since February. The star of her feed was definitely the R1: dull and dinged up at first, then scattered in pieces across the floor of the shop, then whole and perfect, molten silver in the sunlight. Out of habit, I unlike a photo of Max beaming proudly beside the bike just to like it again. As if my sister ditched her phone and is ignoring her email, but still checks her Instagram notifications.

There's a few pictures from Jolene's garage, too. Max arm-deep in the engine bay of a bubblegum-pink Jeep, or racing a coworker across the shop floor, both on their backs on mechanic's creepers. I took that one. I'm here, too, in a selfie of us at the lake, and another of us on her attic daybed, stuffed together into the wearable blanket she got me for Hanukkah. And there's me on the Husqvarna at the track last summer.

But I've seen all of these already. What I'm looking for is the unseen. Some dude I've never met named Riley who, as JoJo said at the farm this afternoon, gives off "dirtbag" vibes. Like a scraggly mustache and a Confederate-flag neck tattoo? Max's judgment wasn't 10/10 (hence the destruction of the Founder's Fountain), but she would never—

"Pass the hoisin sauce, El?"

I snap my head up to find Dad looking at me. Of course, he can't see my screen or read my mind, so I smile through my suddenly pounding heartbeat and shove the sauce across the table. He smiles, too, splattering sauce onto his cold stir-fry. I shovel half of my plate into my face before he goes back to his catalog, and I can safely return to snooping.

When pictures from the last year turn up nothing, I switch over to the photos she's tagged in. I recognize a few of the accounts, like her friends from the garage, or Devil's Paradise, and there's a post from a motocross blog captioned "Where are they now? Teen track stars who never went pro."

Rude.

There's one photo I've never seen, posted from an account I don't recognize: ShellybeanXOX. Max sits in the bed of a mud-splattered acid-green truck, a small crowd stuffed in beside her, all of them flipping off the camera. Which, whatever, it's nothing my classmates haven't done, even if I would never. Colleges look at your social media accounts, and that's a fact. But the boy with the weirdly shaped, scraggly beard crushed up against Max does look a little extra friendly. His arm is across her shoulders, hand fisted in the fabric of her jacket sleeve. The jacket.

I tap on the account, where ShellybeanXOX is definitely the star of her own feed. But Max is there pretty regularly along with the rest from the truck, sitting on plastic lawn chairs on a strip of dirt in front of an average apartment building. Or in the parking lot of a twenty-four-hour diner, posing beside their bikes—Max with the R1, Bad Beard and some of the guys with GSX-Rs (figures they'd be Gixxer boys). It's hard to find pictures where Max is there and Bad Beard isn't. It's also hard to find pictures where they don't all have a bottle in hand, even though I never saw my sister drink. She was like, this fifteen-year-old kid racing star into "eating clean" whenever she wasn't jogging around town or doing chin-ups in the basement.

I mean, she is twenty-two now, and hell, I've had a beer or two at a party in the woods behind Jenni Lynn's house. No big deal. It's just . . . surprising.

Though I don't recognize the people, I actually do know the place where my sister seemed to spend a lot of time—the Piney Bend Apartments in Deerfield, not far from Devil's Paradise. It's across from the 7-Eleven where we'd always stop to get Gatorades and trail mix after a track day. Max never told me she had friends who lived there.

I copy the link to the picture of them all stuffed into the clown truck, then pull up JoJo's freshly saved number and send it along.

**EL:** I think I found something

The dots appear and disappear a few times, long enough for me to anxiously scarf down a whole slab of Mom's garlic bread. Then she replies.

**JoJo:** What, the guy with the knockoff Iron Man beard? Is that Skeezy Riley?

**EL:** Maybe. They definitely hung out, but I never met him

**JoJo:** I bet she wanted to spare you from suffocating on his body spray. Look at him, you know he smells like patchouli and manstank

**EL:** He definitely does

**JoJo:** So . . .

**JoJo:** When can you pick me up tomorrow morning?

It's flattering that she's ready to ride at dawn for me (or like, 10:00 a.m.). Though it's also possible—probable, even—that she's a new girl in a small town with no car, and is just incredibly bored. Either way, I hide my smile by stuffing more garlic bread into my mouth until I can get my face under control. Then I ask my parents, who are busy chewing silently, "Can I take the car tomorrow morning?"

"Where to?" Dad asks automatically.

"Um, to hang out with JoJo."

Mom looks up from her plate. "Who?"

"Just a girl. She joined volunteering club, and I want her to feel, you know, welcome or whatever." None of this is a lie, except for maybe the "just" part.

"New in town?"

"Yeah, but you already know her family. She's Jolene Boyd's granddaughter."

Mom frowns, and I start to panic, because that last part might not help my case. Mom has kind of a weird *thing* about Jolene, who saw so much of Max in the year and a half she was home when my parents saw so little.

Anticipating trouble, I rush to say, "We probably won't get to hang out much outside of the club meetings, since she has a job like me. Did I tell you I picked up an extra shift on Monday? Also, Dad, do you think you could look at the latest draft of my application essay? I know it's not due for months, but I thought since you're in the medical field, you could—"

"Okay, Eliana." Mom cuts me off with a tight smile, but her voice is soft as she adds, "You know it's not that we don't trust you, right?"

Possibly she kicks Dad under the table, because a second later, he echoes, "It's not that we don't trust you."

"Yeah, I know."

"We see how hard you're working," says Dad.

"We know you're not . . . you've never given us a reason not to trust you," says Mom.

Mission accomplished, then, and it should feel good, even if I have to ignore the almost-spoken *We know you're not your sister*, all while I hide the evidence of my plans to follow in Max's footsteps beneath the dinner table.

The Piney Bend Apartments haven't changed since my last track day with Max. Same cluster of squat, plain brick buildings on the corner across from the 7-Eleven, with stained AC units hanging out the windows. Same thin strip of dirt and crabgrass around each unit. But I swear I would've noticed this green abomination in the parking lot if it had been here back then.

"Target fucking acquired." JoJo grins at me.

"I don't know." I eye the truck, two spots up from us, while keeping low behind the steering wheel of the Oatmobile. There's a covered bike beside it, a thick chain snaking under the tarp and winding around a NO PARKING signpost. "That could be anybody's, not just Riley's. And we don't even know if Bad Beard is Riley."

"But whoever that truck belongs to, they definitely know Max, right?"

"Right." Deep breath. "Now what? We could . . . What if we throw a rock at the truck? Not at the windshield, you know, just at a wheel or something, and it sets off a car alarm. Then we run back here to watch who comes out of what door when they hear the—"

"Oh my God, criminal mastermind. What if we knocked on doors instead of getting ourselves jumped in a parking lot?" JoJo asks, aghast. "Look, just pull up those pictures, and we'll check for the apartment number."

I didn't think *she'd* be the voice of reason today, but yeah, that makes more sense.

I have to scroll past some text notifications from Zaynah to get to Instagram; I'll answer when we're not on a stakeout. In one of Shelly-beanXOX's photos, a shot of the truck-bed crowd sitting on a stairwell with Max in Bad Beard's lap, there's an apartment 26B in the background, the party spilling out through the open door. I tip the screen toward JoJo, and when she leans across the console to look, the AC vent blows a strand of pink, citrus-smelling hair into my face. How does she work in a garage all day yet smell much better than me?

For the fiftieth time this morning, I doubt myself. I'm staking out the apartment of a stranger, somebody Jolene said was the worst, with another somebody who, as of a few days ago, was a total stranger to me. Maybe back in Charleston, JoJo was considered the worst. What do I really know about her? Aside from her family's horrible tragedy, and her hopes and dreams, and the smell of her hair . . .

Well, I know she hasn't once judged my sister, no matter what I've said about her, or judged me for wanting to bring her home. And I know I feel a little braver just sitting beside somebody fearless, the same way I used to on the back of the R1, fully believing that Max was strong enough to steer us around any hairpin turn no matter how scary it looked peering out from behind her shoulder. I guess that's enough for me.

Climbing out of the minivan, we cross the heat-hazed parking lot and follow the signs to apartments 15–30 in the second building back from the road. 26B is up a three-flight staircase. We stand on the familiar landing to face the peeling green door.

"Ready?" JoJo asks.

I'm not, but I knock anyway.

When a full minute goes by, I knock again.

At last, we hear low muttering behind the door, and the rattle of various chain locks. When it opens, a guy in frayed pajama pants leans against the frame, blinking in the daylight. No wonder. The living room behind him is still dark, the dingy-looking vertical blinds drawn, even though we got off to a later start leaving Dell's Hollow than we'd planned. Squinting into the gloom, I see bare walls, a collection of mismatched beanbags and chairs, and a shallow sea of trash—mostly fast-food containers, and an overfull cereal bowl being used as an ashtray. A skinny cat picks its way through the debris, poor thing.

"Help you?" the guy asks, not sounding all that eager to help.

If JoJo weren't right behind me, I'd take a step back. Instead, I paste on my "good kid" smile: The one that wears down grumpy senior citizens when I'm volunteering at the nursing home, or coaxes a recommendation letter out of a teacher with way too much on their plate. "Hi, good morning!" I chirp. "You don't know me, but I think you might know my sister, Maxine Blum. Or maybe somebody who lives here does?"

Scratching his hairy jaw, he looks me up and down. "You're Max's sister?" He snorts.

"I—yes, her younger sister."

"Obviously."

"And . . . are you Riley?"

The guy shakes his head. "That's my roommate."

"Oh, great. Could you go get him?"

"He's still in bed. Want to come in and wait?"

As he shifts position in the doorway, I catch sight of a dully glowing fish tank on a TV stand in the corner behind him. The water's only half full, green, and furred with algae. I don't see anything living in the depths. I briefly imagine my parents peering into the water when the cops (no doubt watching the apartment as we stand here) call them to come and collect me, after raiding this place for God knows what. Mom and Dad realizing that I not only lied to them but willingly walked into the home of a man with a tank like that . . .

"We're good out here," JoJo answers for both of us.

"Might be a minute."

She shrugs, leaning against the staircase railing until at last, he shrugs back and turns to go inside.

When the door shuts behind him, I let my smile slip away. "They can't be Max's friends," I insist, keeping my voice low. "She had local bike friends, sure, but that guy? He's like the dudes with mohawk helmets who wheelie through traffic. And did you see the fish tank?"

JoJo frowns. "She wouldn't be the first girl to fall for a loser. Thank

God we both dodged that heterosexual bullet, right?"

Suddenly I'm smiling again, against my will. "I've dated boys, you know. Well, one boy. I went to the winter fling with Aaron Fuller in ninth grade. He was sweet. His mom drove us to Shake Shack after."

"Ah, young love."

"So you've never? Dated a boy, I mean. Or have you, um, ever dated?" I scuff my sneaker over the concrete of the landing, where it catches in a slick of something long dried, but still sticky.

Before she can answer, we both jump as the door swings open again, revealing a bleary-eyed Bad Beard. He's wearing a T-shirt, at least, and a pair of baggy jeans with the knees permanently pinched outward. "You're Max Jr., huh?" he croaks at me, clearly freshly woken.

"Max is her sister," JoJo says defensively, stepping up beside me. "And we're looking for her."

"We're looking for her riding jacket," I hedge. "Brown leather, with a hood, and a zipper that goes like this?" I trace a diagonal line across my chest with one finger, though he isn't really looking at me.

"So, what? You want Max's address, or you want the jacket?"

My heart stutters, then speeds up. "Both, if you have them."

"Do you?" JoJo asks, eyes sharpening.

"Maybe I do. What will you give me for them?" Riley's mean little smirk feels like a challenge.

"Um." Stupidly, I pat my shorts pockets, like I'm carrying a thick stack of cash to hand over instead of a hair elastic and the keys to the minivan. "I get paid next Friday—"

"What about her bike?"

I imagine the R1 tucked safely inside our backyard shed—Max's favorite thing in the whole world, which she charged me with keeping safe for her in her very first postcard. "No."

Riley scratches his beard. "I'll make it fair. I'll race you—you win, you get the jacket and the info. I win, I get the bike. Not like it's yours anyway."

"I can't. That's . . . I just can't."

"Then how about you come back here when you grow up a little and you're ready to take a risk, huh? I'll AirDrop my Instagram and you let me know when you're ready to race." Riley swipes something on his phone, and mine chimes with a notification. He purses his lips to blow a grotesque little kiss through the snarls of his strange beard, and then, snickering, shuts the door in our faces. The bolt clicks, and the chain locks rattle into place.

I stand there feeling lower than dirt—lower than the downward-creeping roots of my dad's vegetable garden—until JoJo takes my hand in hers and tugs me gently back down the stairs into the sunlight, so bright that it hurts.

# CHAPTER SEVEN

## JoJo

El drops my hand as soon as we reach the minivan. Which is a shame, because it felt right there, resting in mine. But she's also dealing with a lot—I can only imagine how shitty she feels knowing her sister was with that guy—not that I can say anything about that. So, I just keep quiet as El unlocks the car. As I open my door, her hand reaches out, resting on the handle.

"Thanks again for going with me," she says, casting a quick glance back at the apartment building. "I mean, you didn't have to. And this could've been dangerous, but I'm glad you're here."

I'm not quite sure what to say, so I default to humor, as always. "Absolutely. That guy was . . . not great . . . which is to be expected, I suppose, based on someone with a beard that bad."

Mercifully, El laughs at this. "He was awful. And did you see that living room? I swear you could've planted crops in the dust on top of the coffee table."

"The fish tank was also a crime. And I wanted to steal their cat away from them. Grandma Jolene always says to never trust a man who can't treat his pets well."

"Amen to that."

A long pause stretches between us. "I'm sorry though," I say, twisting a piece of hair that's come out of my ponytail. "I really hoped we'd find out more about Max."

El swallows once. "Me too." Her voice is wobbly. "But maybe Max doesn't want to be found. Maybe I should give up."

I fight every part of me that is Grandma Jolene's granddaughter and don't offer El a hug or a sweet tea for her sorrows. "Not a chance. If this were a detective show, I'm certain this is where someone would say, 'That guy's hiding something. I can feel it.'"

El scowls. "He definitely knows how to find Max, unless he's totally lying. But how do we get him to tell us?"

I smile, confidence filling me. Feelings are hard, but racing, that's easy. Or easier at least. "We race him for it?"

"With what? I'm not risking my sister's bike; I've never even raced it before."

"Then I'll race him."

"You don't even have a driver's license. Or a car." El looks pointedly at what she calls the Oatmobile.

She's not wrong, but she's not completely right, either. Mom's car isn't running yet, but it could be. "All details we can figure out later."

"Those are hardly *small* details."

"Trust me. We'll come up with a plan. Now, come on. Cheer up. I'm buying you lunch."

"From where?"

"The Shake Shack, of course. I saw one as we drove into Deerfield."

El looks at me through her eyelashes, looking so cute for a moment as understanding dawns on her face. "JoJo Emerson-Boyd. This is not a homecoming dance. There's no need to get so fancy."

I bark a laugh. "What can I say, you're worth it."

El laughs as well and we spend the rest of the ride to the Shake Shack laughing and talking about El's shortish racing career and who's winning on the F1 circuit this season. By the time we get milkshakes and fries to dip in them, El's decidedly more cheerful.

Once we're parked outside Jolene's house, a long silence stretches between us. I want to say something cool, memorable. Something that conveys how much I like hearing her laugh.

"So, see you on Saturday at the nursing home?" I blurt after slurping up the last of my strawberry milkshake.

It is neither smooth nor interesting, but a relieved look flashes across El's face. Because, right, we're just barely-maybe-sort-of friends. Nothing more.

"Yes, see you then. And in the meantime, I'll try to think of a way to get Max's jacket."

"We'll figure it out." I hop out of the minivan and hurry into Jolene's house, forcing myself not to look back.

Have you ever thought about what it's like to sit behind the wheel of an F1 race car? Maybe you know something about the drivers, the teams, the drama, the money, the crashes. But underneath all that stuff, there's a feeling. Gloved hands resting on a wheel. The sick-sweet-heady-broiling perfume of asphalt and exhaust. The enraged roar of twenty high-test, expensive engines and the voices of hundreds of thousands of people crowding the stands. There are the hopes of all the drivers, their nerves, their sweat, the half breath after the last red light is lit and then LIGHTS OUT AND AWAY WE GO—there's the moment everyone pushes their feet into the gas and it begins.

After that, it's a scramble for position and dozens of laps around a track, each one with the potential for glory and danger. Your wheels hug the curves, you check out of the corner of your eye for other drivers. There's a too-tight turn, a miscalculation, a sliver of bad judgment, and the car beside you goes spinning off into the gravel or careening into the wall.

It's a place where milliseconds matter, where death lurks at every turn, and where the sweetest victory can be stolen in the span of an exhale.

I haven't driven anything as supreme as an F1 car, but when I raced I had the sweetest taste of a fraction of what it must have been like for those drivers. God, I miss it.

As I sit at a long table inside the Clearview Senior Center and Nursing Home's leisure and activity room on Saturday morning, stringing beads onto a piece of ribbon and listening to Mrs. Delores Russell, a pint-sized white woman with purple hair that matches her purple lipstick and plum-colored dress, explain why she can only eat peas on Thursdays, I can't help but think of how I used to spend every Saturday at a racetrack, either in my own car or watching Mom race. If I close my eyes, I can almost feel the rumble of the cars shaking the ground as they fly past. There's the hot wind in my hair as Mom pulls into the pit, and the nerve-wracking stress as her crew changes her tires in mere seconds.

She was so good. So fast. So clean in all her driving, always. What had happened the day she crashed? Had it been because she and Dad had argued that morning? Or was it something else, some small thing that—

"Are you sure you want to go with the blue?" Mrs. Delores Russell asks, interrupting my thoughts as she glares at the teal-blue-purple bead pattern I've been stringing.

Before I can reply, a cheer fills the room. Behind Delores, the TV is on and a group of other Clearview residents watch an older episode of the Netflix F1 show *Drive to Survive*, eagerly cheering for every team and arguing whether or not Lewis Hamilton will be world champion this year. I long to join them, since Dad doesn't even let us put racing on at home anymore, but I told Delores I'd help her make jewelry for her granddaughter, so I'm stuck at the table.

"I think the blue works here," I say, holding up the bracelet.

Delores purses her lips. "My granddaughter hates that color. Go for pink."

"What about green?"

This makes Delores glare at me over her coffee. "Pink. And make it quick. We've got a lot of other pieces to make." She gestures to the complete jewelry set she's drawn out in her sketchbook.

Delores used to be an artist, but now her hands are too unsteady to string beads, so she sticks to designing complicated patterns for volunteers to bring to life. Already she's told me three times how disappointing I am at bead stringing and how wrong my color combinations are for this bracelet.

Gripping the already-strung beads, I yank them off the ribbon. They pool in my hand, and I glance up at the clock hanging above Delores's head. It's 12:45, and there's still no sign of El, although the volunteer event starts soon. Of course, it's my own fault for arriving half an hour early, but I thought I might catch El and see if she'd come up with any ideas for getting Max's jacket back from Riley. I could've just texted her, yes, but that feels like a friendship line we're not quite ready to cross yet.

Across the room, a loud gasp cuts through the TV viewers. Delores and I both turn to watch as an F1 car—someone on the Haas team by the looks of it—spins out, cutting across a tight field of other race cars. Three drivers—Ferrari, Aston Martin, and AlphaTauri—smash into each other, and fenders, wheels, and other car bits go flying, but my eyes don't leave the white Haas car. It crunches as it hits the side rail, crumpling in on itself. A fire erupts, and there's a collective intake of breath inside the nursing home.

"Get out of there!" shouts one of the seniors, an older Black guy with white hair and a deep voice. He waves his hands at the driver, as if that will help.

As if anything will help.

All at once, my breath has been stolen. All at once, it's February of this year all over again. I'm at Daytona. There are three laps left in the race when something goes wrong. Mom's in the lead and then suddenly, she's not at all. Where she should've taken a curve easily, she spins out. Her car hits the side of a wall at full speed and then ricochets across the track, flipping and bouncing in a way that makes my stomach churn. Mirrors, parts, and pieces of her car wing off, littering the track. As her car slides to a stop in the center of the track, flames start at the engine. The other cars fly past, still racing, even as flags are waved, telling the drivers to slow down. A safety car is sent out. Dad shouts into his headset. Then, he's running toward Mom's car. I stand in the back of the pit, unable to move, my feet stuck to the floor like they've got magnets on them. There's a TV in front of me, broadcasting live coverage of the race. The announcers are saying something about the crash. I remember feeling out of my body, somehow there but also far away. All of me desperate for this not to be happening. Mom was supposed to take me to get my license tomorrow. It was going to be a celebration—when she won at Daytona, I got my license. Then, we would go to the Caribbean for spring break as a family to celebrate.

But no. It all came apart in milliseconds.

The top of her car was crunched, like a soda can that had been stepped on, but even on the TV, I saw her struggling to get out. There was her arm, her face for just a moment.

"Mom!" I had yelled, my voice lost among the thousands of others. Then, my feet started to move again. I had turned away from the TV, breaking all of my dad's rules by rushing toward the track. Hands grabbed for me, pit crew members and other people on her team—"Don't, JoJo! It's not safe to run out there on the track!"—but I didn't care. I pulled away, surging toward Mom's car. If I could get her out of there, she would be okay. We could be okay. Life could go on as it had before.

"MOM!" I yelled again, but just as I was close enough to see her face, strong arms pulled me back.

"JoJo!" It was Dad. His face was red, his voice frantic. "What are you doing out here?"

"I have to get to her, Dad. We have to get her out!"

He waved toward the safety team. Part of them was trying to put out the fire and the other was working to cut Mom out of the car. "They're working on it."

"They're not working fast enough!"

"We have to let—"

That was when the fire found her fuel tank. A great, heaving blossom of orange and red, it surged upward. The explosion sent us all sprawling. I'd landed hard on my belly, gravel digging into my hands. Dad had flung himself over me, making a dome of his body as metal and fire rained down around us.

Mom never made it out.

The beads in my hand clatter to the floor, spinning wildly under the table and dancing across the room.

"Shit," I swear, dropping to my knees and crawling under the table to pick them up. Tears fill my eyes. This is why I don't think about the crash. Why I work so hard to keep racing separate from that day in my mind. Because if I think too closely about it, I'll never get into a car again.

And that's just not acceptable.

Mom wouldn't have wanted that and she always knew how dangerous racing could be. "That's part of why I do it," she had told me. "Because it makes me feel alive. Even when it could kill me. There's a certain feeling that I'm always chasing."

Another cheer fills the room. I stop trying to catch rolling beads and look up. On the TV, somehow, the Haas driver stumbles out of the still-burning car. He waves his hand, and moves toward the safety crew that's been dispatched.

Lucky bastard. Why did he get to walk away and Mom didn't? Who decides these things?

*Fuck.* It's just so unfair.

"You missed some," a familiar voice behind me says.

I swipe at my tears as El appears beside me on the ground under the table, holding a handful of blue and teal beads. She glances at the TV and understanding crosses her face.

"I was wondering if you still watched races," she says softly.

"Sometimes." There's too much ache in my chest to lie.

"Do you miss it?"

"Always."

"But not the crashes."

"Not the crashes."

She takes my hand, opening my clenched fingers. The beads fall from her palm into mine, hitting the others gently. Her hand lingers as she closes my fingers over the beads. "It's okay to not be okay. I know people always say things like that, but it's true."

Before I can reply, Delores pops her head below the table. "What are you two doing down there?" She eyes the closeness between us suspiciously. "We're making bracelets here, not gabbing all day."

"Be right there, Mrs. Russell," El says. "I brought you some new charms from the craft store." She fishes a small brown paper bag from the pocket of her shorts and holds it out.

Delores takes it eagerly and turns away, leaving me and El beneath the table.

"Did you think of anything yet?" I ask El. "So we can race Riley?"

"Not really. I wish we had a fast car, but I hardly think the Oatmobile will beat him. He probably wouldn't want it anyway."

As soon as she says it, I decide what to do. And I think Mom would approve. Her words whisper in my mind: *There's a certain feeling that I'm always chasing.*

Maybe helping El will bring me that feeling.

I let out a deep breath. "I have an idea of where we can get a car, but it's going to take some planning. And some work, since it currently doesn't run."

El raises an eyebrow. "Want to come over to my house tonight to figure it out?"

I definitely do.

"Yes."

"Come by at seven. My parents are going out to dinner."

"GIRLS!" Delores is decidedly not happy that we're still under the table.

El shoots me a knee-melting grin and clambers out of my space, leaving me a little breathless.

*There's a certain feeling that I'm always chasing.*

As I stand up, too, I know exactly what my mom meant, in more ways than just on the racetrack.

# CHAPTER EIGHT

## El

This is not a date.

One failed stakeout and a run to the Shake Shack doesn't make JoJo and me anything but coconspirators who can finish off three orders of spicy cheese fries. Tonight is just another strategic meeting of the Find Maxine Blum Club.

So ask me why I'm running around my house like an anxious chicken at quarter to seven. Picking stuff up only to put it down an inch to the left, setting drinks on the counter next to the pickle chips just to shove them in the fridge a minute later to keep the cans cold, tucking away anything particularly embarrassing in my bedroom. I plunge my granny underwear to the bottom of my laundry basket. The only moment I stand still is to text Zaynah back, belatedly:

**Zaynah:** What are you up to tonight? Want to go to the Fry Basket?

**Zaynah:** ?

**Zaynah:** Helloooo El?

**EL:** Sorry, my parents want me to stay in. Tomorrow?

I drop my phone back on my nightstand, not sure why I've lied to my best friend, except that I don't think my nerves could handle a bunch of looky-eyes emojis and question marks. And because this is *not* a date.

By the time the doorbell rings, I've worked up a sweat even with the AC roaring to keep up with the heat wave outside. I towel my forehead on the hem of my cropped floral tank—but not like kitchen-curtains floral, like *I don't assume there's anything happening here just 'cause we're girls and we're gay but I can't help it if I look pretty tonight* floral—and catch my breath before opening the door.

Of course, JoJo looks exactly how she did at Clearview this afternoon in cut-off denim shorts and a faded, oversized ringer tee, hair half-fallen out of its jumbo claw clip, a fabulous new beaded bracelet still tied around her wrist. See? This is definitely not a date. But she beams up at me from my porch like she's skipped dinner and I'm a welcome helping of spicy cheese fries, which makes my heart do silly things.

I guess I stand there trying to quiet it for a moment too long, because JoJo has to ask, "Can I come in?"

"Yeah, yeah, of course." Stepping aside, I tug an elastic out of my back pocket and scoop my hair into a super-short ponytail, undoing the half hour I just spent baking beneath the iron to curl it, while JoJo kicks off her sneakers. "Did you eat already?" I ask. "We have pickle chips."

The height of romantic gestures.

"I ate," she says, "but I could drink. I rode over, obviously, and it's hotter than hell's ass out here."

Behind JoJo's shoulder, I see her bicycle on its side on our front lawn. "Oh my God, I should've offered to pick you up!"

"Well, pour me some soda and make it up to me," she says. And then she *winks*.

I wipe my sweaty palms on my shorts as I lead her toward the kitchen. JoJo glances around us at everything I stopped noticing long ago, but now, I wonder what she thinks of it all. The SHALOM cross-stitch in the hallway. Mom's yoga candles (which I'm pretty sure she bought from a white woman's Etsy shop). The bowl on our kitchen counter overflowing with Dad's freshly picked onions, even though nobody in the house likes them very much. JoJo stops in front of the fridge to look at a photo of me and Zaynah that's been there since sixth grade. "Eliana Blum, you were adorable," she declares.

"Look away," I insist, wincing at the version of me in the picture. All braces and elbows and my long, frizzy hair before I discovered leave-in conditioner. "We'll take some stuff up to Max's room—if my parents come home early, they won't bother us up there."

I'm anxious, all of a sudden, about showing her the attic. What if JoJo hates it? What if she sneers at the egg yolk–yellow walls the way she once sneered at Dell's Hollow? I think that might kill me.

But she doesn't. Loaded with Coke cans and snacks, we make our way up the attic's spiral staircase and shove through the shower curtain, and JoJo whistles appreciatively. "Wish I had a space like this. It's pretty tight at Grandma's right now. Like I'd sell my soul for a closet. Or a nightstand that didn't double as a sewing table. But this is really cool."

"It is," I agree, relieved. "And look." I crawl across the daybed to tap the poster behind it, where a few clippings and pictures cling to the wall. "Our girl!"

It is, in fact, our girl: Leticia "Letty" Ortiz, arms crossed and smirking in front of her bike from *F9*—the Harley-Davidson Sportster Iron—against a backdrop of billowing red smoke.

"Why's it in Japanese?" JoJo asks, and laughs.

"They didn't make this one in America. Max had to order it from some fan site, and bring it home from school for me at Hanukkah, but I wasn't brave enough to put it in my room. So she hung it up here and said I could visit Letty when I wanted."

JoJo picks up one of the leftover World Market candles still clustered atop the old bureau by the door, giving it a sniff—that's a good one, clementine and honey. "Do your parents . . . Do they not know?"

"Now they do," I'm quick to reassure her, not that it should matter if they didn't. "Not back then. That was, like, four years ago? I was in my brief Aaron Fuller era. Max knew, obviously. I still thought maybe I was bi?"

"But you're not?" She sets the candle down and picks up another, patchouli and cucumber, which isn't such a good one. Her nose wrinkles cutely.

"I'm pretty sure I'm a lesbian. Like, as much as I can be sure. Anyway, I've had girlfriends since, and Mom and Dad know about them. There was Danielle Pérez for a couple months, and then I dated Abby Bacon for a year and a half." We used to joke about me, a Jewish girl, putting Bacon in my mouth, even though we never went that far. I flush a little to remember it with JoJo so close by. "I don't have a girlfriend now, though. Um, what about you?" It's not a slick segue, but she never did answer the question I asked outside Riley's filthy apartment.

Done with the candles, she crosses the attic and drops down on the daybed beside me, propping herself on her elbows and tipping her head back to let the sun through the skylights shine down on her, like a satisfied cat. "No girlfriends. Not, like, steady ones. No boyfriends, either."

"Now, or never?"

"I was pretty busy with training, and racing, and traveling with my parents and the pit crew." Her closed eyelids scrunch for a second, but she sounds fine when she continues. "I am bi, though, and I've dated boys and girls and nonbinary people. But just like, casually. For fun." Opening one eye to squint up at me, she challenges, "Is that a problem?"

"What? No, why—of course it's not a problem," I splutter. "Not for me." *And why would it be, Eliana, when this isn't a date?*

"Hey!" JoJo leaps off the bed, startling me when I'm already on the back foot, as Dad would say. "Does this thing work?" she asks, crouching over the Wii console on the floor beside the small TV and stand.

"Um, yeah. It's a little old, from when I was in elementary school, but it works. I haven't played in a while. We've got *Mario Kart* for it, though," I say, happy enough to change the subject.

JoJo glances back at me, grinning. "How about a race?"

"Aren't we supposed to be like, scheming right now?"

She waves her hand. "We're excellent drivers. We can totally scheme and race at the same time."

It takes me a few minutes to get things going, plugging in controllers and cables. While I work cross-legged on the floor, JoJo helpfully sums up our situation. "So Riley has Max's jacket for sure, and maybe information about how to contact her. Unverified, of course. But he won't give it to us unless we race him for it. And you said you don't want to race the R1—"

"I *can't* race the R1," I correct, untangling the input cable.

"But I thought Max taught you?"

"She taught me to drive it. She used to take me to this abandoned half-built neighborhood development outside Dell's Hollow, and I drove on the highway there and back. But I can't ride it like she can. I couldn't even race the Husqvarna like she could, and the R1 is so much bigger and faster. And I can't lose her bike—even if we found her some other way, she'd throw me in the Boston Harbor when I told her."

"I bet she wouldn't," JoJo says gently. "But okay, the point is, racing the bike is out. So we ask if Riley would accept different terms. Not bikes, but cars."

*Mario Kart* loads at last, the opening theme blasting louder than I'd expected as Mario and Luigi jostle each other on-screen. "You said you have a car?" I ask, sitting beside her and handing over a Wii Wheel. "But it doesn't run, *and* you don't have a license."

"There are some obstacles, yes," she admits.

We choose our characters: King Boo for me, Princess Peach for her.

"So whose car is this?" Maybe I've made peace with the fact that JoJo is trouble—fun trouble, mostly—but I'm not about to steal a vehicle with her, even if she'd look extremely hot in Letty-style heist getup. I have the volunteering club to think about, and college applications, and good God, my parents . . . I don't even want to picture the looks on their faces. It'd tear down every brick in the wall of trust that took years for me to build, painstakingly convincing them with every perfect test score and responsible choice that I wasn't like Max even before they kicked Max out, because things had been rough between them for a while—since Max set her heart on going pro, at least. And all that time, I knew in my bones that of course I was no Maxine Blum. She's got talent and guts, while I've got . . . prep courses and dental floss.

"It's my car," she insists, "because it was my mom's."

I look at JoJo.

She determinedly does not look back at me—just says, "Pick the Special Cup, not the Star Cup."

I'm terrible at the Special Cup (it's not like my dirt bike skills really transfer), but I switch courses on-screen, then carefully ask, "What kind of car is it?" as our characters materialize in the Dry Dry Ruins.

She shifts on the bed to get in driving position, and her bare leg presses hot against mine, our knees lightly overlapping. Though I expect her to, she doesn't move hers away.

I don't move, either.

We launch off the starting line on the green light and past the Yoshi Sphinx, zooming through the golden sand and dodging falling pillars and a Pokey while JoJo explains herself.

"It's an AMC Hornet SC/360 ."

"Is that a . . . fast one?"

JoJo snorts. "It is indeed."

"Why is it at Jolene's?"

"Mom was storing it at Grandma's garage. It's been there a few years now—like I said, it doesn't run right now. But it was always Mom's favorite. She named it Betty. Mom grew up poor. Like she used to tell me there was dirt-poor, and then there was Appalachian-kid-in-the-mountains poor, and then there was what she had experienced. Both her parents were addicts, and she was raised by her great-aunt Betty, who was always out of work. They spent most of Mom's childhood in a run-down trailer that had no running water, and Mom went to school in the same clothes most days. But she loved her great-aunt Betty. And they loved nothing better than to watch NASCAR at the restaurant where Mom started working on weekends. Then one day, despite all odds, a NASCAR driver actually came into the restaurant. Somehow, they started talking, then they started talking shop. He was so impressed by everything she knew about cars and the circuit, he asked her to join his pit crew for the weekend, then permanently. Mom was sixteen. And the rest, as they say, is history. You can read about it online."

And I have. There were many, many news stories about JoJo's mom's meteoric trajectory from pit crew to practice driver to actual NASCAR racer. She'd come out of nowhere and, the minute she turned eighteen, started beating everyone else almost immediately. Sponsors fell over themselves trying to sign her and she was winning races months after starting out. But none of that explained the Hornet, or why it didn't run.

"Where does the Hornet come into this story?"

"Ahh," JoJo says, her voice soft as she concentrates on *Mario Kart* for a moment. "Right, the Hornet. Mom always promised herself she'd get that car if she ever had enough money. She used to keep a picture of it on her wall as a kid, and Great-Aunt Betty, who didn't live long enough to see Mom race, said it wasn't the most popular, but it was the finest car in the world. Mom bought it for herself after she won her first race, and it broke down once in Dell's Hollow, which was how she met Dad. It's not run in a few years, because we were busy with racing . . . and then Mom was gone . . . and it's still here. But I think I can get it running. We just need to get the keys."

I want to hold JoJo's hand, or thank her for sharing her mother's story with me. But I don't want her to think I'm pitying her; I would hate that, if it were me. So instead I ask, "Where are the keys?"

"In Grandma Jolene's safe, in her office. She'll let me work on the car with them, but she locks them up there, so no one will steal the famous car that belonged to DeeDee Emerson."

"How are we going to get the keys, then?"

"I have some ideas." JoJo shrugs. "But first, I have to get the Hornet running. Once we do that, we can worry about the keys."

"What's wrong with it?"

JoJo's eyes light up as she launches into a gearhead nerd-out about fuel injectors. As JoJo's been talking, I've tried to stay on track while avoiding the Pokeys that flail toward me every time I drive nearby. Meanwhile, as Princess Peach, she's been exploiting every half-pipe and dash panel. Predictably, she speeds through the finish line while I'm still gingerly picking my way across the sand. I don't think I could've beat her, even if I wasn't distracted by her wild plan—and a little bit by the feel of her skin still against mine.

But now, with no game to pretend to focus on, I have to push back. "JoJo, your mom's car isn't a fair exchange for a jacket," I state the obvious. "Or an address, if we're lucky."

"Of course it's not. So doesn't that tell you something? You really think I'd race if I wasn't sure I could beat that guy?" She flashes the cocky smile I remember from the go-kart track: a smile that was well-deserved.

"Maybe not. But still. I'm not gonna let you risk it for Max. It's not worth it."

"Well, *I'm* not doing it for Max; it's for you. Like I said, it's hardly a risk if I know for a fact that I can win. And anyway, I do think you're worth it. So promise you'll consider it, okay, Detective?" She reaches over to press Play on my controller, and we're dropped down onto the infamous Moonview Highway track. The traffic light turns green and, just as with the last game, she hits the accelerator at the exact right moment to take off with a boost.

I don't take off at all.

Instead I do one of the bravest things I've ever done, which is probably a low bar. I mean, I wasn't brave enough to hang a picture of Letty Ortiz in my bedroom. I wasn't brave enough to keep it pinned on the track. I wasn't brave enough to break up with Abby Bacon even when she barely answered a text for the last month of our relationship, or after I saw her at the Cineplex with Charlotte Masciarelli when she'd claimed she was busy helping her aunt wash her dogs. I wasn't brave enough to demand that Max stay with me, or to demand that our parents let her stay, because I needed my big sister and that was all that mattered.

But I'm just brave enough to lean in—slowly, so she can see it coming and dodge if she wants—and ask JoJo Emerson-Boyd once our lips are inches apart, "Can I kiss you?"

She nods, her signature grin dimpling her cheeks.

JoJo tastes like Coke and pickle chips and summer, like . . . I don't know, like that feeling of being a kid and playing outdoors past what should be your bedtime on a night like this, the sky still impossibly blue and bright, feeling safe and excited at once. A feeling you don't even know you're gonna spend your life chasing. I haven't felt that way in a long time, but I do now as I slip my fingers through the hair that's fallen from JoJo's claw clip, and she tosses her own controller aside to cradle the back of my neck and pull me down.

Princess Peach shrieks on-screen as something blasts her off the road.

We break apart, giggling, and JoJo's green eyes shine in the sunset glow of the skylight. She smirks (smirks!) before scooping up her Wii Wheel once more. "Pick up your controller, Blum—I bet I'll still beat you."

I do, though King Boo still hasn't left the starting line. "So . . . *is* this our first date?" I ask, my lips feeling slightly like somebody else's lips, somebody braver and happier and luckier than me.

"No, silly," she says as she laps me. "This is our second."

# CHAPTER NINE

## JoJo

If I close my eyes, I can still feel El's lips on mine and taste her strawberry chapstick. It's 7:00 a.m. the day after our first kiss, and I'm standing in Grandma Jolene's garage. I've got the bay doors open, and a cool breeze that smells of earth and the deep valleys of the Appalachian Mountains wafts in. I run a finger along my bottom lip, wishing I was back in El's room, *Mario Kart* on the TV, the space between us nonexistent as El leans in to kiss me.

It was a terrifically brave move on her part—and one I'd been thinking about making from the minute El took me up to Max's attic bedroom. And then again when she'd sat down beside me on the bed. Our legs touching had been absolutely delicious and unbearable, but I still wasn't entirely sure she was into me like that, so I'd sat as still as possible. Not being brave. Until she'd leaned over and asked to kiss me first.

Fearless.

El Blum is fearless, even if she doesn't know it.

Exhaling sharply, I push all thoughts of El away. Today is about Mom's car, not cute girls who kiss me dizzy. I got up before sunrise this morning, grabbed a Coke out of the fridge, and hurried to the garage, wanting a bit of quiet before Grandma Jolene or anyone else arrived. Mom was an early riser; I can't remember a single morning of my childhood when I got up before she did, and I feel oddly close to her as I sip Coke—her favorite drink and her one sugary indulgence—while birds sing and the morning sky shifts from deep blue to lavender.

Slowly, Coke in hand, I pace around Mom's car, running my fingers over the hood, the driver's side mirror, the wheel wells. I can almost see her, checking her reflection in the rearview as she backs out.

Am I really good enough to repair this car? What if I break it while trying to fix it, and it never works again? I'm a driver, not a mechanic really, and the thought of the Hornet falling apart further under my hands causes me physical pain.

Mom's voice floats back to me, almost as if it's carried on the breeze.

"Most drivers are mechanics, too," Mom had said to me during one of our many talks in the garage at our old house in Charleston. "You can't expect to operate a car at the highest level if you don't understand what's happening inside it."

Dad had been telling me something similar for years and letting me help out in the pit when Mom was practicing. I knew how to change a tire before I knew how to read.

But the night Mom told me this is burned in my memory. It was late October, just a week before Halloween, and Mom had just gotten an antique Mercedes as a gift from one of her sponsors. It was lovely— pale blue with creamy brown leather seats—but it didn't work. On that autumn night, she had the hood open. I'd been thirteen, wearing a cat-eared sweatshirt, and my pockets were full of candy corn. I'd won all of my races that spring and summer, but the last three had been miserable defeats. Mom had brought home a bag of my favorite candy from the drugstore and taken me into the garage for some "race car girlie time," she called it. Her version of girl talk. I had other friends whose moms took them to the salon or the spa—my mom did that sometimes with me, too—but a lot of our most important conversations happened around cars. Getting your period? Over the engine of a 442 muscle car. Kissing and consent? Under a souped-up Honda Civic that a friend had loaned Mom, while she was showing me how the nitrous worked. Breaking up with someone? Inside Mom's beloved Hornet with Dolly Parton on the radio.

But, that particular night, rather than talk about the races I'd lost, Mom had put a wrench in my hand. "Don't think; just take something apart."

"This is a Mercedes," I'd said, not wanting to touch anything in the engine. "I don't want to break your new car."

"It's a new-old car," Mom had said. "Besides, you know what you're doing, JoJo Beans. I trust you."

I'd scowled at my childhood nickname, but then I'd stuffed a piece of candy corn into my mouth and taken the wrench, a satisfied feeling surging through me at her trust.

Slowly, painstakingly, Mom talked me through all the parts to adjust in the engine, all the fluids to fill, and all the gauges to check. She let me do everything, watching over my shoulder as I tested things. My worries about my own lost races faded as we laughed and fixed the car. Eventually, many hours later, my hands were grease stained, and all my candy corn was gone. Dad had gotten home after ten and reminded us that the next day was a school day, but Mom had let me keep working until well after midnight.

"I think it's ready," I'd said, after giving everything another once-over.

Mom had handed me the keys. "You can do the honors."

I'd slipped the key into the Mercedes's ignition, praying it worked. It coughed a bit as it turned over, but then it sputtered to life, purring as I gave it a bit of gas. I cheered and Mom beamed at me.

"See," Mom had said, pulling me into a hug once I was out of the car. "You just need to trust yourself like I trust you. You're more skilled than you think, JoJo."

Swiping at tears that have risen in my eyes from the memory, I put my soda down and pop the hood on the Hornet. The noise echoes though Grandma Jolene's garage.

"Trust yourself," I whisper as I stare at the engine's twisting parts and metal guts. That was easy for Mom to say, maybe, but trust won't fix an engine. "Take it one step at a time, JoJo, not all at once."

I could do that at least. Fixing an engine is like training for, or competing in, any race—if you thought about everything you had to do all at once, you'd fail before you started. But if you took it one turn, one lap, one problem at a time, you'd get through it.

Slipping on my headphones and turning on my favorite playlist, I dig into the engine.

Hours later, my phone alarm goes off. It's almost 10:00 a.m., and I've figured out why the Hornet was rattling so much when it drove—there was a split walnut wedged between the tire and the right hubcap somehow, and the engine is running much better thanks to a full oil change and several new spark plugs.

Grandma Jolene waves at me as she walks into the garage, her bangles rattling and a stack of paperwork under her arm. "Howdy, early riser," she says, walking over to the Hornet. "What have you discovered?"

I update her on my progress, and she pats me on the back lightly. "You can keep at it for another half hour, but then I need you to get the tires off that Chevy that came in last night." She nods toward a mini-van that's on the lift. "And I brought you some breakfast. Soda doesn't count for shit, no matter what your mama used to say." She shoots me a sad smile, and hands me a brown paper bag.

My stomach grumbles as the smell of one of Grandma's homemade breakfast sandwiches wafts out of the bag. I hold it gingerly in my dirty fingers, eager to dig in.

"Will do," I say, finishing the last of my second Coke. I quickly check my texts—nothing from El, not even a reply to my good-night text last night, which makes me feel like a total dork, if I'm being honest. But she probably just didn't check her texts after I left her house, and she might not even be awake yet. And as I do so, an auto-generated collage of photos and videos pops up on my notifications screen, with the title "Good Times at the Track."

It's from February, at my last race, which happened a week before Mom died. Glancing quickly at the office, where Grandma Jolene is settling behind her desk, I swipe to the first video.

It's one Mom took on my phone, and it starts with her grinning into the camera, selfie-style.

"Say hello, JoJo!" she says, aiming the camera at me.

I scowl as I stand beside my race car, holding my teal helmet at my hip. "Mom! I have to get ready, stop filming."

She cackles and just walks the video closer to me. I roll my eyes affectionately as she zooms in. "My daughter, the future F1 champion!" she declares.

The video stops then, and the collage moves on. The next picture is of Mom and Dad on the side of the track, making funny faces at the camera. Then there's one of him kissing her on the cheek. Her eyes are closed, and his attention is fully on her. They were always—always!— so cute together.

I grip the brown paper bag in my hand more tightly, willing myself to look at the next few photos. Then, there's a series of race moments: me getting into my car, the checkered flag dropping, my car pulling away from the pack. Then, there's a video of the last few seconds of the race. The camera bobs around as Mom jumps up and down and her voice and Dad's deeper one cut through all the other yells of the crowd. "GO JOJO! PUSH!" Mom shouts. "You've got this!" Dad shouts.

Of course, I couldn't hear them in my car, but I still remember that last turn, the way I went a fraction too wide, my feet slamming on the gas as I shifted, fighting against velocity and physics as I wrestled the wheel back. On the video, it's a blurry second of footage as my car nearly spins out, and then I surge forward, barreling over the finish line a nose ahead of the next car.

I remember how relief had flooded my system after that win. How I felt giddy and exhilarated and exhausted all at once. But on the video, I just hear Mom and Dad cheering, hugging each other, and then Mom's voice comes in right before the video cuts off: "I knew it! I knew she'd win this one! She's fucking phenomenal! So much faster and such a better driver than I ever was at her age."

Dad's reply is cut off by a roar from the crowd and then the video montage ends. For the second time that day, I wipe away tears. This is why I never watch those montages my phone makes—because even though they're good memories from times of great joy, they're so incredibly hard to see now Mom's gone.

"Hey, you okay?" says a familiar voice behind me.

I spin around to see El Blum holding two cups of coffee. I sniffle, close my phone's photos, and then take a long steadying breath.

"What are you doing here?" I ask more gruffly than I mean to.

El eyes my tears, and then thrusts a coffee toward me. "Inviting you to a race," she says, forcefully cheerful, which I'll take one thousand times over pity.

"What? Now? It's not even ten in the morning." I can't help it; my eyes linger on her lips, which are sparkly with chapstick. I wonder if she tastes like strawberries.

"Motocross starts early," she says, shrugging. "Plus, after you kicked my ass so thoroughly on Rainbow Road last night, I figured maybe I should show you my track."

I look her over—is she serious right now?—and grin. "So, you really want me to skip out of work, so we can go see a race?"

"I guess I really do. You in?"

I'm not sure how I'll convince Grandma Jolene to let me go, but there's no way I'm turning this down. "Of course I'm in. Wouldn't miss it for anything."

El grins at me and my heart gives a little sputter, not unlike the Hornet's engine before I got it working.

# *CHAPTER TEN*

## El

Devil's Paradise is my two-mile-long home track full of sharp turns and bermed corners, tabletops and whoops, doubles and triples, and that goddamn sand section that feels as familiar to me as the topography of my backyard, even after months away. It all comes back in an instant when I pull into one of the grass lots beside the track, smell the race gas, and hear the satisfying *braaap* of the revving bikes in their practice session—one of the best sounds in the world.

We roll by competitors parked along the perimeter fence, unloading bikes and equipment and coolers from their truck beds. As we climb out of the car, Jo nods at a young rider in a bright aqua jersey sandwiched between her parents and her 85cc two-stroke; the top of her head only comes up to their chests. "So that was you, huh?"

"I was maybe a foot shorter than that when I started on a 50cc. My first race, I'd only had my hand-me-down bike for a few months, but I wanted to be like my big sister. I remember being scared shitless at the gate. My kneepads were knocking against the bike, my legs were shaking so bad."

"Oh God, me too. I still get nervous before a race. I was nervous at Putt by the Pond, even."

"You were?" I'd never have guessed; Jo seems so effortlessly sure of herself, just like Max. Not that Max never got scared at the gate—she told me she'd just learned to love that part, like climbing the first hill of a roller coaster and enjoying the fear, and I would learn to love it too. I bet Jo does. But I don't know if I ever will. I got older, and my brain got better at cataloging everything that could go wrong, the mistakes I might make, and the ways I'd never live up to Max's reputation on the track, all while idling at the starting gate. I muscled through with hours and hours of practice, with manuals and motocross autobiographies and YouTube instructional videos. And I do love riding, I always have. I'm not afraid to crash. But if I'm honest, it's only gotten harder over the past year to shut out the part of me that decides a jump is too much for me before I've even tried it.

"Well, maybe I wanted to impress you." Jo winks.

I melt.

"How old were you, your first time?" I turn to grab the picnic back-pack out of the trunk so she won't catch me blushing as I amend, "Your first race, I mean."

"Four and a half."

"You're kidding me!"

"Jeff Gordon started racing at five, and he was winning champion-ships a few years later. Mom wanted me to get ahead of his record early."

"Did you win your first race?"

Jo shoots me a half smile. "Not even close. I could barely reach the pedals, but Mom still hung up my participation ribbon next to her giant trophies."

I laugh. "My parents were the same. I was one of the last to cross the finish line out of twenty-five kids, but we went to Putt by the Pond after to celebrate, and everyone acted like I'd won the Nationals. Best victory sno-cone ever." That was back when they were a little in love with motocross themselves and did what they could to support us on the track (and what they could afford; motocross isn't cheap by any means, and we might not be wealthy, but I know that unlike Jo's mom, we had plenty of privilege just to race at all). They sort of burned out on enthusiasm when Max burned out of the sport . . . but I don't need to be thinking about that today.

We make our way across the lot, and Jo slips her hand into mine like it's the most natural thing in the world. I take extra care not to trip over a wheel rut and bring her down with me.

Walking along the perimeter fence, we pass the rider registration table, and the pit where kids wait under shade tents with their parents and their bikes, stretching and hydrating and strapping on their gear. Helmets and goggles, gloves and jerseys, pants and knee braces and boots. On the one hand, it's strange not to be in the pit, but on the other, I feel as light as I ever have at the track in my cropped muscle tank and cutoffs. Plus it wouldn't hit the same, holding gloves with JoJo.

The bleachers by the starting line have filled up, but they don't have the best view anyway. Instead, I lead her to my favorite spot, a grassy hillock under the partial shade of a small white oak where we can sit between races, with a clear view of some of the most exciting parts of the track when we stand against the barrier.

I unzip the backpack to pull out our lunch: salami and cheese sandwiches, pickle chips, and blue Gatorade, my track day favorites, and something of a sequel to the homemade biscuit breakfast Jo shared with me on the way. Jo tears into her sandwich, peering down at the track.

"Tell me what we're watching?"

"Right now the kids are in a practice session, just learning the track, so they're not gonna ride too aggressively. If they do, they'll probably piss off the vets, who'll smoke them even harder. Everyone knows that jerks during practice get lapped in the race. Pro races last around thirty minutes, but everyone competing today is too young, and none of them are riding anything over an 85cc. So they'll go a few laps, more like ten or fifteen minutes."

"Did you ever want to go pro?" Jo asks, fiddling with her Gatorade cap.

"*Hmm.* I mean, probably as much as any little kid who rides twice and thinks she's Tarah Gieger. For a while, I was riding a couple times a week. I guess I stopped going as regularly when Max came home, though. She didn't seem into it anymore, and I'd gotten pretty busy. Anyway, I've never ridden above B Class—that's intermediate—and you need to be an A Class amateur to ride with the pros. That's what

Max was. She could've done it. She already had her AMA license when she turned sixteen, and she could've had the points to apply for her pro license by the time she graduated—sooner, if Mom and Dad had let her homeschool, or get her GED. But they didn't want her to do that."

"Your parents and my dad would have a lot to talk about."

"Why, have you tried to get your dad to let you go pro?"

She's quiet for a moment, then snorts. "What do you think? He's got me riding a bicycle with a basket."

"Yeah, that's rough. But it's probably faster on hills than the Oatmobile."

We toast sports drinks in commiseration before I point to the track. "Okay, they just flagged them off their practice session. They'll ride back to their tents, refuel and lube, whatever they have to do. Then, they'll race."

Twenty or so minutes later, Jo and I stand at the barrier with the rest of the spectators who line the track, though not nearly as many for the youth races as there might be at an AMA event. We can just see the starting gate, where two dozen riders from the 85 junior class are lined up, revving their engines, billowing exhaust. The gate falls, and every kid drops their clutches, opens the throttle up, and takes off, spraying comet tails of clay and sand behind them.

"Who are we rooting for?" Jo shouts.

"Whoever we like!" I scan the field. A few of the kids are smooth and fast enough to avoid the traffic along the straight and ride to the front of the pack. A moment later, number 34 gets the holeshot; as the first racer through the first corner, they've already got a decent chance of winning, even though the race has just begun. Max was notorious for getting the holeshot. "If 34 doesn't mess up in a big way, they could probably hold the lead," I shout back as the pack rides over the whoops in front of us, then momentarily careens out of view around a tight corner.

Jo nods at number 19—the girl in the turquoise jersey—as she takes the corner in a battle for last place. "I'm rooting for 19."

"She's gonna be struggling to make up the time," I say doubtfully.

Jo rolls her eyes, because *duh*, she knows that better than most. "She got a bad start," Jo says, "but she's holding her line."

The kids come back into view as they ride over the dragon's back—like small whoops that move upward in elevation, ending with a jump—and I remember how hard I had to work as a kid to keep my speed up over those bumps, to commit and just go for it rather than crawling over them.

By the second lap, 34 is still in the lead, and 19 has fought her way up a bit.

By the fourth lap, 34's dropped to third, likely over some mistake we couldn't see, and 19 has made it to mid-pack. But then the white flag is waving at the starting line; they're on the final lap.

When the checkered flag signaling the end of the race goes up, 34 has wrestled back into second place, while 19 finishes just around the middle. Jo screams and cheers for her, and I join in. It was a decent comeback after a potentially disastrous start, and I hope she feels good about that.

If anything, it might feel worse to be 34 right now—so close to the top, and probably spiraling over the mistake they made and couldn't fix. I would be.

"So what do you think?" I ask Jo, settling back down onto the grassy hill to sit before the next race.

She drops down beside me. "Pretty badass! I'll have to find a proper track besides Putt by the Pond to take you to. You can come cheer for me when I finally get to drive again."

"Oh sure. I'll dress up like the flag girls, break out my sexiest coveralls just for you."

Though I mean it as a joke, Jo's gaze drops to my sneakers and drifts up the whole length of my body, leaving goosebumps in its wake despite the scorching heat. "Well, I sure wouldn't stop you," she says.

If we weren't surrounded by various parents, I'd go in for our second kiss. For now, I settle for resting my knee against hers, and finding her hand in the grass, my stomach swooping like I'm riding the dragon's back myself.

# CHAPTER ELEVEN

## JoJo

By the following Sunday, the day of the barbecue at Grandma Jolene's, I'm a mess of emotions. First, there's the family stuff. Normally, for a party like this, Mom and Dad would do all the cooking together, but since Mom is gone, Grandma Jolene has gotten everything catered from a famous place an hour outside Dell's Hollow. Despite Dad's commitment to not driving, he made an exception, since Grandma Jolene, too busy with party setup herself, tasked Dad and me with picking it up, which we couldn't do on our bikes. Now we're en route home again.

And then there's El, whom I've not seen for a week, since she's been busy with work and I've been busy fixing up Mom's car. El reached out to Riley on Instagram, but we've not heard from him yet about a race time. I've been texting with her and thinking about her pretty much nonstop since we kissed in the car after the race at the motocross track. And kissed, and kissed . . .

It's a lot to process while I'm wrapped in the honey-sweet, smoky smell of barbecue, riding along with Dad, who has been tunelessly humming Metallica for the last half hour. I keep checking my phone, hoping El will have sent me something today, but I've not heard from her since we texted goodbye last night, long after midnight. And I don't want to text her again because I already sent a picture from the BBQ place. Yes, I'm excited to see her, but I'm not *desperate*. I've got some semblance of cool self-control left . . . or at least I'm trying.

As we near home, Dad finally stops humming and clears his throat in a time-for-a-Dad-talk-about-your-future kind of way. "So, JoJo . . ." he says tentatively. "It's almost your senior year . . . what are your plans for this next year? And after?"

I inhale sharply, wrenched out of my cyclone of thoughts about El and our kisses and what it will be like to see her again tonight at the cookout and will it be weird and will she like my friends and will we kiss again and—

"JoJo," Dad prods. "Not sure if you heard me, but I asked what your plans are for the future."

"I heard you," I mumble, trying to compose an answer that is more than just blurting out: "I plan on kissing El Blum again, if she'll let me!"

In an effort to buy time, I pull down the passenger side mirror and fiddle with my nose piercing. "I mean, I guess my plans are to get through high school? Do senior year stuff?"

This would be the perfect moment to tell Dad about the F1

Academy, but I don't say anything. Because what if he says no? Better to give myself more time to figure it out than to get rejected outright now.

Dad slows his already glacial pace to let a family of geese cross the country road. "Sure, of course, senior year stuff. But what about after that? Are you thinking college? You could go to one of the UNC schools . . . then you wouldn't be too far from home."

"Dell's Hollow isn't home."

It's an automatic response, but one that rings empty, even to my ears, after the last few weeks. Does Dell's Hollow feel more like home? When did that happen?

*The minute El Blum walked into your life*, whispers a treacherous voice in my head. Or maybe not a treacherous voice, but a true one.

Dad doesn't say anything, his eyes still on the road, but the muscle in his lower jaw twitches, like it does when he's about to cry.

I put a hand on his arm. "I'll keep UNC in mind," I say softly, offering my words like an olive branch. "And I'll let you know my plans as soon as I do. Promise."

The F1 Academy form is still in my messenger bag, which sits at my feet. I'm not sure what I hope to accomplish by carrying the form around everywhere, but I'm hoping the answer will come to me. I got an email this morning from a racing coach in the circuit who'd seen my initial email interest form. The coach and her team had watched my old tapes and wanted to talk. But the same doubts plague me: What if I'm too rusty to race? What if I've lost all my skills, since I've not been on the track since Mom's accident? What if I can't drive anything other than karts at Putt by the Pond these days?

I push all those worries way down and let the scent of ribs and baked beans wash over me. The application isn't due until August 1, meaning I still have weeks before I need to let the academy or any racing coaches know what I'm doing. Plenty of time to figure out my future and get my dad to literally sign off on it.

My best friend CJ, a short, curvy, blond seventeen-year-old, and their boyfriend James, a seventeen-year-old Black trans guy who CJ has been crushing on since we were all in ninth grade, are waiting at Grandma Jolene's house when Dad and I get there. Grandma Jolene has put them both to work in the backyard setting up tables and chairs.

After I drop a tray of ribs on the kitchen table, I rush into CJ's arms. They wrap me in a hug and, for the first time in months, I relax.

"I'm so glad to see you," I whisper, channeling my inner YA heroine and letting out a breath I didn't know I was holding.

CJ squeezes me tight. "I'm glad to see you, too. Now, where is she?"

"Where's who?"

Of course I know CJ is talking about El, because we've been messaging about El and our dates and kisses and *what does it all mean?* this entire week.

CJ releases me and glances around the backyard like El might be lurking behind the shed. "Don't pretend you don't have a girlfriend."

"She's NOT my girlfriend."

"Did you tell her that when you were smashing faces while playing

*Mario Kart* the other day?" James says, a smile spread across his face.

"I hate you both," I mutter.

CJ wraps an arm around James's waist and snuggles against his side. "We love you, too," CJ says, beaming. "And don't worry, I promise we'll be cool when El gets here. James spent at least half the drive from Charleston reminding me not to tell your new lady about that time you peed yourself during a race."

I splutter with fake outrage. "Hey! That was a secret! One that only you, me, and like three thousand other people know, since I was seven at the time and the race was broadcasted on our local public TV station."

James cracks up, and I like him that much more for it.

CJ winks at me. "Every racer starts somewhere. Speaking of that, have you filled out the F1 Academy form yet?"

I pat the messenger bag slung across my shoulders. "It's in here. Already filled out. I just need to get my dad to sign it."

"Promise me you'll ask him?"

"Promise."

"Because if you don't do this, JoJo, you'll be missing out on a huge—"

Dolly Parton's "I Will Always Love You" explodes from the outdoor speakers, interrupting CJ's lecture. Which, okay, I love that CJ is encouraging me. And yes, we've discussed the F1 Academy form a dozen times, but I'm not really ready to confront my missed potential or racing or any other part of that world right now. Thankfully, at that moment, Grandma Jolene and Florence follow the music, bursting onto the porch in a twirling rainbow of silk dresses, clattering heels, gold jewelry, and bottle-red and icy-blond hair. They dance for a moment, swaying in each other's arms, and then Grandma Jolene dips Flo deeply.

"God, I love them," CJ mutters beside me. "Promise me we'll be as fabulous as they are when we're in our sixties."

"Absolutely," I vow, unable to stop a grin as Florence rights herself and then lifts her sunglasses to glance around the backyard. She's a tall white woman with a pouf of blond hair twisted up on her head.

"Where's my favorite almost-granddaughter? JoJo, get over here!" Florence calls out.

I wave and walk toward her. "Hi, Flo. It's good to see you."

She air-kisses both my cheeks and then looks me over. "Well, now, JoJo Emerson-Boyd. Aren't you a sight. You're looking more and more like your sweet mama every day. Which is a good thing because Lord, she was a beauty." Florence shakes her head, making her gold earrings dance. "We all sure do miss her, JoJo."

With these words, Florence pulls me into her ample bosom, wrapping me in a cloud of orange blossom scent that reminds me of a dozen other backyard cookouts like this one. I close my eyes for a moment, just letting myself believe Mom is in the next room, putting out her famous caramel cake and helping Dad in the kitchen.

But of course she's not. And I'm *not* going to start crying now, in front of my friends, Florence, and Grandma Jolene.

"I miss her, too," I say quietly, pulling out of the hug more abruptly than I intended and swiping at my eyes.

Florence pats my shoulder. "I know you do, darlin'." Then she turns to CJ, who she's heard about for years, with a loud, happy exclamation, and gives them a huge hug and shakes hands with James.

"Hey, JoJo!" my dad hollers through the open kitchen window. "Your friends just pulled into the driveway. Can you get the door for them?"

My heart leaps up into my throat like a skydiver in reverse. El is here. Time to let her meet CJ and James and my family.

Dad has set up the kitchen table as a bar, and all of Grandma Jolene's liquor cabinet is on display. He's also mixed up his famous firecracker punch, one of Mom's favorites, and he's placing a large bowl of it on the table as I walk past.

I raise an eyebrow at the bowl. "Is that for all of us?"

Dad sighs. "I'd like to say no drinking for you and your friends, but I was seventeen once, too. So no more than two glasses of punch, fair? And none for any of your friends who are driving." He hands me a glass with a small bit of punch inside. "This one is for tasting purposes."

I throw back the viciously sweet combination of cherry Kool-Aid, whiskey, vodka, Sprite, and a hint of hot sauce. It sizzles on the way down, landing in my stomach like a booze-soaked fireball. "It's perfect. Mom would have loved it."

Dad gives me a watery smile, which I return. There's a knock on the door, and I leave Dad with the punch and hurry to open the door.

El Blum stands on the porch, a box of veggie burgers in hand, with Zaynah at her side. El's short blond hair is in two adorable space buns and she's wearing sneakers, jean shorts, and a black tank top. She's perfect, and I have to fight the desire to kiss her then and there.

"Hi," I say, giving a little awkward wave.

"Hi." El leans in closer to me, and I swear, for a second I think she's going to kiss me right in front of Zaynah.

But no. She points at my upper lip. "You have a bright red mustache."

My hand flies to my lip. "Oh! It's from my dad's firecracker punch. Which is delicious and dangerous."

"I like it," El says.

Zaynah rolls her eyes at that, which reminds me that I should be inviting the two of them into the house, not standing outside flirting with El.

"Come in, please, and help yourself to punch or anything else." I step wide to let them walk past. El's hand brushes mine as she steps through the doorway.

"It's good to see you," she whispers, so only I can hear.

Heat flushes through me at her touch. "I missed you," I admit. And it's true. Texting has been great this week, but I've really just wanted to be alone with El again.

CJ and James appear in the hallway then, and a smug, knowing smile crosses CJ's face as they catch my eye. "El?" they mouth.

I give the smallest of nods and CJ shoots me a thumbs-up. I can feel a blush rising on my cheeks, and I can't stop a grin from spreading.

"Uhm, El, Zaynah, this is CJ and James," I say, wrenching myself a step backward from El. "CJ is my best friend from Charleston and James is their boyfriend and an all-around exceptional human. And this is El and Zaynah, my friends from the volunteer club, who I told you about."

At this, CJ and James both make elaborate, theatrical bows. A laugh bursts out of El, and she and Zaynah return the ridiculous bows.

We all move through the hallway, talking and awkwardly bumping elbows, and then we're at the punch table and everyone except Zaynah, who doesn't drink, fills a red plastic cup with the firecracker punch. Before we can take a sip, Dad shoves us outside as more of Jolene's and Florence's friends arrive, letting themselves into the house without knocking.

The next hour is a blur of older hippies and local folks filling the backyard and greeting Grandma Jolene and Flo, my friends all talking to each other, El and CJ cackling over something but I don't get to find out what because Dad sends me to find more chairs, and then I'm bringing more cups of firecracker punch out for my friends, and then finally, finally, it's time to eat. Everyone fills a plate and my friends and I sit down at the picnic table under a massive oak tree near the back of the yard. My head swims from my second glass of punch, and sweat makes my T-shirt stick between my shoulder blades, but El's squeezed next to me, her bare legs pressing against my own.

"Everyone! Settle down for just a minute, please!" Grandma Jolene's voice rises above the laughter and conversation. She stands on the back deck, her hand in Florence's. "We just wanted to thank y'all for coming out this evening and for helping us celebrate Florence's birthday!"

Florence plants a kiss on Grandma Jolene's cheek, which makes the crowd of people in the yard cheer. Grandma Jolene beams at her and beside me, I swear El scoots closer.

Grandma Jolene continues. "Now, we're leaving for Italy early tomorrow morning, so we might have to head to bed before the dancing stops, but y'all stay as long as you'd like. We're so happy you could make it, and cheers to my family and to the friends who have become family."

It's her yearly toast and it sounds both sadder and sweeter somehow this year.

Grandma Jolene raises her glass of spiked lemonade and says, "To family!"

We all raise our own glasses, and repeat: "To family."

The words catch in my throat as a vision of my mom, sitting with my dad and me under this same oak tree, rises in my mind. Beside me, El makes a small noise as she says it, and without thinking, I rest my hand above her knee and squeeze her leg. Because I'd wager good money she's thinking about her sister, Max.

Family. What a lovely, terrible, messy, heartbreaking, and heart-filling thing all at once.

"We'll find Max," I whisper, leaning in close. "Don't worry, Mom's car is running great, which means we're that much closer to getting Max's info from Riley. If he ever tells us when a race is happening."

"Thank you," El says, her voice scratchy. She takes another long sip of firecracker punch, which paints her lips red.

Before I can tear my eyes away from El's red, red lips, CJ flicks a grape at me from across the table. In one incredibly smooth move, I catch it in my mouth, proving that my reflexes aren't totally a lost cause after all.

# *CHAPTER TWELVE*

## El

I don't need a full hand to count the times that I've been truly tipsy, like beyond a beer in the woods or a plastic champagne flute at New Year's Eve. They are as follows:

**1.** The first Passover seder after my bat mitzvah, when Bubbe and Papa decided I was mature enough to handle actual wine instead of grape juice. Except the thing about seders is you refill your glass four times in the first hour or so of the night while barely munching on matzah and parsley and salt water. I was blitzed by the soup course. I threw up in the back seat on the way home, and my parents were boiling mad at my grandparents. It was Welch's again from there on out.

**2.** My third date with Abby Bacon. We went to a barbecue at her cousin's family's lake house but spent half the night hiding from her (homophobic) grandparents down by the dock, sitting in a pedal boat with the mosquitoes and a bottle of sweet tea vodka for company. We never did find her bathing suit top, which must have floated off into the night while we were, um, pedaling.

**3.** In Jolene Boyd's backyard as the afternoon starts to cool toward evening and, two cups of firecracker punch deep, I *badly* misjudge my cornhole toss, sending my beanbag sailing toward Zaynah's face.

Thankfully, she uses her sober reflexes to duck and cover the top of her root beer can, keeping it from spilling down her shirt. "It's not dodgeball, El," she shouts back at me.

"Sorry, sorry, I'm warming up!"

Zaynah takes her turn, landing a beanbag in the middle of my board for a point.

I line up my next toss as Zaynah steps well out of range, but it flops down in the grass at the bottom of her board, far short of the hole. "Just getting the feel for it," I assure her again.

"This is our second game."

"Well, maybe I'm off today."

"Maybe you're distracted." She raises her eyebrows and stares pointedly in Jo's direction.

Currently playing croquet with CJ and a gaggle of elder hippies across the lawn, Jo has her head thrown back, laughing, the pink-tipped ends of her ponytail swinging. When she bends forward to angle her mallet at her ball, I cannot possibly stop myself from admiring her leanly muscled legs, her tanned shoulders, her ass—

Until I'm smacked in the chest with a beanbag.

"You're leering!" Zaynah whisper-shrieks.

"I'm not, I'm . . . I'm admiring her croquet form."

*"Mmhmm."* Catching the projectile beanbag when I chuck it back, she immediately sinks it through the hole in my board to win her second game in a row. "You know, you could've told me you guys were dating."

That stops me cold. "Huh?"

"Oh, come on. I saw how CJ looked at you when you met, like they already knew who you were. And you and Jo were practically sitting in each other's laps at the picnic table. Obviously, I knew you liked each other, but you never told me you were official." She says this lightly enough.

But the way she isn't meeting my gaze sobers me up a little despite the punch singing through my blood. "I swear, there isn't a lot to tell. And we're not official, I don't think. I mean, we went on one date. Well, two dates now, but I didn't know the first was a date at the time. Or maybe I wanted it to be, but I wasn't sure, and—"

"I'm not mad or anything," Zaynah cuts off my babbling as she crosses the grass to gather her beanbags from the board in front of me.

"You're not mad that I'm dating Jo?"

"I'm not mad that you didn't tell me you two were dating, if you are in fact dating." Now she looks up at me, and she doesn't have the pursed lips of an angry Zaynah Syed trying to seem all right; I think she's telling the truth.

I breathe out with relief. "So, um, what do you think of Jo, then?"

"You clearly have a lot in common. And I like anybody willing to muck out a horse stall. I want you to be happy. Just . . . you can always tell me stuff, okay? Like, I get the feeling that sometimes you don't want to when you think I won't approve, or whatever."

I open my mouth to protest but wonder if that's true.

As much as Zaynah and I have in common, we come from different families with different beliefs. Being Jewish and Muslim has never been a problem—why would it be? We've often been the only two kids in class who wouldn't show up after summer vacation with dramatic Bible school stories to tell. I'd never pressure Zaynah to drink, or date, or do anything she doesn't feel comfortable with. And I've never seen her judge me for any small trouble I've gotten up to over the years. But . . . maybe sometimes, I do hold back. I haven't told her about Max's jacket, or the stakeout, or that I first made out with Jo while we were conspiring to street race Skeezy Riley. Because I know Zaynah loves me, but I also know that she and the Syeds think of my sister the way a lot of folks in Dell's Hollow do. The town might as well have installed a plaque when they fixed the Founder's Fountain, engraved: *It's a real shame about that Maxine Blum.*

Zaynah shakes me gently by the shoulder, tugging me out of that train of thought. "Hey, just so you know, I approve of Jo. Not that it matters."

"Of *course* it matters," I insist, throwing my arms around her in a swell of gratitude, guilt, and for sure some alcohol-induced emotions on top of it all. "You're my best friend. That's almost the only thing that matters."

She drops her beanbags into the grass to squeeze me hard, nearly toppling us both onto the cornhole board. "So," she says, and giggles mid-hug. "If you're dating, then you've kissed, right? And if you've kept dating, that means it was a good kiss?"

"Z . . ." I extract myself to cover my face with my hands.

"Oh, so it was a *really* good kiss!"

"I need more punch for this conversation."

"Then you need more food first." She loops her arm through mine and steers me toward the long folding table by the back door, still set with potato salad and pineapple slaw and blackberry cobbler. Probably a good idea. On the way, I glance over (leer over?) at Jo once more, where she's lining up to tap her ball through a wicket.

Catching my gaze, she pauses before she swings and beams at me, flushed with sun and punch and friends and just *so fucking pretty.*

*It's wild*, I think, *how one girl can turn your whole summer around.*

# *CHAPTER THIRTEEN*

## JoJo

The afternoon after the barbecue, CJ, James, and I drive half an hour north of Dell's Hollow, winding along narrow mountain roads until we're deep in the Appalachians. James parks his secondhand Subaru wagon (a beast of a car passed down to him after being owned by his two older brothers, which means it's covered in stickers and smells weirdly like fast food and sports gear) in a tiny lot beside a metal trestle bridge that crosses the Greenway River. We all pile out and gaze at the river. Sunlight glints off the water, a wide, moss-colored liquid ribbon that runs out of the Appalachian Mountains and curves around Dell's Hollow. There are no major rapids on our local stretch, and today the water moves sluggishly. Cicadas hum, and though a breeze ruffles the dense foliage along the river's bank, the humidity is like a wall.

"I cannot wait to get in the water," CJ says, as they slather sunscreen on their face for the second time in half an hour.

"Don't wait," James says, grabbing CJ's hand. "Race you to the river!"

The sunscreen tube falls to the ground as the two of them dash toward the water, splashing through the shallows and then diving under. Picking up the sunscreen, I stay near CJ's car, looking down the road for El, who should be here by now. A bead of sweat rolls along my collarbone. Today, I'm river-ready in a racerback bikini top and jean shorts, slathered with sunscreen as CJ insisted, and wearing old Tevas that I borrowed from Grandma Jolene's closet. When I'd asked El the night before if she knew any good local things I could do with CJ and James, who were staying the entire weekend after the BBQ, she'd insisted we go floating with her and Zaynah.

"Floating, like down the river?" I'd asked, skeptical. "You mean in like rubber donut tubes?"

"It's amazing, trust me," El had said. "Max and I used to do it all the time, and it's really fun and chill."

Hard to argue with that reasoning, and besides, if it meant more of my friends hanging out with El and her best friend, I was in. The plan was to have El and Zaynah drive separately and leave Zaynah's car a few miles down the river, so we had a way back to the bridge after the float, where James's car and El's car would be. El and Zaynah were bringing all the inner tubes, and they were supposed to be here fifteen minutes ago.

What am I going to do with CJ and James if El doesn't show up?

Of course, why wouldn't El show up? We'd snuck in a goodbye kiss last night after the BBQ, but what if—

Just as CJ tries to dunk James under the water, El pulls up in the Oatmobile. She and Zaynah have the windows down and are blasting music. My heart does a little flip as El waves at me.

"Sorry we're late!" she says breathlessly as she parks the van beside James's car. "We had to get more tubes because one of ours had a hole in it, so we stopped at a friend's house on the way. But we found five!" She opens the side door of the van and several inner tubes tumble out.

My hand darts out to catch one as it rolls toward me. "Thanks for bringing these."

"Of course," El says. "It's going to be great. C'mon."

They're both in their suits, El in a bikini top and board shorts, and Zaynah in a burkini with a hood, carrying a drybag apiece with drinks and snacks inside, as planned.

I want to linger, maybe sneak a kiss in beside the van with El as Zaynah moves toward the river, but El's already turned away, backpack on her shoulders, and gathering tubes. Looping my arm through an inner tube, I follow her toward the riverbank.

After several failed attempts at everyone getting into their tubes, and CJ and James screeching as they flipped on the first tiny set of rapids, we finally manage to get our tubes floating down the river. A lazy, hazy sort of peace settles over me as I trail my fingers through the warm water. Frogs croak from the banks, crows screech from the treetops above us, and CJ, James, and Zaynah belt out show tunes. It's peaceful, and I close my eyes, letting sunlight wash over my face.

A soft bump on my right side startles me. My eyes fly open, but it's just El, holding out a Coke can. "It's pretty, isn't it," she says, nodding at the river and the general landscape.

It really, really is, and seeing it via inner tube, at this pace, makes me appreciate Dell's Hollow and this area that much more. El grabs my tube with one hand, and we float side by side in companionable silence for several minutes as the river bends and gets even broader. My eyes drift over the tree line, watching a hawk soar overhead. On our right, a tree-covered stone bluff rises along one side of the river. It's covered in thick tangles of branches that jut over the water. A rope swing dangles from one of the branches, and a narrow, well-worn path snakes up from the riverbank, disappearing into the trees. There's a pile of beer cans and a picnic table along the bank as well.

"What's that?" I say, pointing at the rope swing.

El glances upward. "There's a super-deep pool—at least ten feet—in the water over there. Max was famous for once doing a double backflip from that rope."

"Is it safe?"

El shrugs. "I've never done it, but no one's ever gotten hurt on it, at least not that I know of."

I track the way the swing moves in the breeze, as our tubes float near the bank. With the bluff and the trees, it's at least as high as a two-story house up there, but it looks fun. Dangerous, yes, but also exhilarating. The thought of jumping off it sends a spike of adrenaline laced with fear through me.

*There's a certain feeling that I'm always chasing.*

If my goal is to be a race car driver again—which it is, at least according to the F1 Academy form in my bag back in James's car—then I have to face my fears. Confront them head-on. Keep moving fast enough so they can't catch up. Which, in this moment, means jumping off the damn rope swing.

"I'm gonna do it," I say as I gently unhook El's fingers from my tube. I start paddling with my hands toward the shore.

"Jo! Wait!" El calls.

But I'm already slipping out of my tube to haul it onto the riverbank. My sandals sink into the muddy bank. "Come with me?"

El swims out of her own tube and sloshes after me. She hollers to CJ, James, and Zaynah, who are farther down the water. They head toward the bank and walk back upriver to join us beside the picnic table.

"I reserve the right *not* to jump," El says as we pile our tubes on the picnic table and start up the path to the swing.

I shoot El a look and thread her fingers through mine, giving them an encouraging squeeze. Of course, it's fine if she doesn't want to jump. This is about my fears, not El's. And having some fun. And maybe, perhaps just a little bit showing off for El.

"I also reserve the right to not jump," Zaynah says, while CJ and James race each other up the twisting, root-laden path to the top of the bluff. She casts a quick glance at El's and my hands and then starts up the path.

Several minutes later, I'm standing above the river, rope swing in hand. I tug on it, making sure it's attached securely to the tree branch.

No problem there. It's fraying below the knot, but it feels sturdy. Besides, it's not like I'm going to be holding on to it long. Below me, the river is dark green, and beyond the deep pool below the bluff, little eddies form around rocks, looking like the lace doilies on Grandma Jolene's living room end tables.

I let out a long, shaky breath as my adrenaline ratchets up. This is nothing like a race, but that same heady anticipation fills me.

"Want to go first or want me to go?" James asks. He's got one hand on the tree trunk and is looking eagerly down at the water.

I glance over at El, who stands between Zaynah and CJ. She offers me a shaky thumbs-up.

I can't help it; I want to impress her. "I'll go," I say.

"Be careful!" El calls out, her hands now fists at her sides, her brow creased with worry.

I shoot her a half smile and then step back, focused only on the five feet of earth between me and the edge of the cliff. I step back, gripping the rope in both hands.

*Be fearless. Run fast.*

*You can do this.*

With one quick exhale, I surge forward, holding the rope. There's a brief, breathless moment when my feet leave the ground and I swing out, hurtling into the air above the river. The rope chafes my hands, and then I release it, plummeting toward the water. Air rushes past my face and adrenaline lights my veins. A whoop of pure joy whips out of my chest because that's right. I love this feeling. This is what racing feels like and why it's worth being brave.

Before I can have any other great revelations, I hit the water with an enormous splash. I plunge deep, sinking into the cool, murky depths of the pool. My sandals hit the pebble-strewn bottom of the river, and I kick off, surging upward. A few seconds later, I break the surface, laughing and spitting out water.

Far above me, James and CJ cheer and whistle appreciatively. Zaynah is also clapping. And El beams down at me, holding the rope swing in her hands.

"C'mon!" I yell out. "It's so much fun!" I swim toward shore, looking upward.

El's eyes meet mine for a moment, and then she pulls the rope back. My mouth falls open as El Blum runs toward the edge of the cliff, letting out a tremendous scream as she flies out and releases the rope.

*Fearless.*

This girl is so brave and I like her so much.

Like I did, El plunges into the water and then breaks the surface a few seconds later, grinning. Her wet hair clings to her forehead and her eyes shine.

"That was amazing!" she cries out, voice laced with laughter.

I swim back to the pool, so I can kiss her right then and there, in front of all our friends.

After many more cliff jumps, we float the rest of the way downriver to Zaynah's car. We wrap up in towels while she makes the drive back to the metal bridge—how had it taken us so many hours to float down the river when it's just a fifteen-minute drive back to where we started?—and we change into clean clothes. As we're packing all the tubes back in the Oatmobile, my stomach gives an almighty growl. I glance at my phone. It's after five already, and I can't face going back to my house, with Grandma Jolene gone and Dad on his computer.

"Want to grab some dinner at Bless My Grits?" I suggest. "My treat?"

Everyone agrees enthusiastically, and we caravan back to Dell's Hollow, passing through the tiny downtown with its two antique stores, florist, nail salon, library, and the Founder's Fountain and park, which is filled with people listening to an outdoor fiddle concert. We find parking spots near Bless My Grits, a small chrome-and-vinyl-decorated diner, which is run by a friend of Grandma Jolene's, and make our way inside. As we slide into a booth, El squeezing in between me and Zaynah, my shoulders twinge with sunburn. But it's been a wonderful day overall, and I'm feeling very loved by all my friends. I feel almost like the me I was in Charleston.

As our cheeseburgers and fries and Zaynah's veggie wrap arrive, El leans in, showing me her phone and a message from Riley.

*Race happening tomorrow night, Benton Creek Airfield. Be there by sunset.*

Excitement surges through me. "This is our chance! Where's the Benton Creek Airfield?"

El bites her bottom lip as she types the name into Google. "About twenty minutes south of here. It's an abandoned local airfield . . . ."

"Perfect! The Hornet is ready to race!"

"Are you sure? I mean, we can always—"

"What are you two whispering about over there?" CJ demands. They flick a french fry at me.

Zaynah eyes us shrewdly. "We'd all love to know."

"It's nothing," El says, glancing at her best friend and then looking away quickly. She seems nervous.

"We're just strategizing," I say. "About how to get Max's jacket back."

Now El looks at me, eyebrows shooting up in alarm. Maybe I wasn't supposed to say anything?

"Who's Max?" James asks, in between bites of his burger.

"My sister," El mumbles.

"What about Max? What jacket?" Zaynah prods, her voice tense.

"We . . . Remember, Z, she sent that postcard from Boston a few weeks back?" El starts twisting her paper napkin into little snakes. "She asked for her jacket back, and JoJo and I are, uh, figuring out how to get it. Her friend said we could have it, if we, um—"

"We're racing for it." I put El out of her misery. And why not? We're among friends. Family, even. Though I notice she didn't mention Max's address as a second potential prize.

CJ flicks another fry at me. "You shouldn't be doing any racing unless it's for the F1 training program."

El snaps her gaze over to me. "What F1 training program?"

"CJ means the F1 Academy," I say carefully. I've still not told El about it. "It's not a big deal. Just something I'm thinking about doing."

Ever the planner and my number one fan, CJ jumps in enthusiastically. "It's a *huge* deal! Like it means Jo will get to travel all over the world, going to all the F1 races and driving in some of them. It could really make her career. She's been carrying around an application for weeks and it's due by August, but she won't ask her dad to sign the form." CJ turns their smile on me.

I scowl back as I pop a fry into my mouth. Maybe if I'm eating, I won't have to answer more questions?

"Will you leave Dell's Hollow if you get into the program?" El asks, a frown between her eyebrows.

I shrug and wash down the fry with some strawberry milkshake. "Maybe? Yes, but the academy doesn't start until the fall. And there's no guarantee I'll get in."

"You'll get in," James says. "CJ has shown me all your races that are on the internet. I've never seen anyone drive like you."

Pride fills me, but it's quickly squashed by the look on El's face. "I've not even applied yet," I remind her. "Besides, the only race I care about right now is the one to get Max's jacket back." The words rush out of me, my tongue loosened by my desire to erase the crushed look from El's face.

"And what race is that, exactly?" Zaynah asks, still fishing for details. *Shit.*

I let out a long breath and look over at El. She nods slightly, and so I fill Zaynah, CJ, and James in about our trip to Riley's place, his demand that we race for Max's jacket (I don't mention the address, since El's apparently keeping that part to herself), and the race that's happening tomorrow night.

"Okay, so even if you did do this illegal race," CJ says, leaning in close, as if the pair of elderly women in the booth behind us is actually listening to our conversation and not arguing about a recent *Love Island* episode. "How would you do it?"

"You *can't* do it!" Zaynah chimes in. "Even if this weren't the worst idea, what are you going to race in, the Oatmobile?" She turns to CJ and James. "That's what we call El's mom's minivan, which is her current mode of transportation."

El rolls her eyes. "No. Of course we're not going to race in the minivan."

I lean in, lowering my voice despite the fact that we're at a loud party and Grandma Jolene is nowhere around. "We're going to take my mom's car."

"Fuck off," CJ says. "The Hornet? No way. I thought it hadn't run in years."

I nod. "I got it working. Now, I just need to get the keys out of Grandma Jolene's safe. She locked them up before she left for Italy."

"Which we're never going to get open," El adds. "Unless you know a safecracker."

"I mean, I do totally have a heist crew I can call." I pull out my phone, scrolling my contacts quickly. "Let's see, to do a heist, who do we need? Hacker, a money person, some muscle—"

"Don't forget an acrobat, for getting into small spaces," James says, with a laugh.

"And a getaway driver . . ." Zaynah adds. "I mean, if you're going to break into Jolene's garage and steal the keys, you'll need someone to help you escape."

"Are you volunteering?" El says, her eyebrows flying upward.

"Begrudgingly. If I can't talk you out of it, I guess I have to help. What's your role in this heist anyway?" Zaynah shoots back. "The muscle?"

"Wild card, of course!" El picks up a handful of fries and pops them into her mouth. "You never know what I'll do!" she manages to say through the fries.

At this, CJ bursts out laughing. "Well, I'm going to be lookout, because I have zero heist skills. And James, you're with me because, well, you're with me."

"And that way we can hide between cars at the garage and make out." James pulls CJ in for a kiss, which makes all of us groan.

Beside me, El scoots even closer, so she's practically sitting in my lap, and I plant an oh-so-quick feather-soft kiss on her shoulder. She leans into the kiss, and a warm, tender feeling along with a heat low in my belly fills me.

This girl.

Good grief.

"What does that make you, JoJo?" CJ says when they pull out of their kiss with James, distracting me. "Who are you in the heist crew?"

"The Inside Woman, of course," I say.

All my friends groan and laugh at that, teasing me and saying it's not a heist if you can easily unlock the safe. Which I totally disagree with because you've still got to break into the garage and get the keys and get out and not get caught. Which causes another round of spirited arguments. And, as we eat our dinner, our plan for breaking into Grandma

Jolene's garage to get the keys to the Hornet quickly goes from a ridiculous notion to an actual plan.

And somehow, as we leave the diner, Motorcycle Girl™ El Blum's hand is in mine, and we're totally doing a heist so we can then do an illegal street race, and holy shit my life is officially a *Fast & Furious* movie, but as El and I sneak a kiss when no one else is looking, that seems just fine to me.

# CHAPTER FOURTEEN

## El

"You're gonna get us pulled over for going too slow, Getaway Driver," I complain.

Zaynah white-knuckles the wheel as though she's smuggling a van full of escaped convicts across state lines and not a couple of sunscreen-and-french-fries-smelling teens, our still-wet hair dripping river water on her dad's car's upholstery. "No, I'm not. Just don't draw any attention to us." She darts a glance at the rearview mirror, in case the cops are in hot pursuit, I guess.

"Well, I was gonna rip off my top, lean out the window, and flash the good people of Dell's Hollow as we go by, but now that you've told me not to . . ."

"You still can!" Jo pipes up from the back seat.

"DO NOT," Zaynah commands.

You'd think we blackmailed Zaynah into driving us when she was the one who insisted, while everyone else left their cars outside the diner; I think she wanted an excuse to stay in the car, rather than actively heisting with the rest of us.

I look back to catch Jo grinning at me. And I wish more than anything that in this moment, I didn't feel a sharp pang . . . of *something*. I mean, what's to be sad about? We're here, we're full of burgers and sun flushed and loopy after a day at the river. I'm still buzzing a little from the rope swing; it took me right back to the drop-off at Devil's Paradise. I remembered the nerves, but somehow after just a few months away, I'd forgotten the adrenaline rush, and how good it can feel to step off the edge of something solid and let yourself fall.

But.

I can't keep from thinking about the application form in Jo's bag, the one I now know exists and can't forget. She told me about her F1 dreams the day we met, and about the academy, and it's not like I expected her to factor me into her future plans after a few dates and a handful of short-but-impossibly-fantastic make-out sessions. That would be irrational. Illogical. I just didn't know she was walking around with the application form filled out already, or that the program would start so soon . . . .

*Stop it*, I scold myself. *Just enjoy this. Quit overthinking and over-worrying. Be fearless like Jo. Be fearless like—*

"There!" Jo shouts, draping herself across CJ in the middle seat to point dramatically at the garage coming up very, very slowly on our right. "Park behind the building so nobody sees us."

"How could they, in this stealthy vehicle?" James giggles.

I pat Zaynah's dashboard and croon, "You're so stealthy, you're doing fiiiine."

With a startling lack of speed, she turns into the garage parking lot and pulls around back, stopping next to a chain-link fence that surrounds the customer cars. The floodlights are already on, illuminating Fords with fender dents and Jeeps up on jacks, their windshields painted pink and orange under the sunset.

"You're sure nobody's inside?" CJ asks.

"Sure I'm sure," JoJo answers. "Grandma's out of the country, and the employee most likely to be working on something after hours is me. But anyway, that's what our lookouts are for, right?"

"Right!" James cheers way too loudly, and Zaynah death-grips the steering wheel again.

Let the heist begin.

While Zaynah waits in the driver's seat and CJ and James station themselves among the shrubs planted along the side of the garage (supposedly prepared to text us if anybody pulls up out front, but probably anxious to smash faces), Jo leads me to the gate to open the combination lock. I shine my phone light on the lock to help her, and we giggle before switching to stealth mode once the gate swings open. By which I mean ducking between the half-repaired cars and crouching down beside the towering wheel of a lifted Jeep.

"Where's the Hornet?"

She points toward a steel-frame car shelter with a waterproof shell in the back of the lot opposite us, out of the way from the cars they pull in and out to work on. I'm tempted to break off to look at it, this piece of JoJo's past and heart. But JoJo is already combat-rolling across the blacktop toward the back entrance to the garage, even though not a soul is outside to spot us. I hover in my squat, watching her turn over and over as gracefully as a banana going downhill with this swelling feeling in my chest. A moment later, I lower myself to the ground to join her, scraping my knees and elbows across the asphalt with every revolution.

Jo groans as, finally, we reach the building and she stands to punch in the back door code. "I think I skinned my hip back by that Camry."

I gasp. "Oh my God, what if they sweep for DNA?"

We lock eyes, then break down in laughter, forcing JoJo to wait until the half-entered code clears and begin all over again.

Once we're inside, it's obvious that she was right. The garage is empty, the lights off and the neon Coca-Cola and Texaco signs mounted to the brick walls grayed out. But we can see well enough with our phone lights. JoJo punches another code into the alarm panel on the wall with plenty of time to spare. Then we pick our way around carts and creepers and a Chevy Silverado with its hood up on our way to Jolene's office. The last time I was here—the first time I'd been in Jolene's office, if the millionth time I'd been in the garage—I wasn't looking for a safe. Now I see a black box the size of a mini fridge beside the filing cabinet, with a digital lock.

"You know the code for that, right?" I whisper.

"I don't. But I'm sure it's written down somewhere."

"Does she have a notebook? A desk pad? We can do a rubbing, find out the last thing she wrote—"

"Chill, Detective." JoJo laughs. "Though you're adorable as ever in PI mode." She plops down in a rolling chair behind her grandma's desk, pulling out the top drawer to peer inside.

I circle the desk, scanning for anything useful on the scattered pink Post-its while floating just a little over the fact that JoJo called me adorable. I don't find a conveniently written out string of numbers. There are neat stacks of paperwork, and two wire pen cups—one with actual pens in it, the other with multiple lipstick tubes in shades from fuchsia to bright orange to fire-engine red.

There's the cluster of little picture frames, too, and I lean forward to look at them. Jolene and Florence a decade or so ago, sharing a whole baguette Lady-and-the-Tramp style in front of a café with a French name, possibly in France. JoJo's mom and dad posed with what must be toddler-her at a backyard barbecue of yore. I recognize her dad, of course, but he looks younger even than I'd expect, somehow taller, and totally happy. Her mom looks just as she did in the many press photos I found in my (very rational and totally not obsessive) Googling. There's the picture I saw of Jo and her mom that first day, and another of teen JoJo from just a year or two ago, standing on the top spot of an awards podium in a red-and-black tracksuit, hair loose and clearly helmet mussed. She looks ecstatic, smile bright and shoulders loose, totally at home on the podium.

Max was like that, too. Is like that. She *belongs* on a track.

"Hey, JoJo?" I ask, already regretting it, but determined to push through. "When did you fill out that application?"

"Huh?" She's busy rooting through the middle drawer now,

apparently to no avail, since she slides it closed and opens the bottom drawer.

"That application, for the F1 training program. CJ said you carry it around, and I just wondered. Did you fill it out in Charleston, or in Dell's Hollow?"

Now, she stops to look up at me. "Um. Well, I didn't think I had a shot at getting my license in Charleston, after—you know, after Mom." As her eyebrows scrunch, my regret doubles and triples and quadruples; this was *not* the time or place for this conversation, which isn't really my business, anyway, and is totally selfish and silly. "When we moved here, Dad and I made our deal about the volunteer program, and that's when I thought maybe I had a shot. But I guess I didn't want to push him too soon."

I deliberately keep my eyebrows un-scrunched, even as I remember the afternoon we met, when she showed up at Putt by the Pond and raced me only to get out of showing up for the program. And at Devil's Paradise, how she told me that she'd never asked her dad about going pro. Which technically wasn't a lie, but clearly, she's been wanting to.

"I don't even know if I'd get in," JoJo continues, "I just . . . it's a possible future plan. Like how you fill out a bunch of college applications, even though you're only gonna pick one school. I bet you have a list of places you're still choosing between, right?"

"I'm applying for early decision to UNC–Chapel Hill this fall," I correct her, "so just the one. Their sports medicine program is ranked fifteenth in North America, they're in the top 10 percent of universities in the country, and I can get scholarships on top of low in-state tuition, if I keep my grades and extracurriculars up, so I could go right into my masters and PhD."

"Oh." JoJo blinks up at me. "That's . . . rigorous. El"—she scoot-hops around to better face me—"is this something we need to, like, *talk* about? Are you—"

"No!" I nearly shout. "Oh my God no, of course not. Forget I said anything, I was just babbling. I shouldn't be babbling during a heist, I know, but . . . ?"

I feel the heat of her gaze on me for a moment before she shoves back from the desk, sighing. "Well, I didn't find anything. But never fear, I bet I can hack the combo."

"By 'hack,' do you mean 'guess'?"

"Naturally." She wheels across the office, then sits cross-legged in front of the safe to inspect the electronic lock, frowning. "Hmm, she mostly uses birthdays in her passwords . . . ."

"Birthdays? Really, Jolene?"

"Grandma's brilliant, but she's still a sixty-something who asks me to explain her smart TV remote once a week. Let's try mine." She punches in the numbers (while I make a note to research the romantic compatibility of Virgos and Sagittariuses) and is rewarded with a flashing of red from the screen. "That's what I get for being egotistical. I'll try my dad's."

"Hold on a sec." I sit beside her to get a closer look at the brand name on the lock, then pull out my phone to Google it, my stomach sinking. "This is one of those locks that shuts you out if you put in the wrong combination four times in a row."

"For how long, exactly?"

"You want me to pause in the middle of a heist to read product reviews?"

"That *would* be wild card behavior." Jo sighs. "We've just gotta go for it." But her dad's birthday doesn't work, and neither does Jolene's. "Crap. Okay . . . Dad's an only child, so maybe it's my mom's." She starts to punch it in, but I catch her wrist.

"Or maybe her longtime partner's?" I gently suggest.

"Oh. Yeah, that's more likely. I just hope I remember Flo's birthday . . . ." After thinking for a moment, she punches in a date—and we both hold our breath . . . .

Until the light flashes green, and the lock clicks open.

We squeal together, and JoJo throws her arm around me, hopefully forgetting all about this awkward half conversation. We pause long enough for a quick-but-life-changing kiss before JoJo scoops a key on an antique-looking American Motors keychain off one of the shelves and closes the safe. Clutching hands unnecessarily, we sprint back through the garage at a half crouch, as though somebody might be peering through the windows. I realize that besides Googling safes, we haven't checked our phones once for a text from CJ and James, and my volume is off, so who knows if our lookouts could have warned us, anyhow.

Some heist squad.

Out in the back lot again, I stop JoJo before she heads for the fence, where Zaynah waits impatiently beyond. "Hold on, I want to see it. Can I see it?"

JoJo grins, like maybe she was hoping I'd ask. "Sure, I'll introduce you to Betty."

Forgoing the combat roll this time, we dart between the cars to get to the shelter in the back. Not only is it a nice shelter, one with sides and a zippered door and all, but the machine inside has a fitted car cover protecting it. Reverently, JoJo begins the process of untucking and rolling it back, then holds up her phone flashlight so I can see the Hornet in its beam. And it's . . .

I mean. It's attractive. Pretty compact for a muscle car, with a long, straight hood and sloping rear. The angles are crisp for a two-door sedan, and even in poor light, the electric-blue paint and black stripe shimmer. It reminds me of the R1 in my backyard shed; JoJo has clearly taken excellent care of this vehicle, even while slowly gutting and repairing it.

But as far as '70s muscle cars go, it's not exactly a Dodge Charger R/T. And we're about to risk an awful lot on a fifty-year-old sedan racing a modern GSX-R.

JoJo must see the doubt on my face, because before I've uttered a word she says defensively, "Look, this car has a *history*. Just because it's not famous doesn't mean it's not fast. It came out of the Hudson Hornet, you know, and that was a stock car racing star. Won all but one AAA race and over 80 percent of the NASCAR Grand National events the year after it came out. Then like a decade after AMC dissolved Hudson, they brought back the Hornet to replace the Rambler. The '71 took the '70 model and put in a 360 cubic-inch V-8 and a 2100 two-barrel carb. It made 245 horsepower, while barely weighing over 3,000 pounds. But *this* model has the Go Package, which bumped it up to 285 horsepower with a four-barrel carb and a ram-air induction scoop, plus dual exhaust pipes instead of a single and a four-speed transmission. It could do a quarter mile in fourteen seconds, and Mom got it down to thirteen. They only made around three hundred of these with the Go Package, which is why it's so rare. You haven't heard of it because it was overlooked and underestimated, not because it isn't amazing. Betty has the heart of a winner," she insists, staring lovingly down at her mom's car.

"And . . . does she still do thirteen?" I ask, afraid to insult the machine she's memorized, just like me and the R1.

"She can, and she will. I can do it, El." She turns her burning gaze on me. "Will you trust me?"

Though it's hard to think under the heat of her green eyes, I know, in some part of myself, that I *don't* know JoJo well enough to justify trusting her completely. Not with this crush like coals in my throat, or with my sister's jacket, or my family's future.

But I deeply, desperately want to.

So I smile and nod. We leave the Hornet behind for now—JoJo will come back to collect it before the race, since she can't exactly park the car in her own driveway. We throw ourselves into Zaynah's car, beckoning wildly for CJ and James to join us as they stroll out of the shrubbery, then shriek at Zaynah to go, go, go! As we cruise out of the lot at a painfully sensible speed of 15 mph, I push down that familiar part of me. The small, scared El who counts herself out of jumps she hasn't even tried and can never keep her goddamn foot on the gas, not once in her whole life.

She's always been the part of myself I hate most, anyhow.

# *CHAPTER FIFTEEN*

## JoJo

The day after our "heist," if you want to call it that, El and I pull up in the Hornet at Benton Creek Airfield, a small, regional abandoned stretch of runways and rusting hangars half an hour away from Riley's apartment building.

"Holy shit," El mutters in the seat beside me. "Is this really the place?"

The Hornet's headlights illuminate a stretch of tall chain-link fence that's been cut open wide enough to let a car pull through. Kudzu vines cover the fence with a leafy curtain, making the open section look like a portal to another world. Beyond the vines, the airfield stretches into the night, the central runway lined by dozens of other cars who have their headlights on to light up the stretch of pavement. Neon underlighting colors the ground pink, green, and blue, and music pumps out of many of the cars, the bass thumping into the night. Clumps of people stand around, laughing, drinking, and making bets and side bets like something out of *Fast & Furious*.

A thrill of excitement electrifies my nerves, and I sit up straighter. We're really doing this. I'm really staking Mom's car. I'm finally—finally—back on the track and racing again. It's going to be so goddamn amazing.

Even as I have that thought, it's immediately chased by another: What if I lose and Riley takes Mom's car? How am I ever going to explain that to Dad? I grip the steering wheel as my stomach flips. I absolutely cannot think that way. There's no way I'm losing this race. Not even an option.

I turn back to El and her question. "Yup, looks like the place."

She frowns. "It looks like somewhere one goes to get killed."

I shift in my seat, gunning the Hornet's engine and cocooning us momentarily in the loud, hungry purr of a V-8 engine. I can't keep a smug grin off my face. I *love* that sound. "It looks like a place where one goes to win a race and get back a bitchin' motorcycle jacket."

That earns me a small, tight smile from El. "Are you sure the car is ready?"

"Betty is in fighting shape, trust me." I run a hand along the steering wheel affectionately, infusing as much confidence as possible into the words.

Late last night, after we'd gotten the keys and said goodbye to CJ and James, who were headed back home to Charleston this morning, I'd biked back to Jolene's garage and taken the Hornet out for a test drive.

It had run beautifully—and quickly, as it should. But would it be quick enough to beat Riley's bike?

It has to be.

The twilight sky is deep purple and orange, though the night is creeping in at the edges. Fireflies dance along the fence line in front of us, helped along by a slight breeze. I'll have to consider that breeze as I'm racing tonight. The night smells like exhaust, summertime, and El. A heady mix that's going right to my blood.

*Racing.*

My heart kicks at the thought.

*That's all well and good*, whispers a voice in my head, *but what's the plan, JoJo?*

*Be fearless and drive fast enough to not get caught*, as my mother would say.

I still don't have my license, but that didn't stop me from picking up El. And it won't stop me from driving tonight. El had given the Hornet one look and insisted on driving us to the airfield, but I'd refused to leave the driver's seat and she'd begrudgingly climbed into the passenger seat.

"Why are you dressed like Letty Ortiz?" she'd asked me the minute she'd slammed her door shut. Her eyes had run over my leather jacket, white tank top, and tight low-rise jeans.

"Good luck. Also, don't you like Letty?"

El's voice came out a little choked. "I love Letty Ortiz with the collective burning passion of all the queer girls out there. But isn't that a little warm for summer?"

"It's not even July yet."

She hadn't replied—merely raised an eyebrow.

"Fine," I'd said, shrugging out of my jacket so I was just in the tank top and jeans. "Better?"

El gave a little squeak beside me, and leaned so close that I thought she was going to kiss me, but she just wiped at a smudge of grease on my cheek. "It's fine. Perfect. Whatever."

And then, she'd pulled away again. I didn't know if it's due to the F1 Academy application form we'd still not talked about and I'd still not sent in, or her nerves about tonight, but I didn't have time to focus on it.

We didn't have time to kiss or talk much, but I had promised her I'd get Max's jacket back, and that was a promise I meant to keep.

I pull the Hornet through the hole in the fence and we drive along a service road that approaches the main runway. The tarmac is overgrown in parts with weeds. There are at least fifty people here, but it's a world away from the big-city illegal street races in the *F&F* movies, where there are girls in teeny-tiny skirts and sky-high boots and whole streets in LA that are cleared by legions of racers.

"Real world versus the movies," I say, as we roll past a lime-green Nissan and two muscle cars. On the main stretch, a Dodge Charger and a souped-up Civic line up at the starting line and tear away, neck and neck as someone drops the starting flag. My heart is going faster than the cars as I pull into an empty spot, close to where Riley has parked his bike. The heat, the roar of engines, the crowd—all of it is so familiar and simultaneously terrifying.

*You can do this, JoJo. You are not going to lose your mom's car.*

Rather than addressing my own fears, I nudge El with my elbow and raise an eyebrow at the crew Riley has brought along. They're a mixed group of twenty-something guys and girls in motorcycle jackets, with a few older Harley riders thrown into the mix. All of them are drinking, and the smell of weed drifts into our open window.

"I can't believe these were Max's friends," El says.

I don't know what to say to that, so I just keep quiet.

As I park the car, I gun the engine again. My heart thrums with the electric energy that comes before a race. A burst of laughter and lots of hoots and whistles rise from the crowd. El scowls and Riley strides over to the Hornet.

He leans down, putting his forearms on my open window. He's got Max's jacket tucked over his arm. His warm, beer-laced breath washes over me as he says, "Can't believe you showed up tonight, little Max and little Max's girlfriend. You sure this sedan can make it to the end of the runway?"

El's scowl deepens and her hands curl into fists in her lap.

"Well, I borrowed it from my grandma," I deadpan. "But my mama and daddy told me this was a real fast car, so I'm hoping it'll be good in a race." I bat my eyes at him, feigning wide-eyed innocence. Really, it's all I can do not to snatch Max's jacket from his arm and tear out of there. But, in addition to the jacket, we also need Max's address. I gun the engine again, letting my annoyance sing through the car.

"Maybe it was fast in the seventies," Riley quips, with a snorted laugh. "But now I doubt it'd make it to the senior center without falling apart." He straightens up. "Welp, might as well get the ass-kicking over with. You're not the only race tonight."

"See you at the finish line," I call to his retreating back.

"If you make it there," he hollers over his shoulder.

This draws another laugh from the crowd, and I feel the smallest smile creep onto my lips. It's going to be so, so good to beat Riley in front of his friends.

I look over at El, who's gripping her seat belt with white knuckles. Touching one of her hands, I uncurl her fingers. "You should get out for this part," I say gently.

She glances at me, a vaguely wild look in her eyes. "Are you sure you can do this?" The concern that laces her voice makes me think she cares about me, and not the jacket or getting Max's address.

"Not to sound like a conceited ass, but I could beat Riley in the Oatmobile."

That surprises a laugh from El. "We should've brought that. What was I thinking?"

"That you trust me, just a little."

A conflicted look crosses her face and then she leans across the space between us and plants a soft kiss on my cheek. "Destroy him for me, will you?"

The kiss warms my cheek and sends a jolt of hope through me. "Happily."

El gets out of the car, and, after flashing her a wink, I drive the Hornet to the starting line. The other cars finish up—the Civic stomping the Charger, and then Riley's there, sitting on a red and white crotch rocket. I'm not a Bike Girl™, but even I can tell the bike has seen better days. The Hornet is going to obliterate him. Or at least I hope it does.

I mean, it shouldn't, as his bike is definitely faster, but this is where driving skill, reckless confidence, and luck come in. Pulling my picture of Jamie Chadwick from my pocket—which I'd not placed on the dash as usual when El was in the car because I didn't want to talk about the F1 Academy or my application or any of that—I put her on the dashboard. There's no room for self-doubt here.

"I believe in you, Betty," I murmur to the car. "I believe in us."

Beside me, Riley says something, but I ignore him. My fingers curl around the steering wheel, all my focus on the stretch of runway in front of me.

There's a difference between race car drivers who are good enough, pretty good, really good, and elite. Some of it's training, some of it's luck, and a lot of it's pure, unbroken focus. That's one of my greatest strengths on the track, and it's led me to countless victories over the last few years.

"Still can back out," Riley says, as he settles onto the bike.

"Wouldn't dream of it," I call back. "See you in thirteen seconds."

He snorts and drops his helmet visor.

In front of us, a girl in short jean shorts and a Guns N' Roses T-shirt holds a checkered flag. Out of the corner of my eye, I see El press her hands over her mouth. Then, my gaze snaps forward.

Three, two, one . . .

The flag drops.

My foot slams into the gas.

# CHAPTER SIXTEEN

## El

Here's the thing.

Even on a dented and dusty GSX-R600, this guy should be able to smoke Jo in a drag race. It's not a super-powerful bike; honestly, the fact that Riley's racing us on a 600 when his muttonchopped, glassy-eyed friend is sitting on the sidelines on a 1000 shows they didn't think much of us even before they saw the Hornet. Still, I know that bike can do just over an eleven-second quarter mile. I don't know if Jo knows, but she has to see that a thirteen-second car up against a modern sport bike on a straight is some real tortoise versus the hare bullshit.

I believe in Jo. I trust Jo. I really do. I'm just trusting her while I stand on the sidelines with the neck of my T-shirt stuffed between my teeth to keep from screaming with anxiety, because it seems simply impossible that we can win in her beloved Betty.

I should've remembered that nothing is simple when it comes to JoJo Emerson-Boyd.

As the girl on the runway drops the flag, Jo roars instantly and cleanly off the line, the Hornet's blue paint flashing under the fading sun.

Not so much Riley.

With reflexes slower than Jo's—fuck yes, Jo!!!—he's still hanging out on the line a second after she's taken off. I can imagine the sweet, sweet shock on his face behind that tinted face shield. He never expected her to launch like that.

JoJo and the AMC Hornet SC/360: underestimated, but amazing.

I know exactly what happens next, and why Riley overcompensates, throwing the throttle totally open in his panic to catch up. He should've held a little back. Instead of streaking after Jo, his rear tire spins on the blacktop, pinning him in place for another valuable second before he's off the line and trying to catch her.

But he can't.

To a chorus of groaning and heckling from his friends and the gathered crowd, Riley crosses the finish line just after my Car Girl™. And now I'm absolutely screaming, sprinting down the runway toward Jo as she turns the Hornet around to cruise back toward me, this dude and his 600 once again in her dust. We meet in the middle where she pulls to a stop. I throw myself on her before she's even got two feet out of the car and on the pavement, flinging both of us awkwardly across the seats.

"You did it!" I shriek into her ear. "You're incredible, Jo!"

She hugs me back, and I feel her arms shaking around my waist, just barely. But she sounds extremely cool and collected when she says, "I've been told."

By the time we work our way back out of the Hornet, Riley's pulled up to idle the bike beside us, the sourest of frowns above his jagged, scraggly beard. Two of his bros are jogging up from the sidelines behind him. I tense where I stand beside Jo, realizing the potential stupidity of our plan. I mean, beyond winning the race, we didn't *have* much of a plan. What if Max's supposed friends don't want to give us what we've fairly won? Or what if . . .

What if Riley was lying? He's got my sister's jacket, sure, but he never gave us proof of her location, and we never asked. What if all of this was for nothing?

But the glassy-eyed Gixxer boy with the muttonchops practically brays in Riley's face as he arrives. "Nice burnout." He barely looks at us as he dumps Max's jacket into my arms.

I hug the familiar amber-brown leather to my chest, burying my nose in the thick fabric hood. It smells like whatever's been simmering in the hot bed of Riley's truck, probably, or beneath his bed. But under the perfume of old-burgers-and-skunk, I still detect a whiff of Max. Like her attic bedroom, it's held on to traces of her all these months later.

"And the address?" Jo demands while I'm busy sniffing and swallowing hard.

Riley pulls a folded piece of paper from his shorts pocket.

Jo takes it, frowning as she smooths it out and scans the handwritten address. "Clark's Gold Star Pawnshop in Richmond? What the hell?"

"That's where she works," Riley says, begrudgingly.

"No," I protest. "She's in Boston."

"She *was* in Boston," Riley says. "But she texted me about a mint-condition Time Walk MTG card from the pawnshop a few weeks ago—"

"MTG?"

"Um, Magic: The Gathering?" Riley sneers at us. "It's only one of the most powerful and rarest cards. Max said her Boston roommate's cousin hooked her up with a job after she moved, and she'd send me the card if I'd Venmo her for it. Probably asked twice what it was priced at, and I doubt she even paid for it, but she knew I'd been looking. Anyway, that's the address it shipped from. You can find her there."

"But . . ." I'm flailing upward through this information, like a swimmer swept off their feet by the breakers. "But I got a postcard from her, just a couple weeks ago. She sent it from Boston."

"Maybe it got lost in the mail, or she had her roommate send it after she left?" Muttonchops guesses.

I can't think of a reason she'd do that.

"We'll call the shop tomorrow," Jo leans in close to tell me. "We'll ask if Max is working, and they'll tell us if she's there at all. This is good, El. This is a clue," she insists.

"Yes. This is good." It is. This is a win. I cradle the jacket in my arms, repeating, "This is a good thing."

And that's when the blip of a police siren cuts through the sounds of idling bikes and revving engines, as two City of Benton Creek cop cars jam through the gap in the chain-link fence, flashing their warning lights. They park to either side of the gap, and we watch as the pair from one car pulls a plastic road barricade out of their trunk. They set up across the only way out, while the pair from the second car climb out into the overgrown grass, bullhorns in hand.

"Y'all know you're trespassing," a cop with a mustache like a Picture Day comb drawls into his bullhorn. "We have to chase you out of here again, it's gonna be a real problem. Now line up, you know what to do."

"Shit, shit, shit . . ." Riley mutters as the small crowd around us shifts nervously.

A guy standing beside his murdered-out Fiesta spits onto the runway, then slumps into his driver's seat and cruises slowly toward them across the grass. Stopping at the barrier, he speaks to the mustache cop, passing what must be his license and registration through the rolled-down window while the other three check his trunk and back seat.

"El . . ." Jo whispers while the crowd around us starts to move.

I clutch sightlessly for her hand, and she takes it.

The cops look more annoyed than angry, and in an unlikely blessing, this crowd of bored small-town gearheads is almost made up entirely of white dudes aside from us. So I don't think anyone's in immediate danger from them. But my parents? They'll kill me. Then they'll ground me until I graduate, and Putt by the Pond will fire me, and I won't be able to show my face at volunteer club with an arrest record, and UNC will never let me in once they find out I've been trespassing and street racing—

*Well, technically, your girlfriend was street racing*, a treacherous, wheedling, familiar little voice whispers inside of me. *You were only standing here.*

God, I hate that voice.

Maybe Jo sees something in my face, because she says, low and urgent, as she disentangles our hands to open the passenger door for me, "You won't get in trouble, El, I promise. They're not gonna bust you just for being here when you weren't even driving."

I start to climb in, but stop to realize aloud, "You don't have a license, Jo."

She hesitates, and I think I see something in *her* face for the first time, a flicker of uncharacteristic fear, before she forces a tight smile. "So they'll call my dad, and he'll call my grandma, and I'll get a lecture from Italy. What are they gonna do, take away my car keys? It'll be fine."

The drivers around us are reluctantly pulling out and lining up behind the Fiesta. It seems the cops don't find anything, because two of them move the barrier to let him pass through the gap in the fence, then walk it back into place before circling a lime-green Nissan. They'll make their way down the line until they get to us, car by bike by car. Tempted as I am to believe Jo, I'm pretty sure that driving a technically stolen car without a license is bigger trouble than she's making it sound. And I'm not the only one with plans for my future.

"Maybe . . . maybe we should switch. Say I was driving."

"*No*, El, just get in the car," she says, gently shoving me toward the passenger's seat.

But I can't. I can't let Jo take the fall for everything she's done to help me. Can I?

I'm still frozen on the asphalt when an engine revs loudly, and we both snap our heads toward the fence. The cops have just moved the barrier for a car to pass through, but before they can move it back, Riley and the Gixxer boys rip out of line and plough through the gap in the fence after it. I can hear the cops swearing and shouting from here as they do. Both pairs pile back into their cars and turn their sirens on, taking off after them and leaving the rest of us behind.

I glance back at Jo. "Should we . . . should we wait for them to come back?" I ask, even as the remaining cars take advantage and tear through the fence toward freedom.

She stares at me as though I've just suggested we hide the evidence of our crimes by eating the Hornet. "Are you kidding?" she shrieks, but she's laughing, too. "Let's go, go, go!"

We throw ourselves into the Hornet and take off, and now I'm laughing, too. She sticks to the speed limit as we thread our way through back roads, but we don't cross paths with Riley or the cops. By the time we reach the highway toward Dell's Hollow, I'm absolutely giddy with adrenaline and relief. Jo and I haven't let go of one another yet; we stay connected, my arm threaded below hers while she keeps a hand on the stick so that we're layered atop one another, my hand resting on the leg of her jeans. As we come up on a familiar exit, I squeeze. "Hey, pull off here?" I ask. It's a total impulse, but the thrill of victory and escape makes me bold. I feel like a completely different person.

Trustingly, she takes the exit without asking why.

I direct Jo down a stretch of rural roadway under a sky steadily darkening to ink, and though she glances sidelong at me, she doesn't question it. At last, we reach our destination: Pemberly Mill, a half-finished housing development in the middle of nowhere. Along the honeycomb of streets marked with 10-mph signs, two-story town-houses in inoffensive shades of sand and taupe and fog stand in various stages of construction on dirt lots or lawns that have turned to mead-ows. Some have no siding at all, only particleboard. Some are missing roofs, their rafters bared to the night like bones, while a handful look move-in ready. Like anybody could be inside right now, living their mysterious lives.

But nobody's around except for us.

"This is where you used to come with Max, right?" she asks, parking beside the dry basin of what would have been a man-made pond. She takes in the rows of dark windows on a darkening street. "To practice riding?"

I'm surprised she remembers. "Yeah. She had me ride for hours, learning the difference between dirt bikes and the R1 so I could get my motorcycle learner's permit. She, um, forged Mom's signature on the forms and took me to do the tests so I could get my endorsement. My parents still don't know. It's the most rebellious thing I've ever done, until today."

"Eliana Blum!" Jo shrieks. "You *are* a wild card."

Maybe I am.

"She was a good teacher," I say, protective of the memory. "Like, she took it seriously. Drill after drill after drill until she thought I could pass the off-street skills test."

"And you aced it, right?"

"Well, it wasn't that different from the Husqvarna, since the controls are pretty much the same. Though the highway is scarier than a track, obviously. And you sit differently, you know, and the turn radius is really different, plus there's countersteering to consider on a street bike, and you can't lean a dirt bike around a curve like that without a low side . . . ." I trail off when I notice JoJo watching me with the same rapt attention I bet I wear on my face whenever Letty Ortiz is on-screen: leaned forward, eyes bright. "What?"

"I just like it when you talk technical."

I flush. "Wait till I tell you about the one hundred points of traction."

"Oof." She bites her lip.

"Lean angle points versus acceleration and breaking points—"

"El, would you get the fuck over here?"

What started as a joke is no longer so funny, and I am *extremely* aware of my hand on her thigh right now, the worn texture of her jeans and the warmth of her muscled leg beneath it. Without a center console between us in the compact cab, it's easy enough to lever my weight and swing my own leg up and over so I'm straddling her lap . . . until I'm perched awkwardly with my back smashed up against the steering wheel. Laughing, Jo reaches down to slide back and recline the seat. Not all the way, but enough that I'm fully braced over her now, my elbows on either side of the headrest, my mouth inches from hers. It's a soupy summer night, and without any air flowing through the AC-less Hornet, it's even hotter in here.

But I don't care. And I feel sorry for the El of one month ago who had no idea what it was like to breathe the same air as the undefeated JoJo Emerson-Boyd. Leaning down to kiss her is the easiest thing in the world; with the seat reclined and gravity working for me, I just have to let myself fall.

By the time Jo drops me off, it's after ten o'clock. I am mostly put to-gether, cooled by the highway wind on the ride back, though I can feel my lips are still redder than they should be as I stand in my driveway, and there's no saving my hair. Tying Max's jacket around my waist to free my hands, I scoop it up into a miniature ponytail. At least my parents should be in bed by now, the porch light left on just for me.

But I'm surprised to see the living room lights on when I wrestle my key into the front lock. I don't even have the door open before my parents appear in the entryway. And at the looks on their faces, any lingering trace of a smile fades from mine.

Mom peers out into the night behind me, where the Hornet's headlights are just disappearing beyond the sweetgum tree that blocks the road from view. "Was that your friend JoJo driving?"

"Yes?" Caught off guard, I'm scrambling to remember what alibi I gave my parents. I told them I'd be with JoJo, didn't I? Yes. And she told her dad that she was meeting me for a volunteer club event. "Sorry, I didn't think you'd still be up. I tried to be quiet—"

"Your friend JoJo," Dad chimes in, "who you're certain has her driver's license, and did *not* steal a car from her grandmother's shop without permission?"

"I—" Shit. *Shit.* "I mean . . . it's her mom's car," I say faintly, because we might've miraculously escaped at the airfield, but now we're caught, and I'm in trouble, probably massive amounts. And now Mom has noticed the jacket knotted around my waist, Max's jacket.

All of the blood drains from her face, and all of the blood is draining from *my* face and fingers and toes, and I am the worst wild card in the world for having no idea how to salvage this situation, and *how the fuck were we caught?*

"Kitchen, now," Mom says, low and cold, as Dad shuts and locks the door behind me.

# CHAPTER SEVENTEEN

## JoJo

I can still taste El's strawberry chapstick on my lips as I pull away, watching her parents basically drag her into their house. I drive away, wishing more than anything that we were still in that housing development she'd directed us to. Remembering how she climbed out of her seat and into my lap. Wishing her body was still draped over mine, her warm mouth smiling against my own as we got tangled up in the seat belt.

Eliana Blum.

A wild card indeed.

I touch a finger to my lips. Worth it.

I hope I didn't get her in trouble—her mom didn't look too pleased as I pulled out of sight—but at least we got Max's jacket back and got her address. What we're going to do with the information is a whole other question, but El has the jacket. Even if she can't hold her sister or find her, that has to count for something.

Once I'm out of El's driveway, I pull over and dig my phone out from between the front seats, where it fell while El and I were making out. Hoping she's texted me something cute or maybe sent an update that her parents aren't going to kill her, I swipe to my messages.

And.

Shit.

There's nothing from El, but there are fourteen missed calls from my dad and three from Grandma Jolene. (What was Grandma doing calling from Italy? She's six hours ahead of us, which means she's been calling since before dawn her time. Shit.)

There are also a heap of texts from both of them. The last one from Dad just reads:

*Don't take the car back to the garage. Come straight home.*

A cold dose of adrenaline—something I avoided when borrowing the car in the first place, driving it through town, and racing it—washes through me now, making my legs weak. Gone are all thoughts of El and her body wrapped around mine. Gone is the thrill of racing. All of those lovely things are replaced by a cold lump of dread. I'm in so much trouble.

Or maybe I'm not. Maybe this will just blow over. Dad hasn't had much energy to parent lately, and I can't see him taking up the charge now.

Right.

Surely I can talk my way out of this.

I take my time driving home, letting my arm hang out the window and relishing the warm evening breeze as it cools my sweat-soaked forehead. At least I'm driving. That's something. Everything slots into place with my hand on the wheel, and the car hums happily as I aggressively shift it and drive through a stretch of farmland between El's house and Grandma Jolene's.

I know I'm in big trouble the minute I pull up outside Grandma Jolene's house.

For one, all the lights in the house are on. For another, Dad sits on the front porch, smoking, which he hasn't done in months. As soon as I pull the Hornet into the driveway, he stubs his cigarette out in a nearly full ashtray and stands. The stale scent of cigarette smoke washes over me through my open window.

Letting out a breath full of nerves, I turn the car off. How bad can it be? It's not like Dad can ground me from volunteer club. And he doesn't even know about the F1 Academy application. And if he tries to stop me from seeing El, then I'll—

"JoJo Lucille Emerson-Boyd, get out of that car this minute." His voice cuts through my thoughts, and his use of my full name makes me wince. There's a controlled edge to his voice, a hint as sharp as a knife in a chef's hand. That edge, in someone who doesn't yell, tells me he's well and fully furious.

*Keep moving*, I hear my mother's voice in my head, reciting one of her earliest racing lessons. *The only way forward is through and the faster you go, the sooner you'll get there.*

I pull the keys from the ignition, retrieve my messenger bag from the back seat, and step out of the car. The door slams softly shut behind me and my boots crunch over the driveway's gravel as I walk toward the porch. "Hi, Dad."

He's in jeans and one of Mom's old racing T-shirts. A car with her number on the front sits superimposed over a bright blue shape of the state of North Carolina. It's such a little thing, to see him wearing one of her shirts like old times, but it makes my heart ache.

"Fun time at volunteer club?" he says archly.

I can't help but smile, trying to push my sadness down. "Fun time with the *president* of the volunteer club. Does that count?"

Dad doesn't crack. "Hardly. Sit."

He points to one of the rocking chairs on the porch, but I climb the steps and plop onto the porch railing. We've not fought or talked much in months and Mom was usually the one to ground me or come up with a punishment when I got into trouble, which was rare. Dad was usually happy to take a back seat to her, and even now, the strain of figuring out what to say makes his forehead crinkle.

Silence stretches between us, a great expanse filled up by the rustle of the breeze through the leaves of the twin oaks in Grandma Jolene's yard and the buzz of thousands of cicadas. The scent of the night-blooming jasmine that climbs a trellis on the far side of the porch floats on the air, delicate and seductive. I lick my lips, tasting El's chapstick again. Somehow I feel like a part of so many stories in this moment—the ones from my past, when Mom and I would sit on this porch and I would catch fireflies; and the one from right now, when I snuck out and kissed a girl after winning a race; and the ones in a future that hasn't happened yet, when Dad I might laugh about this moment someday. Thinking about that hypothetical future reminds me of the very real, tangible one I have tied to the form in my messenger bag. The one I still need to ask Dad about.

I slip the Hornet's keys into my pocket. "I'm guessing you already know where I've been?" I say, prompting Dad. The sooner we get through this, the sooner we can talk about other things.

Dad blows out a breath, finding his voice at last. "Mostly. Your grandmother got a call from Mabel Rae, her head mechanic, about an hour ago. Mabel Rae went back to the garage tonight to get her phone, and when she got there, the Hornet was gone. She panicked—"

Horror fills me, a shot of ice down the back of my neck, as I think of something that somehow hadn't occurred to me yet. "Did she call the police?"

Is borrowing Mom's car going to send me to jail? That would kill all my chances at the F1 Academy and likely mean I couldn't race or go to college—and what would it mean for El? She's going to hate me if—

"Mabel called Jolene first," Dad says, swiping a hand through his hair. "So slow those speeding thoughts of yours. Mabel Rae had a notion that you might have wanted to drive the Hornet. Says you've been working on it all week, so she called your grandmother in Italy first. Jolene called me—and you, I'd imagine."

I hold up my phone, showing him all the missed calls from Grandma Jolene.

Dad nods. "Yep. I told her you were with Eliana Blum. When we couldn't get you, Jolene called El's parents."

Shit. Shit. Shit.

"And El's parents told you I picked her up in the Hornet?"

"They told *Jolene* you picked El up in the Hornet," Dad confirms. "None of which you were supposed to be doing."

Shit.

My stomach plummets. El has to be in so much trouble. Which isn't really fair.

Getting defensive is a terrible idea; I know this. But I can't help it. I can't explain to Dad the real reason why I took the car or how important it was to get Max's jacket back. Or why I had to help El. Or what it means to have a friend or a connection to someone. Or what it was like to kiss a girl like El under the stars on a warm summer night.

"We didn't do anything wrong," I say, crossing my arms.

"That's a wildly untrue statement." Dad sits in a rocking chair and knocks another cigarette out of the pack. "You took a car that doesn't belong to you, from private property, drove it without a license, and did who-knows-what with it."

Ahhh. So he doesn't know about the street racing at least. We can keep it that way.

"Dad. You make it sound like I've never driven a car. Or like Mom wasn't letting me drive the Hornet two years ago when I had my learner's permit. You make it sound like I'm supposed to just sit around this house all the time, not doing anything!" I try to keep my voice level through this speech, but the last part comes out strained. Full of the hundreds of unsaid things I've held back over the last few months.

Dad flicks his lighter on and off. "I know all that, JoJo, but you can't *steal a car.*"

"I didn't steal it."

"You borrowed it then?"

I give a brittle laugh. "It's practically mine anyway! Since you don't even drive anymore. Do you really think Mom would just want Betty sitting in the garage unused?"

Dad makes a choked sound at the car's nickname. His fingers fly to his wedding ring, which he twists around his finger. "Your mother isn't here to have an opinion on that."

"But she is!" I burst out. "She's all around us and you've forgotten all the things she liked!"

Dad's face crumbles at that accusation, but I can't stop myself. I push on.

"She would've hated that we're not racing! That we're not even driving! That all my dreams have had to change! I've not even told you this because I've been too scared to ask, but I've been carrying around an F1 Academy application for weeks, hoping you'll sign it." I pull the form out of my bag and wave it at him.

Confusion crosses Dad's face as he tries to follow everything I've said. One thing really seems to land with him. "You shouldn't be scared to ask me anything, Jo. I know we're not very close right now, but you can ask me anything. I want you to talk to me."

"Does this mean you'll sign it and let me follow my dream to be a race car driver?"

"Absolutely not." He brings the flame to his cigarette and inhales sharply.

"You have to sign it. Please."

"I won't, kiddo."

"This is my chance to make something of myself. To follow my dreams!"

He gets up to stand beside me. "You'll find other dreams, JoJo."

"I won't! This is what I've wanted since I was like five years old."

He stubs out his unsmoked cigarette. "I'm not signing the form."

"Dad, please! Do this for me. For Mom. For the life we had and the things we all wanted."

Tears fall down my cheeks as I say it, and I swipe at them. A long moment stretches between us, full of unsaid things. I turn to look at Dad.

"I can't keep you safe if you drive!" Dad says finally, his voice a jagged whisper. "Don't you understand that? If you race, then I could lose you, too!"

It breaks me to hear the tapestry of his grief in those sentences, but my grief is here, too, sitting beside us on the porch like a living thing.

"If you hold on to me too tightly, you'll lose me as well," I mutter. "Don't you see that? People like Mom and I, we're too fast and we're always furiously chasing something."

"Not if I can help it," Dad says, blinking away his own tears. "Now, give me the keys to the Hornet. You're not driving it again until you have a license." He holds out his hand.

Sullenly, I fish the keys from my pocket and put them in his open palm. "What about signing my F1 Academy form?" I ask, knowing it's an impossible request.

"Might as well tear it up. I'm never signing that."

I bite back all the hateful, angry things I want to say and shove the form back into my bag. "You're ruining my life."

"If that's what it takes to keep you safe, so be it. That's called tough love, and sometimes a parent has to do it. Now, get in the house and head to bed. We'll talk in the morning about the consequences of your actions."

I want to say more, but I don't. There's no point in arguing with him now and I'm only going to say things I regret if I stay on this porch a second longer.

I shouldn't have said those things to Dad, I know that, but unlike him, I'm not afraid of racing. I love the risk and the possibility in every race. I'm not even afraid of losing a race. No, what terrifies me is losing myself and the careful vision of my future that Mom and I had crafted over many, many racing training sessions, long talks about track conditions, and hundreds of mornings spent together, dreaming about when she'd come cheer me on after an F1 race.

The thought makes me get up from the air mattress I'm lying on and dig into my suitcase. Grandma Jolene gave me three drawers in her craft dresser, but a lot of my clothes are still in the suitcase I brought with me for the move. Digging past sweatshirts and winter sweaters, I pull a bundle out from the bottom of my suitcase. It's another of Mom's racing shirts, the twin to the one Dad has on in fact. It's folded around a tiny red jeweler's box that I've not opened in months.

Carefully, I pull back the T-shirt and rest my palm on the box.

Mom had given it to me the morning of her crash. The last morning of her life. Of course, neither of us knew at the time that it'd be her last morning, and we'd gotten up early like usual, letting Dad sleep as he'd been up late the night before watching race tapes. Mom and I had made coffee and eggs and taken them to the breakfast nook in the apartment we were staying in for the race.

"Are you excited to finally get your license?" Mom had asked as she slathered jelly on toast.

I'd shrugged, not feeling any sort of way about it. "It feels almost like an afterthought, to be honest. Like, I've been driving for so long, this is just the official piece of plastic that says I can do it off the track."

A soft smile had pulled at Mom's lips and she beamed at me. "It's a big deal though, JoJo. I still remember when I got my license. Great-Aunt Betty made me a caramel cake and let me drive her around town."

"I wish I could've met her."

"You would've liked her a lot, I imagine. Now, let me give you something before I start crying over Betty and my baby girl being nearly grown up." Mom had swiped at the tears in the corners of her eyes, and pulled the red jeweler's box out from her pocket.

She handed it to me.

"What's this?" I'd asked.

"Open it. You'll see."

Inside the box was a gold necklace with a tiny golden F1 car charm on the end. Its little wheels moved as I put my finger on them.

"It's perfect," I'd said, slipping it on.

"It's something to remind you of your dreams," Mom said, pulling me into a hug. "Even if I'm not always here to remind you, this little charm might do the trick."

We'd eaten our breakfast, gotten ready for the day, and then, a few hours later, Mom was gone in a fireball at the track.

I haven't worn the necklace since.

Slowly, I open the red jeweler's box. The little golden car is there, tangled up in the chain after I'd thrown it into the box on the night Mom died. I slip my finger in the chain, trying to unsnarl it.

"I miss you," I whisper to the air. I'm not sure if I believe in spirits, but I think I might. And in that moment, I feel Mom's arms wrap around me.

Dad might not want to sign the form, but Mom believed in me and my dream. I'll find another way to get to race. With that thought in mind, I untangle the necklace and put it on.

An hour later, after I'm settled in bed and reading, I get a text from El. It's short, to the point, and sends a thrill of excitement through me.

**El:** I'm going to find Max. Want to come?

I fire off a reply immediately.

**JoJo:** Would love to, but I have no ride. Dad took the Hornet's keys

El's reply makes me want to kiss her.

**El:** No worries. I'm driving. Meet me at the bottom of your driveway in fifteen minutes

Not pausing to wonder if this is a good idea or not, and not considering how El is going to drive us to Richmond, Virginia, a town that's a few hours away—in the Oatmobile surely?—I throw a change of clothes, my toothbrush, and my wallet into my messenger bag. Then, I scrawl a note to Dad and leave it on my air mattress—*Be back soon. Love you. ~JoJo*—and open my window. It's nothing to tiptoe across the roof and climb down the metal garden lattice that covers one whole side of the house. I did it a hundred times as a kid and tonight, I don't even flinch when my hand slips and I slide the last few feet to the ground.

When El Blum pulls up on a racing bike ten minutes later, with an extra helmet on the back seat, that's what really makes my heart start racing.

# CHAPTER EIGHTEEN

## El

I sit at our too-long kitchen table, penned in by my parents on either side, and trap my hands between my own knees to keep them from shaking. For all my parents' many expectations of me, I have never seen them look at me as though I've shattered every single one of them at once.

I've never seen them look at me the way they once did at my sister.

"Tell me," Mom starts, "what in the blazing hell were you thinking, Eliana? Getting into the car—the *stolen* car—of a girl you barely know, who doesn't have her license? Her poor grandmother had to call all the way from Italy in the middle of the night to find out where she was. She lied to her father about her plans, do you know that? Neither of you were answering your phones. You could've been seriously hurt, or *arrested*."

As if that's the worse option by far.

"And where did you get that?" Dad chimes in, eyeing Max's jacket slung across the back of my chair. Like it's a feral cat that snuck into the house alongside me and might take a swipe at him at any time.

If only I didn't have the jacket. It's unlikely that I could've lied my way out of trouble, but I could *maybe* minimize the consequences. Say we just drove into Deerfield to the DQ for Blizzards, or better yet, that we never even crossed the town line. But I can't think quickly enough to explain away the jacket.

Still, if I can make them understand *why* we did this . . . If they would just stop looking at me like that . . .

"I was trying to help," I say, and hate how small my voice sounds.

"Help who? That girl?" Mom's eyes narrow. "What kind of trouble is she getting you into, Eliana?"

"What? No, she didn't—I got her in! Just . . . listen. I got a postcard from Max, remember? A few weeks ago?" I ignore my parents' identical winces at the mention of their oldest daughter. "She asked me for her jacket back, and I went to Jolene's shop to see if it was there. It wasn't, but that's where I met JoJo. She was just being a good person, trying to help me track it down. And then one of Max's friends said he had it, and that he knew her address—"

"What were you doing, talking to your sister's friends?" Dad cuts in, looking horrified.

"I just told you. He said he knew where Max was, but we had to meet him or he wouldn't tell us, and—"

"So." It's Mom who cuts me off this time. "Not only did you girls steal a car and drive it without a license, you arranged to meet up with a man you don't know at all, who could've been a serious danger to you both, in a random location that he picked?" Mom sums up, pinching the bridge of her nose. "Please tell me, Eliana, how we're supposed to trust you again after this series of unbelievably poor choices."

The worst thing is, I can't argue with her. Those were the choices I made, and on paper, they were pretty poor. I see how this looks from the outside.

But instead of feeling guilty, there's this anger growing steadily inside me, like magma rising toward the surface. The more I think about it, the greater my fury. Because don't I get any credit for seventeen years of careful choices? Seventeen years (give or take) of studying on weekends, and volunteering at the Hebrew school, and weeding the garden beds as soon as I'm asked, and flossing twice a day and wearing my nightly retainer post–middle school braces, and keeping tabs on Max when my parents couldn't, and *never* putting a foot off track?

It's suddenly so important to me that, for once, they look at me for the kid I am, the kid who's been here and been reliable, the kid who's planning on going to the sports medicine program at UNC, and not as some miniature version of the kid they tossed away.

"I wouldn't have done any of it if *you* were looking for Max," I insist. "You never want to talk about her, but for all we know, she could be hungry or in trouble. Maybe she wants to come home, but has no money to get here. Somebody had to find out." I lean back in my chair, arms barred across my chest, trying to keep my gaze as cold and steady as Mom's, and trying not to notice how wounded Dad looks. Actually, my mother's lips seem to be trembling, too.

But that's probably rage. Because when she speaks again after a long silence, she sounds politely icy. "There's nothing any of us can do to bring Maxine home," Mom says, as if it's an indisputable fact.

"How do you know?" I demand. "Have you even tried? Do you even care?"

I jump in my seat as Dad pounds a fist down on the table, snapping, "Enough, El. Enough of this. You're grounded."

After I recover from the shock of Dad losing his cool, I snap back, "I have the volunteer club. And work."

"Quit."

"I can't—it's my club! How will that look on college applications if I quit my job and the program I started halfway through my junior year summer?" Not that Putt by the Pond itself was going to get me into college, but it's the principle.

"How will it look if you wind up like your sister?" Mom bursts out, the ice cracking at last. "You're sneaking around, stealing, hanging out with the same people who dragged her down."

I don't know what she's talking about—yeah, Max drove our parents' car into the Founder's Fountain, but she didn't steal it, and I don't see what Riley or any of those skeezballs had to do with it, since Max was alone when it happened. But I'm so swept up by the fight now, it's practically an out-of-body experience, and I truly can't stop myself. "So instead of picking her back up, you tossed her out."

Dad is up now, pacing the room. But Mom is cool and calm again when she says, "We did not. Your sister left."

"That's a lie. She'd never leave . . . she wouldn't have left her bike," I insist.

A ragged laugh bursts out of Dad, who's halfway across the kitchen. "If your sister cared about us as much as she claimed to care about that bike." He scrubs a hand down his flushed face. "We need to let go and move on, El. We should've sold that bike months ago—"

"No!" I nearly scream, bolting up from my own chair.

"It isn't doing her any good," Mom agrees with him, "and it isn't doing us any good. If you can't understand that this is *for* you, Eliana, then I just hope that someday, even if it isn't until you have a child of your own, you will. I won't lose another daughter by making the same mistakes all over again." She folds her hands on the tabletop and stares down at her knuckles, evidently done with looking at me.

"The bike goes," she pronounces, "and you're grounded. You can keep your phone tonight to let Zaynah know she'll need to take over the club for a while, and to tell your boss you won't be in tomorrow. And I suggest you separate yourself from this girl JoJo while you're at it. Because I don't think she's a good influence on you at all."

I'm too furious to name the ways my parents are, as a united front, burning my life to the ground before my eyes. Instead, I rip Max's jacket from the back of my chair, not intending to tip it over. But as it starts to fall, I let it. The chair hits the floor with a heavy crack. I'm out of the kitchen a second later, and my parents don't call me back.

It's another twenty minutes before I hear them climb the steps and pass my locked door on the way to their own, barely pausing outside of my room, where I lie on my floor (petty as it sounds, I'm way too angry to want to be comfortable). I wait another half hour, counting every second, then ease open my door to creep down the hall to *theirs*. The lights inside are off, and I don't hear any murmuring voices or restless creaking of the mattress.

Time to move.

I change into jeans and the work boots I'd put in the back of my closet for the summer, and slip on Max's jacket. The last time she let me try it on, I swear it was too big. Now, it's a little tight across the shoulders. But it'll do.

I shove a few things into my school backpack. A jumble of toiletries scooped from my bathroom counter. A fistful of T-shirts and sports bras and socks. A pair of pajamas. My wallet. My postcard collection. I hover over the retainer case on my nightstand, throwing it in at the last moment; I am who I am.

It's easy enough to sneak out the sliding door in the kitchen, back to the shed where the R1 waits. I already have the keys, and among Max's bagged-up gear in the corner where I expected to, I uncover a pair of helmets—hers and the spare she kept for me—along with her hard-shell motorcycle backpack. My school bag squeezes inside it with the spare helmet. I put on my sister's helmet and backpack, and then comes the first tricky part: walking the R1 down to the street, where I have a chance of starting it and taking off without my parents hearing. From the left side of the bike, I pull the clutch in and use a foot to put it in first, then lift the lever with my toe to put it in neutral. I push it forward with a hand on each bar, leaning it slightly toward me so if it falls, it doesn't fall away. It's tougher to muscle the bike across the grass, but I send a silent prayer of thanks to the Husqvarna for my upper-body strength. Once I've steered it around the house—it's not far to the driveway—I push it all the way down to the street.

Out on Cider Lane, I pull my phone from Max's jacket pocket, but I pause just a moment before I text Jo, to consider *not* texting Jo.

I could still put the gear and the R1 back. Go inside. Seethe in my dark bedroom. Wake up to a world where I have no parental trust, no job, no club, and no girlfriend (at least, not practically, because after tonight, Mom and Dad will hardly let Jo into the house while I'm grounded, which might be until school starts).

And absolutely no chance to find my sister and bring her home.

I press Send on the text.

Then, for the first time ever, I straddle the bike and shift it into drive without my sister's watchful gaze nearby. Panic flares up in me, but I push it down, deciding to be fearless instead.

# CHAPTER NINETEEN

## JoJo

We stop for gas about an hour after we leave Dell's Hollow. El pulls off the highway and steers us through a small town whose name I forget immediately. We pass rows of Victorian houses with peeling paint and wide porches and several trailer parks before reaching the edge of town. A streetlight illuminates a two-pump gas station under a broad metal awning and a falling-down motel next door.

I haul myself off the bike as soon as El parks. My back and legs ache from sitting behind her the whole way, holding her waist, but I have zero regrets. The feel of her body in front of me and the smell of her hair has fully wrapped me in a delectable cocoon of full-on crush, hunger, and exhilaration. I take off my helmet and stretch. The sound of cicadas fills my ears, dense as the summer night air. "Nice driving," I say to El.

"Nice hanging on," she says, lifting her visor and grinning at me.

There's a wildness to her right now, a recklessness that was clear in how quickly she hit the throttle on the bike as we pulled away from my house. She was still safe enough on the road as we drove—because you can take the honor student out of the volunteer club, but you can't make her totally rash—though there were definitely some turns where I held on tighter than others.

It's nearly midnight according to my phone, and there's no word from Dad yet. Around my neck sits Mom's necklace, cold and comforting at the same time.

"I'll get gas," I offer, pulling my debit card out of my wallet. All my many years of race winnings are in this checking account, and I know El makes almost nothing at Putt by the Pond.

I slip my card into the machine, and El takes off the gas cap and sticks the handle into the bike. As she's pumping gas, I stretch again and look around.

The gas station would be sketchy if there was anyone in it, but it's empty. Likewise, no cars drive through the tiny town's main street, and there's not even a dog barking. We're out of the mountains and nearly into Virginia, but my phone says Richmond is still at least two hours away. A huge yawn—the kind that makes my ears pop—splits my face.

El's looking at me and my yawn snares her, making her do the same. We both laugh through our yawns, as nerves, elation, and the thrill of the unknown yawn back at us.

A light rain has started since we pulled into the gas station and it whispers against the metal overhang above the pumps.

"So, what now?" I ask, looking up at the rain and the dark road in front of us. Suddenly, the thought of my warm bed feels incredibly enticing. The race, kissing El, the fight with my dad, and now this surprise road trip have left me exhausted. I'm not sure I can hang on to the back of El's bike for another two hours as we drive to Richmond. Not to mention we have no plan for what we'll do once we get there.

El looks up at the sky. "Can you check the weather? I looked before I left my house, but it didn't seem too bad—"

Of course she checked the weather before sneaking out and stealing a bike, because El Blum might be a wild card, but she's a prepared one. It's a little thing, but one I adore about her.

I swipe to my weather app. "It looks like it's going to rain for the next three hours, maybe more. And there's a thunderstorm warning."

El swears softly. "That's what I was worried about. I'd hoped we'd avoid it, but I think we're going to get drenched." She finishes pumping gas and puts the handle away.

I look over my shoulder, at the small roadside motel next to the gas station. There's one car in the parking lot, and the neon sign by the office says It'll Do Motel.

You've got to be kidding me.

As if hearing my skeptical thoughts about the "It'll Do," a crack of thunder splits the night and the rain goes from a whisper to a roar.

"Well, we can't stay under this metal awning for the next three hours," I say. "Unless we want to get hit by lightning. And I don't think we should drive in this storm."

"Are you seriously considering the It'll Do Motel?" El says, looking around like a better plan will materialize in the night.

"How bad can it be?" I ask. "It's probably like the motel in *Schitt's Creek*."

El darts another nervous glance my way. "This place makes that motel look like it's four stars at least."

She isn't wrong, but what other choice do we have?

"C'mon," I say. "It'll be an adventure."

Ten minutes later, a sweet old lady whose name tag says FLORA has checked us into our room and explained some of the history of the It'll Do Motel, including how the name was a joke at first, then a bet, and then somehow became the permanent name for the place. She would've told us more about it, but we pleaded exhaustion. When I'd tried to get two rooms, El had protested.

"I'm not sleeping in this motel alone," she'd hissed.

Which, fine with me. I just hadn't wanted to presume, but I was more than good with sharing a room with her.

After El parks the bike under the covered concrete porch in front of our room, I unlock the door, flick on a light, and suck in a breath.

"Well, this is . . ." I pause, my words utterly stolen by the sheer amount of floral in the low-ceilinged room. The walls are papered with a green-and-pink roses print, the bedspread on the queen bed is covered in bright yellow daisies, a bright pink-and-blue carpet bursting with minia-ture flowers has been spread over most of the dingy gray motel carpet, several large floral needlepoints are framed on the walls, and there are no less than three fake flower arrangements on the bedside tables and beside the TV.

El leans against my back, peering into the room. "Wow," she breathes, her voice a whisper beside my ear. "Flora wasn't kidding about the renovations she's been doing."

Before checking us in, Flora assured us that she'd been busy visiting craft stores to spruce up the It'll Do, which had been in her late husband's family for years and is now hers. She'd shown us the tiny blue flowers she was hot-gluing to a vase, and told us she'd give us the best room in the place.

"Wow, indeed," I echo, forcing myself not to lean backward against El's body.

Her closeness absolutely evokes the way she sat on my lap in the Hornet after I won the race. The way our lips grazed each other's. The hand she shoved into my hair to pull me closer to her . . .

I take a step forward, putting some distance between El and me. Outside, the rain hammers the pavement, and the lone streetlight beside the It'll Do Motel's sign flickers. When El closes the door behind her, there's a long stretch of quiet between us.

Right. We're just two girls alone in a motel room. Two girls who were kissing a few hours ago. And there's only one bed. And we're wearing rain-soaked clothing (well, maybe not soaked, but wet clothing). And I desperately want to kiss El again . . . .

"This is like a rom-com—" I start to say right as El blurts out, "You can have first shower."

I nod at that, clamping my teeth down on my dorky rom-com comment and, to shake off my nerves, fiddling with one of the fake flowers that's fallen out of its arrangement. Maybe it'll be easier to talk to each other when we're cleaned up.

I take a quick shower in the floral-heavy bathroom (tiles painted with flowers, flower art on the walls, flower shower curtain), and then slip into the long T-shirt and boxers I normally sleep in. When I come out of the bathroom, El's sitting on the edge of the bed, still wearing Max's jacket, looking at her phone.

A pang shoots through me, starting low in my belly but ending somewhere around my heart. She looks up when I close the bathroom door, her eyes lingering at the place where my T-shirt stops on my upper thighs, and then her gaze moves upward.

A laugh bursts from her when she gets to my head, where a hot pink flower-themed towel is wrapped around my wet hair.

The laugh chases some of the tension from the room. I curtsy and pull the towel from my head, making my wet hair cascade around my face. I wave the towel in El's direction. "Flora has not been shy about embracing the florals."

El smiles at me, meeting my eyes. "Entirely. I love a woman with a passion." I hold her gaze for a moment and a briefly panicked look crosses her face. She clears her throat hurriedly.

"You know what I mean," she says. "With the flowers and all. I didn't mean anything about women, or passion, or like your passion for racing, and oh my God, why am I still talking?" She buries her head in her hands with a groan.

A wicked thought runs through my head but it's chased by me taking pity on El and not making her tell me more about how much she likes passionate girls.

I sit down on the edge of the bed next to her. The mattress lets out a groan and sinks at the middle, making me slide nearly into El's lap. My thigh brushes her wet jeans. She looks up in alarm. "Got it on the flowers. Any word from your parents yet?"

Not moving away from me, El gestures with her phone. "They probably think I'm still asleep in my room. Since tomorrow is Sunday, I'm betting we've got at least until noon tomorrow before they figure out I'm gone. What about your dad?"

I pick up my phone, scanning through its apps quickly. "Nope, nothing. He hates confrontation with me, and probably won't even check on me until dinnertime tomorrow night."

She nods, shifting her leg against mine. My bare ankle brushes her calf.

"Well," El says slowly.

"Well . . ."

She hops up suddenly. "Well, I guess I need to go shower!" With that, she grabs her backpack and hurries into the tiny bathroom, slamming the door as she goes.

Huh.

I run a hand over the indentation her body made in the bedspread. That moment of closeness was painfully uncomfortable. Does El not want to be around me? The way she kissed me in the car says yes, as does her calling me to go on this trip. But maybe she's not really thinking clearly. Maybe she just wants me here for moral support and I'm reading too much into her kisses. Maybe I'll put a pillow between us in the night, just so I don't accidentally roll over and start spooning her. Or maybe that would be a great thing?

The air conditioner kicks on then, sending a blast of freezing air across the tiny room. With it comes a dusty, floral scent that makes me believe Flora has been crushing rose petals and dropping them into the air conditioner. The air makes goosebumps rise across my bare legs, and I grab my messenger bag and scramble under the covers, burrowing deep in the floral sheets. My toes find the warm spot where El was sitting on the bedspread and I dig them into it.

The shower starts in the bathroom and El's voice floats through the thin particleboard door. A smile pulls at the edge of my lips. El Blum sings in the shower. Who knew?

Outside, rain snickers against the windows, and thunder sounds in the distance. I'm so glad we got off the road. For tonight, it feels like we're in a secret pocket of the world. One where none of the adults in our lives know where we are, and where we can be whoever we want to be. I inhale, taking in the scent of roses, dust, and freedom. This is what I crave—little spots of time where I'm answerable to no one and the world unfolds with mystery and promise. Thinking of that, I rifle through my bag, looking for the F1 Academy application.

It's not there. My hands fly over my toothbrush, my extra socks, the tampons I threw into the bag in case my period surprises me, and my wallet, but there's no application.

Panic flares in me, sweeping my breath away, and I grip the strap of the bag. Did the form fly out somewhere while we were driving? Is my dream lost to the winding roads between here and Dell's Hollow? I could reprint it, yes, but I'd not saved the handwritten sections I'd labored over for days. It would be awful to have lost that form.

My mind flies back over the events of the evening, landing on when I pulled out the form and showed it to Dad.

Oh.

That's right, of course.

After I got back to my bedroom, I took the form out and threw it on Grandma's craft table. I'd almost torn it up, but I couldn't quite bring myself to do that. But what was the point of saving it anyway? It's not like Dad was going to sign it. What had he said? *"You'll find other dreams, JoJo."*

I doubt that, but maybe it is enough to not worry about it tonight. This is the time for existing in the weird rose-scented bubble of Flora's crafting fever and sharing a bed with El Blum. Which is something I'd not even let myself dream about. I drop my messenger bag to the floor and grab my phone.

I'm deep in a TikTok hole by the time El comes out of the bathroom. She's wearing a tank-top-and-sleep-shorts PJ set that's printed with tiny elephants. It's adorable and she gives me a shy smile as she turns off the bathroom light.

"Ready for bed?" she asks, coming over to the side opposite me. She turns on the bedside lamp and pulls back the covers. She slips under them, bringing with her a wave of heat from the shower.

I put my phone and the necklace from my mom on the bedside

table with shaking hands. This is it. I'm officially in bed with El Blum for the first time.

I'm not a virgin—I've had sex lots of times, but with exactly two people. First there was Caitlin Walters at summer racing camp last year when we shared a cabin, and after Cait, there was Paul Morris, my boyfriend of a few months last fall. Those times with Cait and Paul were fun, sure, but this feels different. Everything about El feels different. Cait and Paul were casual hookups with lots of flirting. El feels substantial somehow. With her, I know the places where she might break if I don't hold them carefully. I've seen her grief over her sister, and I don't want to cause her more pain.

But I also desperately want to kiss her.

She turns toward me, propped up on one elbow. "Hey, Jo," she says.

I turn toward her, and the mattress sinks again, making it so our noses are nearly touching. "Hey, El."

She scoots a little closer. Our knees touch and I hold absolutely still, trying to control my racing heart.

"Is this okay?" She places one hand on the place where my hips dip into my waist.

"Most incredibly okay," I breathe.

El scoots even closer, tangling her legs with mine. Her thigh grazes my knee, sending heat through me. "And this?

"Also okay."

I lean in, planting a featherlight kiss on her lips. She closes her eyes, and the small hungry noise she makes nearly undoes me.

She pulls me to her, so our breasts touch, and that's it—I'm officially all in. Our kisses deepen, growing more fast and furious with each touch. We're shoestrings wrapped around each other and everything in this moment is our hands, El's hair on my cheek, her warm breath, and—

And then she stops kissing me abruptly, pulling away in one quick motion.

"Oh no," she whispers. She covers her mouth, and her eyes widen in horror.

"What?"

I swear, if El tells me this is a mistake, I'm going to spend the night under a floral towel in the bathtub.

"I'm wearing my retainer." El groans and pulls the covers up to her face. "I cannot believe I'm kissing the hottest girl I've ever met, and I forgot to take out my damn retainer."

Her voice comes out muffled from beneath the blankets, but I can't help but laugh in relief. She wants to kiss me.

I pull the covers down and kneel in front of her. "For what it's worth, I didn't even notice," I say, brushing a piece of her blond hair behind her ears. "What are the chances I could get you to spit out that retainer and we pick up where we left off?"

"High," says El, turning her head and removing her orthodontic hardware. She plops it on the bedside table and turns off the light.

A thin strip of light from under the door is enough to show me El's eyes as she snuggles under the covers next to me.

"Hey, Jo," she says, her lips right beside my ear.

"Hey, El," I whisper back, stealing a quick kiss.

"I'm so glad you came with me on this trip." She cups my face with her hand, and I lean into the touch for a moment.

"I'm so glad you asked me, Motorcycle Girl™," I say softly. "Now, can we please stop talking?"

El leans in for a kiss at that and I pull the covers over us, shutting out the storm, the scent of dried roses, and the rest of the world. Just for tonight.

# *CHAPTER TWENTY*

## El

The sun is so bright through the wax-paper-like motel curtains the next morning, it feels as if I fell asleep in the attic again and the harsh rectangle of sun through the skylight is beating down on me. I think that's a romance cliché: waking up the morning "after" and for a moment, not remembering where you are or who you're with. Except that JoJo's warm back is pressed against my chest and our legs are braided like a loaf of challah, which makes it impossible to forget. I hate to move an inch, but I'm usually a stomach sleeper, and lying curled forward has my spine cramping. I stretch slowly, without moving my arm looped over JoJo's waist.

But she shifts, yawns, and turns over to face me anyway. "Hey."

"Oh, fuck . . ." I clap my hand across my mouth.

"What?" JoJo's eyes widen inches from mine, awake and alarmed. "What's wrong? Are you . . . is everything okay?"

"I forgot to put my retainer back in." I drag my tongue across my front teeth, tasting shamefully unlike metal.

"El!" she shrieks, punching me in the shoulder as best she can at point-blank range. "Don't scare me, you jerk." But she's laughing now.

"You should be scared. I never sleep without my retainer. If my overbite regresses, my parents are gonna be pissed."

And that's when I remember my parents. Rolling away, I scoop my phone off the particleboard nightstand, where it's been charging overnight. Now, it's after eight, and no angry, panicked texts from them yet, just a text from Zaynah asking if I'm opening today at Putt by the Pond, which I thumb past—I'll answer her later. Weirdly, even as I let out a breath of relief, my stomach sinks. It makes sense that they haven't noticed I'm gone. Dad heads to the gym earlier than I get up during summer vacation, and Mom has yoga on Sunday mornings. Unless I have an early cleaning shift at Putt by the Pond, they'd have no reason to see me in the morning, or to check in on me.

Except we had that fight last night, probably the biggest we've ever had (we're not a screaming-match kind of family so much as a silent, two-day-freeze kind of family) and I guess they still didn't feel the need to check on me.

Whatever. It's good. It gives us time. Today, we'll make it to Richmond. Today, we'll find my sister, and I'll bring her home. And when I get back to Dell's Hollow with Max—or when Max gets back to Dell's Hollow on the R1, and JoJo and I follow behind on an Amtrak train or whatever—our parents will have to forgive us both. Everything will be okay again, like it was before. Better, even, because Max and my parents won't fight like they did when she dropped out of school, and now I have JoJo.

I roll back over to face her.

"Still in the clear," I say, pasting on a smile that turns real the longer I look at her.

Because I am so lucky, and JoJo is so pretty, her shower hair dried wild, with her eyes golden-green in a slice of pure sunlight that cuts between the crappy curtains, and her leg both soft and strong as granite as she slides it between my ankles to hook around my calf and pull me closer. "We're good, then?"

"Yeah," I say, suddenly feeling shy again. "That wasn't, um, you've done this before, right?"

"Yeah." She's smiling back at me, but there's a quirk between her eyebrows. "Not for a while, though—like months before we moved out of Charleston. And I was always safe, and um, should we have talked about this before? We should've talked about this."

"No, that's okay! I knew you'd dated and everything. I don't mind. Not that it's like, my business to mind. Can you tell I've never done this?" I wedge my arm up between us to cover my eyes.

"Like, you've never had this exact conversation, or never . . . ?"

"Never had sex." Sliding two fingers apart, I peek at her from between them. "Is that okay? I've had relationships, like I said, we just never did . . . this much. Was I—"

"Eliana Blum!" JoJo grabs my wrist to peel my hand from my face, wrapping it back around her waist. "You were fantastic." She says it like she means it.

My cheeks heat, but not with embarrassment this time. "You too." And she was. Asking where it was okay to touch me and what I wanted, telling me where she liked to be touched and what she wanted. Like, in hindsight, it seems pretty clear I didn't totally know what I was doing, but if she says she had a good time, I choose not to doubt it. I choose to believe this, even as I can feel my inconvenient brain wanting to buzz with questions, with doubts, with what if, what if, what if.

"And you're okay?" she asks.

"Yeah. I'm good. We're good," I echo her words.

We're good.

JoJo grins, sliding her leg farther up, her knee between my knees, and I ignore my brain and our commingled morning breaths completely as I lean in to kiss her again, and this, too, feels like relief.

Day two on the R1 is a whole different game. For one thing, it's a bright, clear morning instead of midnight. While that should make things easier, it means more traffic—a constant flow of cars and big rigs on all sides, instead of the occasional pair of headlights streaking past me like twin stars in the dark. Other drivers were always the most nerve-wracking factor in my brief trips on the highway with Max to reach Pemberly Mill. And now there's no Max to fall back on, no big sister ready to take over if I panic and need to pull onto the shoulder.

With a deep breath, I steer us out of the motel parking lot.

We only put about eighty miles behind us yesterday, stopping in a place called Butner. The short ride to the I-85 on-ramp, which we'll take for the next two hours until the Richmond exit, is mostly fast-food places and the gas station we filled up at. I spot an old hulking water tower in the distance beyond the trees. This isn't super cinematic as road trips go, which is kind of a shame. I've never been to Butner before, even though it's so close to home, and who knows if I'll ever come back?

Still, I'm almost excited to be on the highway again. Because riding gives me little time to think of anything *but* riding. I can't daydream like I might in the Oatmobile, cruising the backstreets after our traffic lights turn to blinking red late at night. Which means there's no time or brain space to spiral over what waits for me back home. Or what I'll say to Max when we find her. Or whether Jo is daydreaming about a training program in London, even as she clings to me; whether last night has changed any of her plans, or has changed nothing at all.

There's just this: the road ahead, the bike beneath me, and the body in which I'm more rooted than I've ever been, because I need every part of me to ride. I work the clutch and turn signal with my left hand, the front brake with my right. My right foot is constantly poised to work the rear brake, and with my left I shift the gears up and down. I accelerate, I brake, I lean—carefully, with JoJo on the back. I smell *everything*, the way I wouldn't even in a car with its windows down: the grass and butterfly weed in the roadside ditches, exhaust and hot asphalt. I *feel* everything, like the slight drop in temperature when we drive through a tree-lined stretch of I-85 and the early sun is off our backs for just a moment, and the rumble of every minor patch in the road, and the warm wind scraping against my throat. I feel awake and alive and afraid.

Which, look, I'm not unused to being afraid of everything all the time, but it's different on the R1, as I'm now remembering that it was different on the Husqvarna. Like I have permission to just feel it, without having to muscle myself back under control.

The 130 miles seem to take forever and fly by at once, but we merge onto I-95 North almost exactly two hours later, as expected. As we cross the bridge over the James River, the skyline of Richmond rears up in front of us. Skyscrapers are gleaming in the noontime sun, and I'm grateful for Max's tinted visor even as I start to sweat, caught in exit traffic. As we take the turn onto East Canal Street—as far into the directions as I'd memorized—JoJo takes over, like we planned this morning. We're going slowly enough that she can lean forward and direct me to a parking garage on the other side of the canal, where we pay for entrance and find a spot on the third level. Hopping off the bike at last, I twist to crack my spine, and strip gratefully out of Max's jacket and helmet. Even in the shade, I'm baking without a constant wind.

JoJo takes off her helmet and rolls up the sleeves on her gray *Fast & Furious* T-shirt. When our eyes meet, she laughs, a little wild.

So do I, giddy with disbelief. "We actually did it!"

She beams back at me. "*You* did it. You drove a whole-ass motorcycle to Richmond." Jo leans across the cooling bike to kiss me, and I feel like I've just won first in my category at Loretta Lynn's, or something. I feel heroic. Unbeatable.

And then I remember the next part of the plan.

JoJo's already on her phone, checking the distance to Clark's Gold Star Pawnshop and how much an Uber will cost us. For now, we'll leave the R1 in the relative safety of the garage; no sense driving it all over Richmond and trying to find parking at each stop. Once we find Max, we'll all come back for it together. Hopefully she'll forgive me for the bugs and dust now plastered to her previously spotless prized possession.

"There's a car seven minutes away," JoJo announces, "and we can be at the pawnshop fifteen after that." She looks up from her screen and asks gently, "Are you ready?"

"I . . . don't think I should think about that," I admit, "'cause I honestly don't know. But we've come this far, right?"

"Right."

We're so close now, either to my sister, or to the helpful coworker that will direct us to her. We're *so* close.

All we have to do is keep it pinned.

# CHAPTER TWENTY-ONE

## JoJo

El grips my hand as soon as we climb into the Uber. I snake my fingers through hers. "We'll find her," I whisper. "Don't worry. We made it here; that's the hard part."

She doesn't reply, just squeezes my hand.

The driver takes us through Richmond, past shops and restaurants. Then, the city starts to change, going from bougie hipster neighborhoods into distinctly more frayed-at-the-edges ones.

"Are you sure this is the address?" the driver, a middle-aged Black woman named Rita, who has a collection of soccer ball stickers with her kids' names and player numbers on them covering the back of her minivan, asks us as we pull up outside the Clark's Gold Star Pawnshop. We're in the middle row of the minivan, and the entire back row—the non-professional riding area according to Rita—is filled with kids' shoes, uniforms, toys, and a booster seat.

We all pause for a moment, taking in the bars over the grimy windows, the collection of guns hung behind the counter, and the two skinny white men outside the shop, smoking and eyeing us warily.

The Gold Star is no less sketchy than Riley's apartment, but it doesn't feel right. Rita frowns, looking like she wants to give us a juice box and deliver us to school play practice, not leave us at the doorstep of whatever trouble El's sister is tangled up in.

El pulls out her phone, swiping to the address Riley gave us. "This is the place," she says, showing Rita the phone.

Rita raises one eyebrow, saying everything with that small gesture. Like: How did you two get into this mess? What are you doing here without parents? Why are you stopping at this pawnshop? Who are you looking for? Should I really drop you off here, even though it's my job?

All very, very good questions.

"Do you think Riley was just fucking with us?" I ask in a low voice. "How do we know Max works here?"

El bites her lip, her confidence visibly evaporating under my question. She was magnificent this morning as she drove us here to find Max, but the Gold Star has left her stumped.

"I don't know . . . for sure . . ." she says. "But Riley was so wildly specific. He could've just said she was in Richmond, but he said Clark's Gold Star Pawnshop, on East Oak Street. He even wrote down the Harley-Davidson garden gnome in the window."

I peer at the pawnshop window, and, sure enough, beyond the grimy glass and collection of for-sale knickknacks sits a small ceramic gnome in a Harley vest and leather chaps. It's hideous, but certainly memorable.

"I don't think Riley is smart enough to lie in such detail," El adds.

That is probably true.

"Do you think you can wait for us?" I ask Rita.

"I don't normally do that, and I can't afford to miss another ride," she says, eyeing her watch.

I pull a twenty out of my wallet and hand it to her. "I'll give you another when we get out," I promise. "But, please, just wait? We won't be long."

With another eyebrow raise, she takes the money. "Five minutes, girls. Be back in five or I'm coming in after you. This isn't a place for kids like you."

"Or a place for Max," El mutters beside me.

Even from inside the minivan, I can see Max isn't in the shop. Not unless she's suddenly turned into a bulky white guy with tufty gray hair and a fondness for pinkie rings.

"Be careful in there, girls," Rita calls as I open the door.

"We will."

Once the door is slammed shut behind me and Rita has locked the doors behind us, I turn to El. A strand of her hair has popped out of her half ponytail and I smooth it behind her ear. She exhales softly at my touch.

"Ready?" I say.

"I think so." She has Max's jacket draped over her arm and there's a hard glint to her eyes.

"Do you need to go into the shop alone?" I ask.

"Not even a little bit. We've come this far together; we're not splitting up now."

Ignoring the guys on the sidewalk, we push open the pawnshop door. A bell jingles as we walk in, and the guy behind the L-shaped counter just grunts, not looking up from his phone. Behind him, next to the guns, hang rows of acoustic and electric guitars, looking like they miss their owners. On another wall are rows of designer purses, some of them in bright colors and all of them secured by a loop of metal wire and padlocks. For a moment, we look around at the display cases, running our fingers over them. Beneath the glass are watches, rings, earrings, and necklaces.

"You here to sell something?" the man behind the counter booms at us, still not looking up from his phone. "I take gold, silver, coins, some stamps, designer bags—but no fakes—only on the days when my bag girl is here. Also, we buy guns, guitars, electronics—"

"Your bag girl?" El interrupts. "Who's that?"

It's clear from the note of hope in her voice that she's hoping this is Max.

The man finally looks up at us at El's question. "Not in the habit of talking about my employees to customers," he says.

"She's not just an employee!" El bursts out. "I'm looking for my sister. Max. She's supposed to work here."

The man's eyes narrow. He looks toward the back room quickly in a way that's utterly suspicious and then scratches his nose with one paw of a hand. "How do I know you're not lying? Max told me she got into some trouble. How do I know you're not here to turn her in to the cops?"

"Do we seriously look like the cops?" I ask, gesturing between us.

My comment is lost, however, in El's triumphant "AH-HA! You said someone named Max DOES work here."

The man scowls at her. "She might. Still doesn't mean I believe she's your sister."

With a huff, El starts tapping at her phone and then she brandishes it at the man. As it flashes by me, I see a picture of El and Max, standing by the R1, grinning.

"Is that her?" El demands. "Is that the Max who works here?"

The man grunts.

"And as you can see, that's me," El continues. "Standing by my sister, whom I've not seen in months."

"Maybe she is your sister, but it seems to me if she's not been around in months, maybe she doesn't want to be found."

"If she didn't want to be found, why did she send me these!" El pulls a handful of postcards from her bag and flings them onto the counter.

"Not my business," the man says. "My business is buying and selling. Now, if you want me to give you cash for that gold necklace your friend has on, I can do that."

My hand flies to the gold race car charm hanging from the chain around my neck. I'd rather put the Harley gnome in my room than sell this guy the necklace my mom gave me. "It's not for sale," I manage through a surprising surge of emotion. Just the thought of a random stranger wearing this last gift from my mom makes me weepy.

El squeezes my elbow. "We're not here to sell anything," she repeats.

"Buy something then," says the man. "Or get out. I'm not telling you anything about Max."

El's face falls, crumbling like a piece of paper that's been discarded.

"At least tell us if she's here!" I say, pulling out a twenty-dollar bill from my quickly dwindling stock of cash. "Can you do that?"

The man holds out a hand for the cash and I put the bill into it. He closes his hand around the bill and goes back to his phone. "She's not here right now. Not on the schedule for a few days. Now get out."

Right as he says it, one of the guys from outside comes through the door. "Who's not here?" he asks, moving around us to slip behind the counter.

"This one says she's Max's sister," grunts the other man. "Wants to know where she is, but doesn't want to buy anything."

The younger man eyes the twenty-dollar bill in my hand. "I'll tell you where she might be for twenty bucks."

I slip him the bill.

"Check Mama Maple's Bacon and Eggs. It's a diner just a few blocks from here. Walking distance really. Max is usually working there if she's not here. Or she'll be at the racetrack."

The other man gives him a fairly murderous look, and gestures for us to get out.

"What racetrack?" El says as I grab her arm.

I wrack my brain, trying to think of what NASCAR tracks are around here.

He makes a face at us, like we know nothing about racing. "The Richmond Raceway."

"It's our local track. Super popular with fans and drivers. We have NASCAR here two times a year."

Of course. I remember now. Richmond was one of Mom's favorites. But there are twenty-six tracks in the circuit and she'd had many favorites. Somehow, in the rush of sneaking off with El, spending the night together, and looking for Max, I'd forgotten about their racetrack until now. My stomach flips as I remember that I'd missed Mom's last race here for a school thing. And now I'll never see her race again.

El presses the guy for more info. "What would Max be doing at the Raceway?"

The guy shrugs. "Beats me. Said she had some mechanic experience. Not sure if she's working there, but I've got a buddy who works there and I put them in touch. But try the diner first. That's where she usually is this early in the week. Not a lot of action at the track on a Sunday afternoon."

El opens her mouth to ask another question, but the big guy has had enough. "Get out. Now. You're going to scare off other customers."

There's not another customer in sight, but still, I grab El's hand and pull her out of the shop.

"Well, that could've gone better," El says, once we're outside again.

We wave to Rita, who taps her Apple Watch.

"What do you want to do now?" I ask, wanting desperately to see the track again. But also knowing El might want to go to the diner.

"I think we should split up," El says tentatively. "If that's okay with you. I mean, what if Max is in one place, but we both go to the other, and then we miss her?"

"It makes sense to split up," I say, weirdly relieved somehow. "I'll take the Raceway. I mean, unless you want it. But I sort of know my way around tracks, and I wouldn't mind seeing it again. And—"

El puts a hand on my arm. "Jo. It's fine. Go to the Raceway. I'll find this diner. I bet Max is there anyway. She's probably got a proper job and is making good money. I bet this pawnshop job is just a temporary thing."

Her voice shakes as she says it, as if she's convincing herself more than me.

"I bet that's it," I say gently. I wrap her in a hug. "We'll find her. Don't worry."

Rita honks at us, and unrolls a window. "It's been way more than five minutes. I've got to get going. I've got another fare to pick up. I can drop you girls off at one place, but that's it."

"We're going in different directions anyway," says El, holding up her phone. She turns to me. "Mama Maple's is just a few blocks away. I'll walk. You get a ride to the Raceway and let me know what you find."

I look around the slightly rough neighborhood. "Are you sure? I can go with you."

El shakes her head emphatically. "I'm fine. Really. It's super close and it's run by like some famous chef. It's got great reviews and is probably crowded even at this time of day. Don't worry about me. Now, get to the Raceway."

She pops a quick kiss on my cheek, and then turns away, walking with determined strides down the street.

I should go after her. I really should. But she's right that we're more likely to miss Max if we don't split up. Plus, El might need some time to clear her head. A lot has happened over the last twenty-four hours—no, less than that. It's been less than twenty-four hours since we raced Riley and I won.

Just that thought makes my hands itch for a steering wheel. For the feel of track under my wheels. For going so fast, I don't have time to think or miss my mom or worry about the F1 Academy application or what's happening between El and me or the trouble we're going to be in when we get home.

"Your friend isn't coming with us?" Rita asks as I climb into the front seat of the minivan.

I shake my head. "She has something to do at Mama Maple's."

"That place is amazing. We should've asked her to get us some takeout. Where are you headed?"

I buckle my seat belt. "The Richmond Raceway, if it's not too far."

Rita turns the key in the ignition. "We've got time, hon. Don't worry. I'm a fast—but safe—driver. My kids like to tease me and tell me I should be driving a race car."

I close my eyes, leaning against the seat. "My mom was a race car driver," I say softly.

"She is not!" Rita exclaims as she pulls away from the pawnshop.

"Was," I say, opening my eyes. I turn around and look for El, but she's already turned down another street and out of view. "My mom was a race car driver. She passed away a few months ago in a crash."

"Oh hon," Rita says, placing her warm hand over mine. "I'm so sorry. Want to tell me about it?"

I shake my head.

"Want a juice box?" She opens the center console and pulls out a juice box and a granola bar. My stomach rumbles at the sight, reminding me I've not eaten for hours.

"That would be great, thanks," I say, taking both with a feeling that could be relief, but might be something else.

"We'll get to the Raceway soon," Rita says. "But in the meantime, want me to tell you about the time I drove a famous F1 driver around Richmond for the day?"

"I'd love that," I say, taking a long sip of sugary juice. "Tell me all about it, please."

# CHAPTER TWENTY-TWO

## El

Mama Maple's Bacon and Eggs is an improvement over the pawnshop, and not just because Gold Star set the bar in the sewer. When I push through the double doors, I find a brightly lit '50s-style diner with shiny checkerboard floors and cheerful turquoise booths. It's one of those postcard places: You know, the slightly unique local attractions they put on postcards and keep stocked at welcome centers and tourism offices. The kind Max has been sending me these past four months. This is a sign, I decide.

Though the diner feels cozy, there's a corridor of booths long enough that I spot an empty one despite the lunch rush. The chalkboard by the door instructs me to TAKE A MENU AND SEAT YOURSELF, HONEY so I hustle toward it, dropping onto the squeaky bench cushion that smells of bacon and onions and coffee in a good way. Maybe we got kicked out of the pawnshop, but nobody will kick a customer out of a diner. I'll just order iced tea after iced tea until Max turns up for her shift. Though honestly, Jo and I only stopped long enough to grab a plastic-wrapped muffin apiece from the It'll Do Motel's "continental breakfast" and scarf them down quickly in the parking lot. I should get a to-go order for Jo . . . unless the Raceway's concession stand is open? We always brought coolers to the track during my and Max's events, but maybe this is a whole different scene.

I picture JoJo carving an expert path through the crowds in her search, smelling the old smells—burnt rubber and burning nitro and barbecue that drifts all the way from the RV campgrounds outside the track. I imagine her lingering, watching the cars roar by and missing the pit like a childhood home. But I do *not* text her just to make sure her head is in the game, or to remind her that I'm here, waiting, wishing we hadn't split up in the first place. I will not hold on to JoJo so tightly that she spins out the moment my fingers slip.

I won't . . .

"Well hi there, sweetie!" a waitress chirps as she appears with her order pad. Around Jolene's age, she reminds me a little of JoJo's grandma, with her carefully applied fruit-punch lipstick and coiffed hair, although she's wearing much more practical white sneakers. "I'm Hazel, and I'll be looking out for you today. What can I getcha?"

"Oh. Can I have the, uh . . ." I speed-read the specials menu I've been clutching but have yet to glance at. "The Mama's Waffles Plate, please, with the Easy Cheesy Loaded Grits? And an iced tea."

"Coming right up." Hazel is that experienced waitress combo of friendly and efficient; so much so, I almost miss my chance.

But just as she turns away, I remember the mission. "Um, hey!" I call after her. "I wanted to ask . . . Do you know when Max will be in today?"

She stops, pursing her painted lips as she glances back and looks me over, more shrewdly this time. "What do you want Maxine for?"

I'm startled by the decidedly unfriendly question, and by my sister's full name. Is she going by Maxine here? I only ever called her that to annoy her, and likewise she with Eliana. But Hazel might just be old-fashioned, or formal. "She's my sister. Maxine Blum? I thought she had a shift today."

Hazel softens again, her thin shoulders lowering. "I'm not sure. Tell you what, sweetie, I'll ask in the back."

"Thank you!" I call, though she's already striding away toward the kitchen.

With that done and my waffles in progress, I can't avoid checking my phone any longer. I peel it out from the inside pocket of the leather jacket I've draped across the seat beside me, dreading my missed calls. There's little chance my parents don't know I'm gone yet. They'll be fuming even if, fingers crossed, they haven't discovered the missing R1. And if they have, then what? Would they call JoJo's dad, or skip straight to the police? I try to stop that panic-spiral in its tracks. They might not know about the bike; though they're disappointed in me, maybe more than they've ever been, I'm *not* the daughter who takes out a bike in the middle of the night and drives it across state lines.

At least, I wasn't until I was.

I peek at my phone, and Missed Call notifications pop up as I tilt the screen. Shit. *Shit.*

There are two from the house, two from Mom's phone, and one from Dad's. So yeah, I'd say they know I'm gone. Only one voicemail from Mom, though, which doesn't seem like "our daughter stole a sport bike" behavior. My thumb hovers over the Play button, but then I see a fresh voicemail from Zaynah as well, left just an hour ago. And scrolling over to recent calls, I see that she's tried to call me six times today.

I'm not prepared to talk to my parents—and honestly, I'm not confident that I won't crumble under their questioning and make this worse—but Zaynah will be easier. Maybe she can even help me buy time until I find Max.

Leaving the jacket in the booth to reassure Hazel that I haven't ditched, I find the bathroom, cotton candy pink and blessedly empty. Tucking myself into the farthest stall (like they're soundproofed or something) I take a breath and call back my best friend. "Hey Z—" I'm barely able to whisper before she explodes.

"Where *are* you? Are you okay? Your parents called mine, they said you weren't there when your mom came home for lunch, and it didn't look like you'd slept in your bed?"

Oh, hell. That's on me; Max would've rumpled up the sheets or thrown a pillow on the floor if she'd snuck out during the night, so she could claim she only got up early. "I—"

"And they said you were out with JoJo yesterday, and she was driving her car without a license?!" Zaynah plows right through me. "You never told me that! I didn't even want to do the heist, but if I knew she wasn't supposed to be driving—"

Now it's my turn to interrupt. "What do you mean, you didn't want to do the heist?" I tuck my feet up against the stall door, as if that'll stop my words from traveling. "You asked to come. You offered to be our getaway driver."

"Yeah, to keep you guys out of trouble if you were gonna do it anyway. And now I'm in trouble, because I couldn't lie to my parents and say I didn't know anything."

"Oh. I'm sorry, Z—"

"And you're definitely in trouble. Where *are you*?"

"Um. Richmond?"

Silence, then, "Are you with JoJo?"

"I . . . yeah."

"Of course you are." It almost sounds like she's sneering on the other end.

Zaynah and I haven't seriously fought since eighth grade, when we couldn't agree on which movie to see at the Cineplex—I wanted *Godzilla*, she wanted *The Secret Life of Pets 2*. We both thought the other was being ridiculously stubborn, which stirred up wounds as old as elementary school, and didn't speak for a week and a half. I'm getting the feeling that this will be worse.

"What does *that* mean?" I ask, already knowing I shouldn't.

"You're always with JoJo, and you hardly even talk to me. We haven't seen each other all summer except for work and volunteer club. I didn't even know you two were dating until the barbecue, when I saw you kissing, and you haven't said anything since. It's like now you have her to get in trouble with, and you don't want me around. We have a club event this afternoon, remember? At the nature center in Deerfield? I'm guessing since you're with her, you won't be there."

"Oh my God, so? I'm always showing up. I show up for work, I show up to tutor, I show up for every school event, I show up for the club. I'm allowed to have more important stuff to do," I hiss back as quietly as I can.

Another wrong move.

"More important than the volunteer club, or more important than me?"

"That's . . . I didn't—"

"Whatever," she cuts me off coolly. "I was calling because I was worried. I shouldn't have been. You've done this before, you know. When Max came home? I know she's your sister and I'm just . . . me, but I hardly saw you until she left. And then we weren't even supposed to talk about her, no matter how worried I was. So I guess we'll talk again when JoJo leaves, right?"

"Zaynah, stop, I—"

The call ends.

I sit there in the stall for a long moment, steaming. Because I've seen Zaynah plenty this summer. We talk all the time, practically every day, and I definitely told her about JoJo before the barbecue.

Didn't I?

With shaking fingers, I go into our text thread, stretching back and back and back. Her text this morning went unanswered, sure, as did a few increasingly unhinged "where are you?!?!?!?" messages since.

But then, dread trickling down and pooling in my stomach, I see a dozen unanswered or barely answered texts before that, from the last week alone. Including an "OMG, you and Jo!!" she sent during the party, probably typing beneath the picnic table, which I never did respond to. And there's no mention of The *Mario Kart* Kiss in anything I've sent since that night in the attic.

Well, fine. I fucked up. This is another thing for me to fix when I get back to Dell's Hollow. Make up with my parents. Make up with Zaynah. Apologize to the club, and to my Putt by the Pond manager for missing my opening shift. Promise everyone that I'll do better, be better, become the girl everyone can count on all over again.

But first: Max.

By the time I slow my breathing enough to leave the bathroom (with a few customers coming and going in the meantime), I arrive just in time to find Hazel setting my plates on the table.

"Everything all right, sweetie?" she asks, seeing my face; maybe I'm not as under control as I thought I was when I left my bathroom stall cocoon.

I paste on a happy customer smile, which gets a little easier as I slide into the booth and the steam from my cheesy grits wafts over me; I really am starving. "This looks so great, thanks. Did you, um, find out when my sister comes in today?"

"Ah, I thought maybe somebody else here told you, and that's why . . ." Her forehead puckers, and her voice is soft as she tells me, "Maxine isn't coming in."

"Like, she called out today?"

"My manager says she was let go last week, sweetie. She—can I get you something else? On the house. We make a great buttermilk pie."

I shake my head, smile pasted in place until Hazel leaves. Then I text Jo call me, and wait and wait and wait for her to answer while my grits grow ice cold in front of me.

# *CHAPTER TWENTY-THREE*

## JoJo

The Richmond Raceway is a few miles away from downtown. Even with traffic, Rita makes it there in less than fifteen minutes. As she did last time, when she dropped El and me off outside the pawnshop, Rita looks at the Raceway and raises an eyebrow. It speaks volumes.

"You sure about this, JoJo?" she asks. We're on a first-name basis now, and I also know the names of all her kids, her cat's favorite spots to sleep in, and where she's going on vacation later this summer. I've also told her too much about my family, my mom, and my racing aspirations.

I nod, taking in the mostly empty parking lot. "I've been around raceways my entire life. This feels more like home than home, honestly."

"Just be careful, hon, okay? I'll wait for you here."

"You don't have to do that. I can call another car."

Rita shakes her head. "Nope. I'm invested now. Go find who you need to and hurry back. I'll be waiting." She pats me on the hand and then pulls a book out of her bag.

It's such an ordinary Mom-type thing to say that it brings tears to my eyes. "Thanks," I whisper as I get out of the van.

Since it's Sunday, there's not a race today, but my quick Google search about the Richmond Raceway revealed the track is still open for fans to tour and to buy tickets for races later in the season. Heart in my throat, I hurry away from Rita's van. My sneakers squeak as I move toward the ticket area. The warm June sun beats across my shoulders. Even though there's no official race, track sounds fill the air. Engines growl as a pair of drivers do a stunt lap and shop tools buzz in the pits. The smell of asphalt baking in the heat fills the air, and I inhale sharply, taking it in. Memories come flooding back with the smells and sounds.

Blink.

Suddenly, it's February of this year. Mom, Dad, and I are headed into Daytona before sunrise, avoiding the crowds and RVs already filling the parking lot, and we pull into the drivers' entrance. Dad drives and Mom has a tight, nervous smile on her face. Incongruously, a Rachmaninoff symphony is playing through the car speakers, the music being one of Mom's favorite pre-race rituals. Dad's hand is laced through hers over the center console, their fight at breakfast long forgotten. I'm wearing my gold race car necklace. There's a moment of perfect family happiness as the three of us wait to be waved through the gate, and the sun breaks over the horizon line, spilling orange-pink light across our faces.

Blink again against the tears welling in my eyes.

Now, I'm seven years old, getting ready to race a division up on the junior kart circuit. Mom is braiding my hair and reminding me that although I'm the smallest one there, I'm also the one none of them will expect to hug the turns like we've been practicing.

Blink one more time—this time tears fall from my eyes and trail over my cheeks—and I'm standing at the main entrance to the Richmond Raceway. I run a hand over the cool metal of the ticket counter and take a steadying breath.

A white man in his early twenties peers at me through the plexiglass ticket window. He's got a baseball cap on backward and a long beard that skims his collarbones. He could be Bad Beard Riley's brother. "Can I help you? Next tour starts in thirty minutes. If you pay extra, you can even sit inside a real race car. It's a cool experience. Totally worth the two hundred dollars."

He gives me a leering look, which I shut down immediately with the scowl Mom taught me early in my racing career. It's a mean look, all drawn-together eyebrows and hard-shell eyes that say without a word: "Fuck-you-don't-ogle-me-you-have-no-idea-who-I-am-no-I-don't-think-you're-charming." Mom told me she perfected it in her days as a teenage waitress, and then used it often as she joined the mostly boys' club of NASCAR.

"I've been sitting in race cars since before I could walk," I say to the guy behind the counter. "I'm here looking for someone. Maxine Blum, maybe you know her?"

Recognition flicks across the guy's face fast enough that I know he knows who I'm talking about. But he shrugs back. "Never heard of her. Do you want a ticket to the raceway's self-guided tour or not?"

I buy the ticket, not wanting to linger at the ticket counter. I'm not counting on finding Max in this enormous raceway, especially since I know there are many hallways and rooms that the public never sees, but I owe it to El to at least look around.

Moving away from the ticket counter, I walk toward the closest entrance to the stands. Bleachers tower above the track and I climb them, taking the steps two at a time. When I reach the top, I shield my eyes and watch a car slide into a pit across the track. It's a messy entrance, and one where the driver fumbles the stop. I would never have waited that long to brake. That's how accidents happen.

I think of Dad, sitting at home, working on filling orders for online car parts. It's surreal that he's not been on a track since Mom died. He used to live on racetracks. Knew everything about every one of them, and even now, if we were speaking, I bet I could call him up and ask him stats on the Richmond Raceway and he'd be able to rattle them off, no problem.

I exhale, sitting on the edge of one of the seats. The metal is boiling from the sun, but I make sure my bare legs aren't touching it.

Being here reminds me of so much—how my family used to be, what we loved, and all we've lost.

But we didn't just lose Mom on that terrible day in February. We lost our family unit. We lost all the memories we might make together. It kills me sometimes to know that I'll never take another picture with Mom. That the ones we have in our home or I have on my phone are it. There will be no more photos after that last selfie we snapped of the three of us, right outside Mom's car before the race.

More tears fall at that thought, and on this already weird day, a day where I've woken up beside a girl I've only known for a few weeks and been to a super-scary pawnshop, I sit all alone at the top of a grandstand in a strange city and at an unfamiliar track, and let myself really, truly sob for the first time in months. Great heaving spasms of grief break through my careful control. I bury my head in my hands and weep—for my mother and the sunrises she'll never get to see; for my dad in his loneliness and the half life he's living; for our family, which was so strong and now is like a tree pulled up and left exposed and broken after a storm; for me and the fact that my mom will never see me win another race; and for my own dreams of racing that feel so very fucking far away.

I sob until I'm nothing but a ragged husk of myself, as empty as the waxy popcorn bag caught between the seats in front of me.

A loud roar pulls me back to the present. I wipe my face on my shirt, trying to find my calm again. Trying to remember why I'm at the Richmond Raceway in the first place. Far below where I sit, the two cars still race around the track, caught in an endless, roaring loop of trying to reach a place they can never arrive at. Each lap is a desperate scramble for position, or a frantic attempt to shave a few extra seconds off their times. I close my eyes, letting the thrill of the race fill me. It rushes into my empty corners, a cocktail of adrenaline and hope and furious need.

I want so very badly to be down there, behind the wheel of my own car, driving against the best in the world. It won't bring my mom back, but it might help me feel her presence somehow. It might make me miss her less. It might help me heal or move on. My mom's words rise in my mind: *Most of us think if we keep running fast enough, we'll stay ahead of whatever scares us. There's a certain feeling I'm always chasing* ....

My eyes fly open, moving to the place where the cars are now. They're holding close to the wall, pinning each other in place around a curve, and then the blue car—the car that's the exact shade as the Hornet, Mom's favorite car ever—breaks free, twisting slightly to the left, and pulling ahead.

My breath snags raggedly in my throat as the blue car speeds forward. It feels like a sign. Like Mom is there with me now, pushing me forward.

I have to keep going with my dreams. I know it in that moment with such clarity, it nearly knocks me over.

Yes, my family has changed. Yes, my dad might not sign the F1 Academy form. Yes, I'm in Dell's Hollow and feeling increasingly complex things for El Blum, but that doesn't mean I have to give up on my dreams.

"I'm not afraid, Mom," I whisper out loud, even as more tears form in the corners of my eyes. Unlike my soul-breaking sobs, these are tears of hope and promise and the sheer exhausted exhilaration that comes from being on track again.

Before I can swipe at my tears, a loud whoop rises from the bottom of the stands. A small, wiry girl with blond hair stands near the track, roughhousing with a pair of guys. She's wearing a mechanic's jumpsuit and waving as the blue car thunders past.

Max!

I pull out my phone. There's a message from El—Call me!—which I'll do in a minute. Snapping a quick picture of Max, I send it off with an I FOUND HER!

I start hurrying down from the stands, skipping stairs. I miss the last one and tumble down three, landing hard on my left knee. Pain shoots up my leg, but I get up. Max has left the railing that overlooks the track and disappeared.

Ignoring the pain on my knee, I hurry in the direction she went. Up ahead of me, she's joined by a guy and a girl, also in mechanics' jumpsuits, and they move toward the exit.

Out the door they go with a wave to the guy in the ticket booth. They're talking with each other, laughing, and Max has an arm slung around the guy's waist.

A little breathless—I really have to start training more—I follow them into the parking lot. They move away, toward a row of cars. The three of them pile into a royal blue Nissan, which looks very much like the one Paul Walker drove in *The Fast and the Furious*, but can't be the GT-R model because those aren't legal in the US yet. The car peels out of the parking lot with a screech of tires. I knock on the passenger side window of Rita's van, startling a little shriek out of her.

"JoJo?" she says, unlocking the door. She takes in my bleeding knee and my I've-clearly-just-been-sobbing eyes as I climb into the front seat.

"I'm fine," I say quickly. "Just tripped on some stairs. Now, please, follow that car!"

Rita waits until I'm buckled before speeding out of the parking lot. Despite the Nissan's hurried exit, we catch up to it at the light outside the Raceway.

I check my phone as we drive. While I was hurrying to the car, a bunch of texts have come in from El.

> **El:** OMG THAT IS HER!
>
> **El:** Where are you? Did you talk to her?
>
> **El:** Don't talk to her without me
>
> **El:** Where are you going?

I snap a picture of the blue Nissan and then write back: We're following them. I'll text you the address.

El immediately sends me a string of emojis—hearts, fingers crossed, cheering megaphone, crying face, and more hearts.

I send a few back, hoping that this goes as well as El has been dreaming it will.

Rita keeps enough distance that the blue Nissan doesn't seem to know we're following them, while still managing to stay on their tail. The car stops outside a row of apartments near downtown, and Rita parks a few spaces behind where the Nissan parked. I watch as Max gets out in front of a dingy, split-level unit with dirty brick on the bottom half and dog-puke-yellow siding at the top. Green mildew slicks the white metal front door and parts of the window frames are falling off. A concrete stoop sits in front of the apartment, set into a tiny yard full of dry grass, weeds, and cigarette butts. A scraggly oak tree that's seen better days casts a little shade on the stoop, and a pair of rusty, mismatched lawn chairs are tumbled under the tree.

I check my phone—we're close to the diner, which means El is nearby. I text her the address and then turn to Rita.

"Thank you for everything today," I say, a little sad to be saying goodbye to her. "I appreciate you rolling with this weird day."

Rita smiles. "Never a dull moment on this job. Now, you two girls be careful. Get home to your families soon."

"We will," I promise while I pay Rita for the ride and include a huge tip. By the time I get out of the car, El is strolling up the street at a clip.

"Hey, JoJo," Rita says, rolling her window down as I hop out of the car. "I'll be sure to keep an eye out for your name in the news for winning races. Don't give up on that dream."

She pulls away before I can thank her.

El pulls me into a hug the moment she reaches me. She smells like sweat and waffles and I bury my head in her neck for a moment. This girl feels like home somehow already.

"I can't believe you found Max!" El pulls out of the hug, looking me over. "And oh my God, what happened to your knee?" She fusses over my bloodied knee, but I brush her hand away.

"It's just a scrape. I'm fine, really. How are you? Ready for this?"

El bites her bottom lip, pausing long enough to tell me that she's really nervous. "I have to be, I guess. We came all this way, and we found her."

I lace my hand through hers. "I'll be right beside you as long as you need me. You're the bravest girl I know."

She kisses me then, quick and shaky, and I kiss her back, trying to put everything I can't say into the kiss.

*I'm going to leave to chase my dreams. I like you a lot. You kiss me like I matter. There's a certain feeling I'm always chasing . . . .*

El pulls away first. Hand in hand, we walk up the concrete step to the apartment door. El rings the bell and we wait a long moment. Her breathing is shallow, and I squeeze her hand.

"Fearless," I whisper.

"Fearless," she whispers back.

We wait and El rings the bell again. Still nothing. A long moment passes.

"I saw her go in there?" I say, not sure what we should do if Max doesn't open the door.

Before I can say anything else, the door flies open. On the other side stands a blond woman, about El's height, who glares at us.

Her face softens when she sees us. "El?" she says, her voice higher than I'd expected and full of surprised delight.

"Hi, Max. Um . . . This is JoJo, my girlfriend."

Max's eyes dart to me and then back to El, but I'm only looking at El. Her girlfriend? Something in me flutters at that word.

"Huh," says Max, a smile at the edges of her lips. "Well, I guess you better come in."

She moves aside and El drops my hand. "If you don't mind, I think I'll go up alone."

"Uhm, okay," I say, wanting to ask about "where you ride, I ride," but also knowing that she's not seen Max in a long time and it might go badly. "I'll be right here," I say, gesturing to the stoop.

"Thanks, JoJo," El says, turning away, "for everything." Then, leaving me alone outside, she follows Max up the stairs.

# CHAPTER TWENTY-FOUR

## El

For months, I've been picturing this moment over and over again, like a movie scene I'm constantly rescripting. Max opens the door of her hotel room/apartment building/ramshackle but charming houseboat in [insert city here] to see me standing on the stained carpeting/sidewalk/quay. She blinks in the sunlight (or under the moody glow of streetlights), unbelieving. *El*, she gasps, *what are you doing here? How did you find me?* Until last night, my answer wasn't so clear (sometimes a train, or hitchhiking, or horseback, in one admittedly unlikely scenario) but after mumbling through an explanation, I deliver my line, which never changes: *I'm here to bring you home.* Face crumpling, Max throws her arms around me. *Okay, El.* She sobs. *Let's go home.*

The reality is a little different, it turns out.

For one, I never imagined JoJo waiting for me on the sidewalk. I hope I didn't hurt her feelings. I love Jo (oh my God, I think maybe I love Jo!?). I just knew that this scene had to happen between Max and me, alone. But I thought Max would be different, too. As she goes ahead of me up the cramped staircase, she almost skips up the steps. And she's humming. Off tune and frantically, like a song playing at 1.5 speed. Which doesn't seem like the behavior of someone about to be rescued from exile.

Okay, maybe my script was kind of melodramatic. It can still have a happy ending.

Max stops on the second-floor landing to unlock a scuffed front door. "This is me. We just have to keep it down, 'cause my roommate works nights."

"Yeah, sure. How, um, did you two meet?"

She shrugs as the door rattles open. "Friend of a friend. Let's go to the kitchen—it's the farthest from her room. Plus I'm dying of thirst."

I follow her into an ordinary apartment, stepping over a jumble of shoes and boots in the entrance hall to get to the kitchen. It's small, with old dark wood cabinets. There are unwashed pots stacked on the yellowed stovetop, and unrinsed glasses in the sink. Which is fine! Mom used to get on Max's case about leaving dirty plates on the counter, or a peanut-buttery spoon in the sink when the dishwasher was empty and *right there*. When I'd come home from school, or a club meeting, or tutoring, or work, I'd head to the kitchen and clean up any debris before my parents got back from work. Now, I have to stop myself from attacking the cups and bowls. I remind myself that Mom and Dad aren't here for her to fight with.

My sister follows my sight line. "Best part of being a grown-up. Well, one of the best." She shoves aside a pile of magazines and mail on the counter and hops up to face me. "Okay El, spill. Are you in Richmond for a field trip? Are you running away from home with your cute little girlfriend down there? What's up?"

This is it: time to deliver my line. *I'm here to bring you home.*

But I'm blushing too hard at her suggestive smirk. "No, we're not, we just started . . ." I feel like last night in the hotel room is written all across my face.

She laughs, that familiar Max cackle that lights up rooms and racetracks alike. "I bet. Hey." Her eyes fall to my waist. "Is that my jacket?"

I hurry to untie the thick leather sleeves knotted around me. "Yes! You asked me to get it for you, and . . . here I am." I offer the jacket up in both hands.

"When?"

"Huh?"

"When did I ask?"

"The postcard. The one from Boston? You told me your jacket was at the shop. And I went, and that's where I met JoJo. She's Jolene's granddaughter, isn't that wild? But it wasn't there, and Jolene said your friends might have it. So we found them, and they made us race for it—it was seriously fucking cool, Jo is amazing, you'd love her—and we got it back, and they told us about the pawnshop. So I . . . I brought it back to you. Because you asked." God, I'm rambling.

But Max is still looking at me like I'm some kid she went to high school with and ran into at the grocery store, whose face and name she can't quite place. "Boston. Oh. That was kind of a weird time. I hated that city. It was too cold, even in summer, you know? I was ready to leave as soon as I got there."

"You wanted your jacket, though, right?" I insist. My arms are starting to shake a little, holding it out in front of me.

"Of course I did. Thanks." At last, she leans forward to take it, cradling the leather for just a second before setting it down into a pile of crumbs around the old-fashioned toaster. "Jesus, El." She shakes her head. "You're a good little sister. Better than I deserve."

"That's not true! You're the best."

She snorts, picking at the edge of the countertop where the Formica's peeling off. "I think our parents would disagree. Do they know you're here?"

I shake my head.

"Don't worry too much. I'm sure they'll blame it on me; I'm the Bad Kid, and you're the Good Kid."

"Maybe I was, but I'm not anymore."

She squints down at me appraisingly. "Well. Sorry about that, I guess. Or not. It's a lot of pressure being the Good Kid, huh?" she asks, sounding more like the big sister I love than she has yet.

"Mom and Dad just . . . sometimes it feels like I can't breathe when I'm around them, you know?" I confess in a rush.

"Sure I do. Like they're so busy telling you how much potential you have, but then you have to carry that potential around with you *all the time*, and God forbid you trip, and sometimes you want to throw it all away just so you can set it down."

Embarrassingly, my throat starts to feel hot and swollen, my nose runny. I nod in case I sound like I'm about to cry, because crying is not part of the script.

"I bet it's gotten harder since I left. Sorry about that, too." Max bears down, and a whole chunk of Formica crumbles away and falls to the floor.

"It's not your fault," I insist.

"I don't know about that, El. I made a lot of mistakes."

"So did I. I stole a car!" I blurt out. "We broke into a safe, and we stole a car so we could race it without a license."

She lifts an eyebrow. "That, I never did. You get caught?"

Again, I nod.

"Shit. Does that mean *I'm* the Good Kid now?"

It shouldn't be funny, but suddenly, neither of us can breathe for laughing.

"*Shhh*, my roommate!" Max gasps helplessly after a minute. "Now I definitely need a drink. How about you?" She hops down, leaving the jacket behind on the counter.

"Yeah. Sure," I say, palming the tears from my cheeks.

The last of my laughter dies as she digs through the fridge, because I realize she looks smaller than she used to. She's lost some of the muscle from her competition days, of course. That's not new. Max barely rode in college, and she wasn't exercising for hours a day just to ride the R1. But I don't remember her shoulder blades poking at her T-shirt like that, or her twig-like fingers wrapped around the handle of the fridge.

"There's something else," I say.

"Like, besides stealing a car?" she asks, still deep in the fridge. "Did you rob a bank on the way to Richmond?"

I pry the bike keys from my back pocket. "Actually, I brought you the R1. I drove it here from Dell's Hollow, and it was . . . really fucking scary, but I did it. And I was good at it. It's parked across town, so maybe we can go and get it together?"

Max stiffens. Then, slowly, she emerges with two cans of something called Irish Goodbye Stout. "You shouldn't have done that, El." Her eyes settle on the key in my palm, still attached to her old mini eight-ball keychain.

"I know. I'm pretty sure Mom and Dad will bury me under the vegetable garden when they find out, if they don't know already, but when they see why I did it—"

"Why *did* you do it?" she cuts in, blue eyes narrowing.

"I'm . . . I'm here to bring you home." It comes out so much smaller and weaker than I'd hoped. "If you drive the R1, Jo and I can find a train station or a bus station." Maybe there's a train or bus to a town nearby Dell's Hollow, where we can transfer. I'll keep looking until I find a way.

Max blinks back at me. Then she says, simply, "No, El."

This is not her line.

This is not the plan.

"But if we talk to Mom and Dad together—"

"I said no. Like, come on. I thought you got what it was like for me there, how I felt like I couldn't breathe in that house."

"Yeah, I know, but . . ."

"Fuck the whole town." Max cracks her beer, and the can crumples a little under the force of her grip. "Maybe you got in a little trouble, but you still don't get it. The hoops I had to jump through, the pressure—"

Now it's my turn to interrupt. "*I* don't get the pressure? Are you kidding me? The way people watch me, waiting for me to make a mess because . . ."

"Because of me. See?" She smirks, infuriatingly. "You're better off without me around."

"No, I didn't say that!" I feel my voice rising to a shriek. "I'm the one everyone's mad at. My best friend hates me right now. I'm grounded forever, so I have to quit my job. I might not get to see JoJo after this, for who knows how long. It's all my fault. I drove my whole goddamn life off track to find you."

"I never asked you to!" Max shouts. "Am I supposed to be happy you messed up? Am I supposed to be grateful? I didn't tell you to do any of that. I wrote something I can't even remember on a gas station postcard, El. So maybe you're right; maybe it's not my fault you fucked up your shit. You made your own choices, just like I made mine. That's life. You make choices and you don't look back."

In the hallway, a door bangs open against a wall. "Maxine, shut *up!*" someone hollers. The door slams again.

Max closes her eyes and hisses, "My roommate."

The big sister I love is fading away again in front of my eyes, and I just want to stuff her into her forgotten jacket so I can grab her by the collar and drag her back to the bike she loves so much. Maybe then she'll remember all of the good things she had in Dell's Hollow, the things she

241

had no choice but to leave behind. There has to be *something* I can do, something I can say. "I . . . Okay, yeah, we both made choices," I whisper hoarsely around a lump the size of a Putt by the Pond mini-golf ball. "But you're my sister. We can fix it together."

"El." She shakes her head. "Look, I need to shower. I have a thing tonight."

"Not at Mama Maple's diner, though, right?" I practically sneer.

It's something Mom might've said to Max during one of their worst fights, those screaming matches after Max quit college. But this time it's coming out of my mouth.

My sister's eyes turn to ice. "Hang around here if you want—this isn't a great neighborhood—but I have to leave by seven. And don't wake up my roommate again."

Standing in the empty kitchen after she goes, I find I'm still holding the key to the R1 in one hand, and the Irish stout in the other.

I remember those nights when Max was restoring the bike at Jolene's after hours, while I was doing my calculus on one of the scarred workbenches. She'd hand me a beer from the shop's mini fridge to match hers. Mine inevitably warmed to room temperature unopened, as we both knew it would, leaving condensation rings on the battered wood. That didn't matter. It was just nice to be in the same space, to be as much like my fearless champion of a big sister as I could possibly be.

In my whole life, that's what I wanted most.

I set the key on the kitchen counter next to Max's forgotten jacket, along with the parking garage receipt. Now she knows how to get it back if she wants it—the thing I've taken painstaking care of for the past five months. Her last reason to come back home.

Then I leave her apartment.

JoJo is waiting under the tree outside, looking at her phone and sitting in a lawn chair to get a bit of shade. When she sees me come out, she jumps to her feet, an encouraging smile on her face. It starts to falter as she stares at me. "What happened?"

I plop down on the burning-hot concrete stoop, staring at the can still clutched in my fist. "I don't know."

Jo sits beside me and says again, "El, what happened?"

What *did* happen? I came all this way. I followed my script. Where did I go wrong? My body feels both heavy and hollow at once. Like my heart is a boulder in my chest, but also a cave. How did today begin as a rescue mission and end like this?

It can't end like this.

"What did Max say? Is she coming home?" Jo bumps my leg with her knee.

"She just needs time. I need time to make her listen. She's going somewhere tonight. I left her the bike key, but we can get another Uber, follow her, and I can try again—"

"What did she say?" This time, Jo's voice is painfully soft, just like Zaynah's whenever she talks to me about Max. Just like Jolene's, and like Mr. Keegan, the faculty adviser for the volunteer club. Just like everyone else.

I clutch the can more tightly. "It doesn't matter. My sister's stubborn, and she's probably afraid Mom and Dad won't let her come back.

Maybe . . . maybe I can stay here for a while, prove I'm not going without her."

"El, have your parents called you yet?" JoJo asks, still stingingly gentle. "My dad and Grandma left voicemails."

"I'm sorry I got you in trouble again."

"No, that's not the point." She waves her hands. "We're in this together, and I'll stay awhile if you need to stay. But do you really think Max is gonna change her mind?"

"We aren't giving up on her."

"I'm not saying that, El." Jo scuffs her sneaker on the sidewalk. "I was at the Raceway just now, you know, and I was thinking about . . . about the stuff we have to let go of if we want to move on."

"I'm not *moving on*, Jo. She's my family," I insist. "She's having a hard time, and what am I supposed to do? Forget about her? Everyone else thinks so, and now you do, too? You don't turn your back on family."

We sit in silence under the burning Virginia sun for a moment that becomes eternity. And when Jo speaks again, it's no longer soft. It's the sound of something gone wrong, just before you crash.

"You don't think I know about family, El?"

# *CHAPTER*
# *TWENTY-FIVE*

## JoJo

*"You think I don't know about family, El?"*

My question sits between us, filling the space more than our bodies on the tiny stoop outside Max's house. Anger swells within me, white-hot, with spiky edges. How dare El ask such a question? How many times has she been around my family? How many times have I told her about my family? Wasn't family one of the things that brought us together in the first place?

El swipes at her eyes clumsily because of the stupid can of beer still clutched between her hands. "That's not what I meant!" She puts the can down and then picks it up again. "I just mean it's not the same thing. I know your mom is—" El stumbles over her words, the way everyone does when they don't want to say the hard, true thing. "I know she's gone—"

"But she's never coming back so it doesn't count?" I interrupt, unable to keep the bitterness out of my voice.

El blows out a breath, putting down the beer can again. "It's just not the same," she repeats. "You don't know, because you don't know Max and me."

I sputter at that for a minute, unsure of what to say. Because it sounds a lot like El's saying I can't speak on family or grief, which is bullshit. And of course I didn't know *her and Max*, but I felt like I knew El. Hadn't I? We'd spent so much time together this summer. And she had called me her girlfriend when I met Max. And I'd snuck off with her on the back of a stolen motorcycle, all the way to Richmond, shitting, Virginia. And when I hugged her, it felt like home, and I've been looking for something that felt like home for months now. And maybe Eliana Blum was that for me in Dell's Hollow, when nothing was familiar.

I let out a long breath, trying to release my anger. Trying to pull upon all my years of training to grant me the ability to keep emotion at a distance.

I fail miserably and my next words come out through my teeth, snarling like a dog's been let off its leash. "You're right. I don't know Max, and I'm not even sure I know you. I mean, we just met a few weeks ago. It's not like I'm looking to marry a girl I just met. What I wanted to be was your friend. Or maybe your girlfriend. Or at least that's what I thought we were doing. You know, on this trip. Or this morning. Or even like fifteen minutes ago, before your precious sister rejected you and you decided to take it all out on me!"

God, this morning in the motel feels like ten years ago. El's crying now and I just want to reach out and hug her, but when my arm brushes hers, she shoves it off and stands up.

"Just don't," El snaps. "I shouldn't have dragged you here to see my 'precious sister.' I should've come alone. Maybe it would've worked if . . ." She chokes back a sob, and the noise quells my anger. I wrap my arms around my knees, pulling them close.

"It was good to try and find Max at least. Maybe you can have some closure now?" I offer, feeling bad about my ferocious words and somehow wanting to salvage all this in some way.

"Closure," El spits out viciously. "Sure, great. That's fucking fantastic. Having closure is so much better than having a sister."

"I—"

As much as I want to fix this, I bite off what I was going to say. Part of me knows it's too late. El and I are now like two race cars locked together around a tight turn, careening toward a wall that we can both see, utterly unable to stop moving forward.

El pops the top of the beer can and dumps the frothy amber liquid on a patch of parched grass. "What do you even care? You're leaving anyway."

I stand quickly, as some of the beer El's pouring out splashes on my shoes. "That's not fair at all."

El flings the now empty can toward the door of Max's apartment building, where it clatters and smashes against the wall. "It's true. You're just like Max."

"What are you talking about?" I pick up the discarded can, because El Blum, good girl and cofounder of the Dell's Hollow Volunteer Club, is littering. Picking up the can feels like the least I can do to restore the balance of the universe. "I'm nothing like her!"

Confusion flits across El's face for a moment at my words and then she scowls. "You're gonna leave like her. Like Letty." She gestures wildly.

I drop the smashed empty beer can in a trash bin next to the front door. My mind and my heart are racing, but even still it takes me a minute to place who El's talking about and what she means. In the reflection from the front door glass, I catch sight of the *Fast & Furious* T-shirt I'm wearing and something in my brain clicks. "Letty? Ortiz? As in *Fast & Furious* Letty? What does she have to do with any of this?"

El makes a frustrated noise. "She's the template, Jo! For you, for my sister, for any girl who's going too fast and who doesn't give a shit about who she hurts along the way."

I draw in a ragged breath, brushing drops of spilled beer off my fingers and onto the side of the apartment building. I turn around. "Firstly, that's blaspheming Letty. And—most important—I'm not a fucking fictional character or your sister! You can't compare me to them!"

My words might as well be flung into the trash because El's still stuck on Letty Ortiz. She stands up, turns around, and crosses her arms. "Remember the movies when Letty was hunting Dom?"

"She had amnesia! She wasn't herself! Why are we still arguing about Letty Ortiz?"

"Because it's important!"

We're yelling at each other now, and this is so clearly not really about me and El but rather about her and Max, but fuck it. If El doesn't want me in her life or if she somehow thinks I'm like Max because we both race, and because we have better places to be than with her, that's fine. I don't need her, either.

I swipe at my own face—when had I started crying?—and say, "We have to go. We can't just hang around here, hoping Max is going to change her mind. That's pathetic even for you."

Ouch. Those words were not what I'd meant to say at all, and they hit El like a blow. She rocks back on her feet for a minute.

Then, she steps closer to me, her eyes dangerous. "If you think I'm so pathetic, then why did you come here with me?"

I step backward, and now my back's against the door of the apartment building. "Because I thought you were different from this irrational person who's yelling at me outside her sister's shitty apartment! I thought you were fun and kind and that you liked me. I see now that you've just been using me to find your sister, and that you were completely delusional about that, too. She doesn't want you here, clearly, so let it the fuck go already."

El steps away from me. "Fine." She pulls out her phone. "You're right. Thanks so much for all your help." She starts stabbing at her phone angrily.

"What are you doing?" I ask.

"Calling my parents back. I gave Max the key, remember? I don't have a way home. And it turns out there's not an Amtrak or bus back to Dell's Hollow; I checked while I was sitting in the diner. The one time I don't do my research . . ."

Even as she dials, I know I could still fix this. I could apologize for the cruel words I've said or try to bridge the space between us, but this isn't my fault. I shouldn't have to apologize when El's the one being an asshole.

"What does that mean for me if you call your parents? How am I supposed to get home?"

El shrugs and starts to walk away. "I guess we're stuck together for a couple more hours."

Well, fuck. What else am I supposed to do? Call my dad, who's barely capable of driving around Dell's Hollow, much less all the way to Richmond? I'm too young to rent a car, and I have money in my checking account, yes, but I can't take an Uber all the way back to Dell's Hollow. That would be a fortune.

Fuck's sake.

Hating myself just a little bit, I run after El.

El's parents arrive a few hours later. It turns out that Zaynah texted them after the fight she had with El and they were already on the road to Richmond by the time El called them. El and I spent the entire three hours we were waiting for them to arrive not saying anything to each other. We don't talk on the way home, either, during what has to be the world's most awkward drive. And El's parents don't talk to her because I'm in the car, which leaves us all drowning in silence. Which is fine. It's all fine. I don't need El. Maybe I don't even really like her—I'm not sure. All I know is that we're broken and I have no idea how to fix us and it's time to focus on myself, my goals, and get away from everything to do with El Blum as fast as possible.

# *CHAPTER TWENTY-SIX*

### El

Dawn on Monday breaks obnoxiously bright, another hot, sunny summer day in Dell's Hollow. I wake early enough to watch the light seep through my bedroom curtains, even though I have no place to be. Yesterday's excruciating ride home was probably the last time I'll leave the house as a minor.

When my parents got to Richmond, they met Jo and me on the curb outside Mama Maple's Bacon and Eggs, the only friendly place I could think of to wait in Richmond (in separate booths, of course). My parents barely said a word to us, just "Are you girls okay?" and "Do we need to pay your bill at this restaurant?" We then got in the back seat of the Oatmobile and stared out our separate windows for the three-hour drive. With no radio, I might add—my parents' first of many punishments to come. The scenery whipping by the Oatmobile's windows was nearly identical to our ride up, but it felt impossibly different. *Everything* was different. I was no longer riding toward the person who mattered most to me, but leaving her behind. Just like she'd left me.

Jo didn't say a word to me when Dad pulled into the farmhouse driveway. She only thanked my parents and muttered a quick "I'm sorry, Mr. and Mrs. Blum" as she climbed out of the minivan. Then I watched her walk away, too, toward the distant figure of her own father waiting on the porch. She never looked back at me. And the worst part about our long ride home?

I'd had enough time to figure out that that was my fault, too.

How did I set off for Richmond convinced that I'd lost everything, only to come home with less? I roll over without bothering to check my phone, tucking in under the blankets; since I don't have a job, a volunteer club, a best friend, a girlfriend, or the R1 to take care of, maybe I can just stay here for the last month of summer vacation, cozy in my self-loathing.

Something creaks overhead.

I bolt upright after the moment it takes me to place the sound—it's been months since I've heard anyone moving around the attic besides me. I leap off my mattress to look out my bedroom window, which overlooks the driveway, and find it empty. Maybe Max parked by the road? She might've gotten here late and wanted to let herself in through the back porch door rather than wake everyone with the rumble of her bike.

As I sprint from my bedroom to the spiral staircase down the hall, a new scene unspools before me, scripting itself. My sister would have driven through the night to get here, plagued by regrets over the last words we hurled at each other. I picture it as I pound up the steps. She'll be sitting on the daybed in her old yolk-yellow room. She'll apologize, and then I'll apologize, and everything will be—

Perched stiffly on the edge of the daybed, Mom startles when I burst through the shower curtain into the attic. She's still in her pajamas and pilled, short summer bathrobe instead of the put-together athleisure that is her usual summer uniform, and has yesterday evening's coffee mug clutched between her hands. She went right to the coffee maker the moment we walked into the house, before Dad quietly banished me to my bedroom, telling me we'd talk tomorrow. I wonder how long she's been up here, if I missed the sounds of her climbing the staircase. I wonder if she ever went to sleep last night.

"El," Mom says when she recovers from her shock.

Still frozen in the doorway ("curtainway"?), I don't know what to say back.

She sighs. "I was planning to wait till later to talk, once your father was up. Or hell, once he was home from work. But I guess we can't put this off forever, huh?"

"I guess."

It's strange to hear her speak to me like . . . like she's a person, and like I'm a person. Mom pats the bed beside her, and I drift closer, though I stop just short.

That seems good enough for her, for now. "What were you thinking?" she asks, again, not as a parent might, but softly, as if she actually wants to know, and plans to listen.

Which makes me want to tell her the truth.

"I—I was trying to help Max. I thought if I could see her and talk to her, I could get her to come home. And maybe . . . if it was both of us asking, then you'd let her stay."

Mom stares down into what has to be a room-temperature mug of coffee, processing. "You made some pretty poor choices, El."

"I know."

"You could've been badly hurt, you and your friend."

"My *girlfriend*," I mutter instinctively, and then, "ex."

Mom looks up at that, raising an eyebrow. "Really? Well. I'm sorry about that."

I snort. "You didn't even like her."

"I didn't know her. I would've liked to have the chance. But I think I know why you didn't feel you could talk to us. To me. And I know it's because of my poor choices, too."

"So you're not mad?"

Mom blinks back at me. "Of course I'm mad, Eliana. I'm extremely mad. You drove a motorcycle across state lines without a license—"

"*With* a license!" I insist. "I—Max helped me get it, she . . ."

Mom winces at my sister's and my machinations, which are probably not helping my case. "*And* with another minor on the bike. That's on top of everything you two did to get in trouble in the first place. That was an appalling series of decisions, and you both might've been seriously hurt, in any number of ways. *But.*" She sighs. "Your father and I have made some stinkers, too, starting with leaving you out of the conversation when Max went away. And God, before that. I can't tell you how many regrets we have over your sister and the choices we made."

Though I'm scared of the answer, I force myself to ask, "Do you regret kicking her out?"

"El . . . we didn't kick your sister out."

Wait, that's not true.

That can't be true.

"Max was furious with us when we told her that going pro was off the table until after college. She never even wanted to go to school. She would've kept riding forever. But we truly believed she wasn't able to handle that life without burning out. Even when she was your age, she was getting into trouble, falling in with trouble. You were just a kid then, so maybe you didn't see it, and we sure didn't want you to. But there were nights when she never came home, places she went that she never told us about, and we . . . We told her no, that she had to go to school. We wanted to keep her safe. That was our mistake, too, because she was miserable there."

"You think you should've let her go pro?"

Mom sets her mug down on the floor to clasp her hands together and prop her chin on her fists. "No. I don't know. I still wonder what we could've done differently, how we could have kept her safe without holding on so tight. Maybe there isn't an answer. When she dropped out, she came home and fell back in with the same crowd anyway, the same bad habits. I thought working for Jolene might keep her straight; that's a good woman, and I know she was there for your sister when Max didn't want me to be. In the end, though, after she crashed the car and got her DUI—"

"She *what?*"

My mother winces. "Like I said, we didn't want you to know. Another mistake, because it seems you've been walking around with the idea that we 'tossed Max away.'"

Now it's my turn to wince, as my words from our fight come back to haunt me. "Dad said you didn't," I remember, though I was too caught up to listen at the time.

"We gave her a choice. Get clean, get it together. We would help her, give her any support or resources she needed. But we told her that we had another daughter to think of, and that we couldn't allow her to put you in danger with her choices. You thought the world of your big sister, and we wanted that for you, but we were terrified you'd be with Max some night, and things would go bad. So we told her she had to pick: the track she was on, or—"

"Me," I offer around the pound of gravel in my throat.

"*No,*" Mom insists. "All of us. Her family. But she wasn't in a place to make that commitment, and . . . and you know what happened after that."

I don't know what to do with this, where to put this information. Max was never kicked out. She had a choice. She told me to take care of her bike, all the while knowing that she wasn't coming back for it, or for me. Whatever I thought I felt on the sidewalk outside of her apartment, it's nothing compared to this: not just losing my sister, but this idea of a sister I never really had. "I must've looked so fucking stupid, telling her I came to bring her home," I realize aloud.

"Listen to me." My mother turns on the daybed to face me for the first time. "Maybe Max will come home one day. Or maybe we'll all have a relationship from afar. I have to believe we will, because she's my daughter, and I love her. But that's not your responsibility, El. And if we're comparing mistakes—which, yes, you certainly made a few—then your dad and I made the same mistakes we made with Max all over again, holding on to you so tightly. You're a good kid, but before that, you're my daughter, and I love you, and all I ever want for you is to be okay."

I sink into my mom and she wraps her arms around me; it's a little stiff with lack of practice, but I could stay here forever instead of facing the mess I've made.

Unfortunately, that's not a choice I can make.

"I fucked up with JoJo," I mumble into her shoulder. "A lot. And with Zaynah."

"Well. Now you have the chance to fix things."

I suppose that's true. "So am I not grounded?" I sniff.

"Oh, El. You are absolutely grounded. And you will not be driving anything with an engine for some time."

"So what, I'm just walking to school in the fall?"

She hugs me a little closer. "Have you considered a bicycle?"

# CHAPTER TWENTY-SEVEN

## JoJo

I shouldn't be surprised that Dad is waiting for me on the porch when I get home late on Sunday night. It's like a repeat of the scene on Saturday night—God, how was the race with Riley only a day ago?—when I brought the Hornet home, but this time, as soon as I'm out of the car, he leaps off the porch and pulls me into a hug.

"I was so worried," he whispers into my hair. "Thank you for coming home."

"Of course, Dad," I say back, hugging him hard. Behind me, I hear El's parents' car pulling away, but I don't look back. I am so done with her, her family, and that entire mess.

"Let's go inside and talk about this," Dad says, letting me go at last. He swipes at his eyes.

Although he's not really an angry guy, I'm a bit surprised that he just seems relieved I'm home, not angry that I ran away.

It helps maybe that I texted him back on the long, awful, awkward car ride home with El and her parents. I answered the one voice message he left me, where he just said, in heartbreakingly halting tones: "JoJo. Not sure where you went . . . but I'm sorry. Please come back. We can talk. And . . . just. I'm sorry."

His message brought tears to my eyes, and I had sent him a message back, saying I would be there soon.

I follow Dad up the steps and into Jolene's house, throwing my small bag by the door. I wanted to burn every part of it that had to do with Eliana Blum, but even I knew that was just being dramatic.

Dad pours a whiskey and Coke and then takes a second glass out of the cabinet, fixing me a drink as well.

"Not a normal thing," he says, stirring the drinks. "But just for tonight, to take the edge off. Now, tell me what happened?"

We sit down at the kitchen table, and Dad gently pushes aside a photo album I'd not seen since we moved. It's the one of his and Mom's wedding pictures, and there's a photo of them smiling in their wedding clothes on the cover.

I cup my own drink between my hands and exhale. It's only been about twenty-four hours since Dad's and my last fight, but it feels like an age. The story of everything that's happened since then comes pouring out of me—about El looking for Max, and El and I growing closer, and how we talked to Riley, and how we eventually learned Max was in Richmond. I take a long sip of my drink, letting it soothe my nerves just a bit.

"So you all decided to sneak out and go find El's sister in Richmond?" Dad asks. "On a stolen motorbike? In the middle of the night? Without telling anyone where you were going?"

I nod, staring at the ice cubes in my glass. It sounds ridiculous now that he says it. Like I should've known better. Of course I should have.

Dad blows out a breath. "Well. I have to admit, it's probably what I would've done. And it's most certainly what your mom would've done."

That admission startles a laugh out of me. "Are you serious?"

"Do you really want to know where my nickname comes from?" He smiles at me, making his eyes crinkle at the edges.

"Absolutely not."

Dad raises his glass at me. "Fair enough, but let's just say that there were some outrageous years for both me and your mother. Especially when we first met. We were utterly wild for each other, and a little wild in general. There was no lakeside cliff we wouldn't leap off, no street race we wouldn't enter, no dare that went untaken."

"Huh . . ." I say, swirling the liquid in my glass. This is a new side of my parents, though one that's not totally unexpected.

"Your mom used to say you couldn't know how to have absolute control on the track if you didn't know how to let go sometimes."

"That's good advice . . . as always . . ."

Dad smiles again, softer this time. "She was full of good advice. Most of the time at least. Sometimes, like all of us, she was just full of shit, too."

I laugh again, remembering how she would absolutely make up unbelievable answers to questions just for fun. I went to kindergarten thinking that Saturn was ringed by donuts and that there were aliens who stopped by the rings for snacks.

"She was amazing," I say softly.

Dad clinks his glass against mine. "She was. And I miss her so much." His voice is tender, full of tears waiting to fall.

"Me too. I miss her all the time. But I think when I'm driving, I feel closer to her, you know? Because racing wasn't about danger to her. It was about joy and freedom and so much more."

Dad exhales sharply and his tears fall. "You're right of course."

I put my glass on the table, pulling a ticket stub out of my pocket. "I went to the Richmond Raceway, too, while I was on this trip with El. She didn't come. Just me. I was looking for her sister at the track—and I found her there—but that's not really the point. When I was there, it was just like old times with you and Mom. There were the pits, the noises, the smells, the cars doing practice laps . . . and . . . it was sad, of course, but it was also kind of good, you know? Like by being in a place like the ones Mom loved, I was closer to her. I don't know. Maybe that doesn't make sense, but I felt her so strongly, just for a moment, when I was there . . . ."

Dad drains his glass. "That makes perfect sense, JoJo. And, since you took off, I've been thinking a lot about how much like your mother you are. Which, of course, terrifies me. But you were right to say DeeDee wouldn't want me holding you back from your dreams. She would've loved for you to try for the F1 Academy. "

My heart picks up at this. Is Dad really saying what I think he's saying?

"Do you want to know something really, really nerdy, Dad?"

He nods.

I pull the folded picture of Jamie Chadwick, the one I always carry with me, out of the pocket of my jean shorts. Opening it up, I put it on the table between us.

"Who's that?" he asks, peering at the creased picture. It's been folded and opened so many times, her face is barely discernible.

"Jamie Chadwick. First W Series winner. I've been carrying her picture around for years now, just as a reminder of what I want to do."

Dad shakes his head. "Unbelievable." He grabs his own wallet from the bowl in the middle of the table and opens it. He pulls a small folded picture from it and places it beside the picture of Jamie Chadwick. It's a photocopy of an old black-and-white photo.

In the photo a white woman in a button-up shirt and white hat sits inside a car. She's seriously side-eyeing the white guy outside her car window, who looks like he's giving her advice. On the top of the car, over the curve of the window, is written "Sara Christian" in big letters.

"Who is she?" I ask, moving my gaze from the picture to Dad.

"Sara Christian, the first female NASCAR driver. Your mom was obsessed with her, from before she was younger than you. She told me about her on our first date . . . hang on, I have a picture here somewhere. Your mother insisted on putting it into the wedding album."

Dad pauses, flipping open the photo album to a photo of him and Mom in front of her Hornet, which is parked outside a Burger King.

"You went to Burger King on your first date? Very classy, Dad." Even as I say it, I remember El and I going to Shake Shack, and dipping fries into milkshakes and laughing and talking about anything and everything. An ache goes through me at the thought and I shove it away. El Blum and I are done. No more fries and shakes. No more kisses. No more races or road trips. Which is fine.

"It was your mom's favorite," Dad says softly. "You know her great-aunt Betty used to take DeeDee to Burger King on her birthday every year, so I think your mom always associated it with celebrations and new beginnings. Least that's how she explained it to me."

I knew that, of course. Mom had told me the same thing the first time she took me to Burger King for my birthday.

Dad goes on, tapping the picture of Sara Christian. "I can still hear DeeDee telling me, a Whopper clutched in one hand, 'Did you know Sara Christian competed in NASCAR's first car race on June 19, 1949, at the Charlotte Speedway?' And she always carried this picture in her wallet. I'm surprised. She didn't tell you about her?"

I search my memories—Mom and I had talked about so much; how could I have forgotten something like her favorite female racer? But in a lifetime of conversations, things were bound to slip through.

"She might have told me, but I'd forgotten," I admit. "It's funny, I can remember Mom's laugh, and the way she burnt grilled cheese every time, but I can't really remember all the things we talked about."

A lump rises in my throat and I try to swallow it down. Am I forgetting Mom? Is that what's going to happen over the years?

Seeing my distress, Dad puts a hand on my arm. "It's okay, JoJo. Truly. Much as I hate to admit it, I'll tell you I can't remember everything about her, either. But you taking off for Richmond made me realize we can't always hold on to the people we love. Whether we like it or not, they'll go away. Or we'll lose them, or they'll lose us. That's just life."

He was talking about Mom, and I was thinking about Mom, but I was also thinking about El and our fight and how, even though I was angry at her, I was still devastated to lose her, too. Grief is a terrible, hollowing thing, and something all of us have to face.

A breath wobbles its way between my lips. "That may be true, but I don't have to like it."

"You don't," Dad agrees. "But you can't fight it too much, either. I think the biggest lesson in my grief is that the present is the only time we have. Yes, we can miss people who are gone, but we have to be in the moment. We have to keep living and trying new things and moving forward . . . just not too fast."

He's right of course, and I'd been thinking about just these sorts of things at the Richmond Raceway.

I run a hand along the picture of Sara Christian. "Where did you get this?"

Dad smiles again. "It was in your mom's wallet, like I said. I've been carrying it around since I went through her things. I never thought you'd be carrying around your own version of this picture. DeeDee would've liked to know that about you, I think."

"I think she'd like that, too," I say. "Can I have it?"

Dad nods, and I fold the picture of Sara Christian in with the one of Jamie Chadwick.

"I'll sign your form," Dad says, finishing his drink and standing to make another one. "And let you get your license this week. In case you didn't get that from my deep philosophical musings on living in the present and following your dreams."

"Dad!" I say, leaping to my feet. "Are you serious?"

"Absolutely. It's your life and you've got to live it. I'm proud of you, JoJo, and I know your mom would've been, too."

I hug him. "Thanks, Dad. For signing the form and for telling me about Mom and for letting me fuck up, just a little."

Dad hugs me back and then drops ice cubes into his new drink. "Always. Though this doesn't mean you get a free pass on stealing your mom's old car or running off to Richmond with El Blum. You're definitely grounded for a few weeks and I'll have some extra chores for you, but those are the consequences of your actions. I'm not going to punish you for being your mother's daughter and needing to race."

"You're the best. I love you, Dad."

"Love you, too," he says, giving me another quick hug. "Now, please, go to your room and don't sneak out. I've been worried all day and need to sleep." He lets out a weary sigh.

"Good night, Dad."

"'Night, JoJo. I'm glad you're back home."

"Same, Dad. Same."

I leave him in the kitchen with his whiskey and the photo album and make my way upstairs. All of a sudden, I realize how much I smell like sweat and road dust and El's skin, and I just need to shower. Immediately.

After my shower, I curl up in bed with my phone. There's no message from El, though I don't think I was expecting one. There's just a bunch of pictures of us from the trip. El beside the bike, grinning. El in bed from this morning, the light making her hair golden for a moment. A selfie of El and me on the bike, my arms around her waist, and my chin tucked against her shoulder.

A deep sense of loss fills me.

It had all felt so real, so good. And even though El had absolutely been a jerk, I will miss her. A lot.

I swipe my photos closed and pull up Netflix. I may have lost El Blum, but at least we had the summer. And the *Fast & Furious*.

With that thought, I pull up movie one, *The Fast and the Furious,* and hit Play, happy to lose myself and my broken heart in heists, one-liners, and Letty Ortiz stomping around gleefully in motorcycle boots.

As it turns out, life without El Blum in it is both easier and harder than I could've ever expected. I spend the weeks after we got home working in Grandma Jolene's garage, helping Dad around the house, and avoiding the places where the volunteer club would be. Oh, and also Putt by the Pond. I keep as far away from there as possible. I don't hear from El—not a text, phone call, DM, or anything—which hurts more than I'd like to admit, but it also helps me realize how truly over we are. More than once I start to text her, but then I stop, not sure what to say.

Dad is true to his word. He signs my form and we send it in. I'm still waiting to hear back, and one week stretches into the next with no word from the F1 Academy.

Grandma Jolene gets home, and she doesn't even ask me about El or the Hornet or our road trip to Richmond. She just hugs me and says, "Life is weird, JoJo, but you'll get through it. Keep yourself in the moment and also keep your eyes ahead at all times."

I'm not quite sure how to do that, but I'm trying. If I'd been a hermit at the beginning of the summer, it's nothing compared to my life after El Blum smashed into it.

Which is fine with me.

# CHAPTER TWENTY-EIGHT

## El

A month after my rock-bottom return to Dell's Hollow, I sit down at my desk with a blank postcard. I picked it up at Fresh Fare, our local grocery store, and the only place I've been allowed besides the house to help Dad with the shopping, at least until my first shift back at Putt by the Pond later today. Fresh Fare's got a limited selection, admittedly. This one has a kind of sloppy photo collage of eastern gray squirrels—our state mammal—but whatever. The picture isn't the point.

I could probably fill a hundred postcards with everything I wish I'd said to Max in Richmond. That she's not the person I thought she was, not the hero I wanted her to be. That I wish she'd told me what was going on and how complicated things were between her and my parents. That she'd been wrong, and mean, and selfish. That I'd been wrong, and mean, and selfish. That I wish I could be the me again who'd believed Max was perfect. That she didn't need to be perfect to be my big sister. That I was mad at her. That I hoped she'd come back. That I hoped she'd stay gone until she found what she needed. That I was, seriously, so fucking mad at her.

But in the end, it takes me an hour of staring listlessly at my corkboard of accomplishments to write two sentences:

*I love you. Your sister forever, El.*

I fill out the address of her sketchy split-level and, after pausing to grab the meager collection of postcards from Max I've kept in my desk cubby, I sneak downstairs as quietly as I can so as not to wake my parents. In the kitchen junk drawer, I find the booklet of stamps, as well as the keys to the padlock on the backyard shed. Peeling off a stamp and pocketing the keys, I slip out of the house.

I stick the squirrel postcard in our mailbox and raise the flag just as the sun is rising bright and orange over the poplar trees in our front yard, promising another hot and soupy August day. Then I walk around through the side yard to reach the shed. Inside, I pat my old Husqvarna on my way to the bags and boxes of Max's forgotten things stashed in the corner. I grab the nearest one—the box of her motocross trophies—and tuck the six postcards sent from her travels through Pigeon Forge to Boston inside, retaping the flaps after them.

Back in the house, I climb the spiral staircase up to the attic, keeping my footsteps soft. I haven't been up here since my talk with Mom, and I don't linger now. I only stay long enough to peel the poster of

Letty Ortiz off the wall: The one my big sister hung up years ago because I wasn't ready to do it myself.

I carry it back down the staircase with me, cradling the paper gone a little brittle with time and temperature fluctuations. After I shift my own various medals and certificates around on my corkboard to make space, tossing out the sillier ones (perfect attendance awards are crap, anyhow), there's just enough room to keep Letty down here with me.

If Max comes back, I think she'll be proud, but I'll have to be enough for me in the meantime.

As I pedal up to Putt by the Pond later that morning, I regret every ill thought I ever had about the Oatmobile. Yeah, it has a top speed of 30 mph when driving uphill, and yes, it has about the same turning radius as the *Titanic*. But I never arrived for work plastered in sweat at 8:30 a.m., and with a few fresh mosquito bites from biking around the pond.

Coasting into the metal rack in the parking lot, I fumble with the chain lock I probably don't need. Since my old Husqvarna isn't road legal, and since there isn't a bicycle shop in town, I had to turn to the July edition of the *Dell's Hollow Daily* to find the one bike for sale within walking distance of my house. Someone four streets over was selling a twenty-year-old Specialized Rockhopper for a hundred. *Needs a little cleaning and tune-up*, the ad said, and it wasn't lying. I've actually grown fond of my little red road-capable mountain bike in the weeks it took me to fix it up with Dad in the backyard shed.

But wow, do I miss the Oatmobile's AC. And the convenient cup holders for iced coffee. And its windshield.

I guess I can't complain when I'm surprised to be here at all. The night I got back from Richmond, I figured I wouldn't see the outside world beyond my driveway until school starts again. But my parents kept to Mom's word; if my manager would let me come back after my immediate grounding was over, and if I could get myself there without the van, I'd be allowed to finish out the summer.

Volunteer club is another story.

I haven't seen Zaynah since the heist, and we haven't really spoken since Richmond, though we did exchange a few texts just after. I pull out my phone to read through them for the hundredth time:

**EL:** I'm sorry

**Zaynah:** OK

**EL:** I know you're mad

**Zaynah:** Are you?

**EL:** No!

**EL:** It was good that you told my parents

**Zaynah:** Glad you're OK

**Zaynah:** I gotta go

**EL:** Can we talk later?

**Zaynah:** OK

Maybe I should've been braver and called her, but I know when Zaynah needs time, and it felt right to wait. Now I'm doubting myself (what's new?) but the plan remains the plan. I knew we were both opening today, so I biked to work half an hour early to meet her in the parking lot, when *she* inevitably arrives early, already dressed for her shift. Zaynah's always had it together like that.

Sure enough, ten minutes later, her dad drops her off in the family pickup. I'm partially hidden by the shrubby dogwoods that border the lot, and she freezes when she comes around them and sees me sitting on the curb in front of the bike rack. She's never looked so intimidating, all five feet of her in her bright red work polo shirt and watermelon-striped hijab, eyes wide as she blinks down at me. I hug my knees to my chest, feeling a little sick, fighting to keep my breakfast hashbrowns down; we've never gone so long without seeing each other, not even during the Cineplex Incident.

And this one's all on me. I let my best friend become a stranger.

"Hi," I croak out. "Hey. I—how are you?" Smooth as deep-fried butter.

But at least Zaynah unfreezes. With a sigh, she gives up the high ground to sit on the curb beside me. Or rather, on top of her messenger bag to protect her khakis from the crumbled asphalt and ragweed pollen I'm surely sitting in. "Are you back?"

"At Putt by the Pond? Yeah. Maryanne let me start my shifts up again."

"I wondered if she would."

I pick anxiously at my shoelaces. "Me too. I've been pretty bad at a lot of things this summer. I wasn't a good best friend."

Zaynah doesn't disagree—how could she, when it's the truth—and has never been one to lie to make things easier. "I figured you had a lot going on. I didn't *know*, because you didn't tell me about any of it."

"Yeah." I can't disagree, either.

"Like, you met JoJo, and then you were always together, even during volunteer club meetings. And I was happy for you! I know you've been sad over Max, and I was glad you had somebody like that, who's into what you're into."

"Lesbianism?"

"I meant racing." Zaynah smiles just a little. "But that, too."

"If it makes you feel better, it turns out I wasn't a good girlfriend, either."

This is the wrong joke to make, and after softening slightly, she stiffens again beside me. "Why would that make me feel better?"

"I—I just meant, it wasn't you. I messed up. I got that postcard from Max and got it into my head that if I found her, and got her to come home, I could put everything back the way it was before. And I think . . . Maybe a little part of me already knew that wasn't possible. And if I went to you about it, I probably would've had to face that, because you knew it, too."

Slowly, Zaynah nods. "So you went to JoJo instead."

"She didn't know my sister. She just believed me."

"But you liked her, too. It wasn't just about Max."

"No. She probably thinks it was, because I fucked up." I wipe away the sweat from the back of my neck as the sun beats down on us. "But uh, we don't have to talk about JoJo."

"El, I *want* you to talk to me. I want to know what's going on with you. That's what this," she waves wildly between us, "is all about. And I feel like I've been chasing you for months to try and find out."

So I talk to Zaynah.

In the time remaining before our shift, I tell her about all of it. How JoJo and I tracked down Max's terrible friends together to find her address in Richmond. How we kissed in my sister's attic bedroom over *Mario Kart*, and it felt like the best and bravest I had ever been. How my parents were waiting for me after the race. How I stole a whole-ass sport bike and drove me and JoJo to Richmond (I fade to black through *some* of the trip up, in sharing mode but not oversharing) only to have Max send me away again. How my mom finally told me the truth about my sister leaving. And how Jo is strong, and funny, and fearless, and special, and she made me feel like maybe I could be, too, but then I messed it all up by unloading on her outside of a shitty apartment complex. "So," I finish up. "How was your summer?"

She laughs, one of the sounds I know and like best in the world. "Well, we got a new rescue goat. Tater Tot. She has three legs and hangs out in Pickles's stall."

"Tater Tot the goat!" I squeal. "Maybe I can bike to the farm to meet her."

Zaynah turns to look up at the Rockhopper behind me. "These are your wheels now?"

"Probably until I die."

Unbelievably, she scoots in to knock her head softly against mine. "You're a Bike Girl™ anyway."

I lean into Zaynah. Everything is not instantly put right, but we're family. As long as we're both willing, we'll find a way to work it out.

If biking to work at 9:00 a.m. was unpleasant, it's nothing compared to biking home in the early afternoon through the clinging late July heat. I'm half-standing on the Rockhopper, pedaling hard to get up Magnolia Street, the steepest hill in Dell's Hollow, I swear, and right on my route, when I hear the rumble of a V-8 slowing behind me, then beside me. Electric blue paint ablaze in the high sun, and a beautiful girl in a bright green jumpsuit leaning out the driver's window.

"Need a ride?" JoJo asks.

Because I know her, I can see that her grin (which I would've called cocky if we'd just met) is glass-fragile, like my heart when I look at her. It would be safer to shake my head and keep us both from shattering.

But I think JoJo Emerson-Boyd is worth being brave.

# CHAPTER TWENTY-NINE

## JoJo

"Sure." El grins back at me, her smile slowly unfolding. Her face is red from biking up the hill and her sweat-slick hair clumps on her forehead under a bulky bike helmet, but she's beautiful.

A pang of relief shoots through me at her reaction, considering the stony silence that's persisted between us through the last four weeks. And the fight we had the last time we were around each other. And all the other millions of ways she could have just told me to fuck off.

But she said yes. It's all I can do not to cheer.

Pushing my sunglasses onto my head, I pull over, turn the Hornet off, and nearly leap out as I open the door. El waits a bit farther down the road. She gives me a little wave as I walk toward the back of the car. We don't talk as we do this weird dance around and toward each other.

Hands shaking with nerves, I drop my keys, and fish them out of the roadside gravel. She scuffs her shoe against a mangy dandelion that's growing along the road. I try to help her wheel her bike, but we end up making the pedals collide with the Hornet's back bumper. I fumble my keys again as I slip the right one into the trunk's lock. Both of us lift El's bike, and the front wheel smashes into the side of my head. Still not talking, we take the front wheel off and cram the bike into the Hornet's trunk, where it barely fits in, but we manage to wedge it awkwardly by taking off the front wheel.

Then, too fast almost, El is getting into my car, and settling into the seat. She pulls a water bottle from her bag and downs all of it. I slip into my seat, buckling my belt and inhaling.

I'm still not sure why I called out to her. I could've driven past, pretended I didn't see her. Revved the Hornet's engine and sped away, rather than slowing down. But as soon as I saw El, standing on her bike pedals, pushing hard to make it up the hill, little dots of sweat tracing the shape of her spine down the back of her T-shirt, a rush of feelings went through me. It was longing, loss, and excitement all at once.

But I clearly didn't really think it through because now El Blum is in my car, and I have no idea what to say to her.

She smells like Putt by the Pond and nachos and sweat and her coconut shampoo. It's all I can do not to bury my nose in the spot between her neck and her shoulder and just breathe in the scent of her.

I hold myself back, gripping the steering wheel.

"Hi," she says after what feels like a year. She buckles her seat belt and turns to me.

"Hi," I echo.

"Nice car." El pats the dashboard, nodding toward the pictures of Jamie Chadwick and Sara Christian I've wedged into a spot near the radio. She bops the little plastic cat hanging from the rearview mirror with her index finger. It swings back and forth between us, its plastic eyes goggling like it can't believe El Blum is in my car, either.

"Thanks," I say, pride in my voice. It is a nice car. My favorite car, which El knows of course.

El catches the cat mid-swing and looks over at me. "What I mean of course is, nice car and I can't believe you're driving. I got grounded until the end of summer."

"Which explains the bike," I surmise. "Instead of the Oatmobile."

"Exactly."

More silence stretches between us. I want to ask her all the questions I've been wondering about: How much trouble did she get in really beyond the grounding? Did she hear from Max at all after we left Richmond? What did her parents say? Did she miss me even a little bit? I want to fill her in on everything happening with me, but I don't know where to start. So, I just sit there, breathing in the scent of El and the grassy smell of summertime in North Carolina. A pickup truck races past us, making the Hornet shake.

I'm just about to put the keys in the ignition when El says, "Wait."

Unzipping the front pocket of her backpack, she pulls something small and dark purple out of it. It's a tiny car, dangling from a key chain.

"What's that?" I ask, though I recognize the car instantly.

El smirks at me. "I thought you'd know. It's a 1969 Dodge Charger on a key chain."

"That's Dom Toretto's car, right?" Of course it is.

"Correct."

"Why do you have Dom Toretto's car? Are you planning another heist?"

El nods, very seriously. "That's exactly it. You've figured it out. I've managed to steal a shrink ray and I need your help pulling off a heist in this teeny-tiny car."

"Where you ride, I ride, right?"

El laughs at that, and then places the tiny car on the dashboard. "I found it on Etsy pretty soon after we got back from Richmond. It's for you and I've been meaning to bring it over to the garage or your house since it arrived at my place. But . . ."

But.

But we weren't speaking. We weren't going out. We weren't even friends anymore.

I reach for the little car, turning it over in my hand. The details are perfect, and the wheels actually move. "Why are you giving it to me?"

El swallows hard. "Well, you see, it's not just a regular 1969 Dodge Charger on a key chain. It's an apology 1969 Dodge Charger on a key chain. I couldn't think of any other way to say I'm sorry for what happened in Richmond, and for being so awful—about Max, and your mom, and Letty Ortiz, and all of it—and I was pretty sure you'd be grounded like me or wouldn't have a car, so I saw it and it seemed like something you'd like."

I wrap my hands around the small car as El's words wash over me. "It is something I like. Thank you."

El fiddles with the Hornet's radio dials. "I mean, you don't really need it now, though, do you? Since you have this car? How do you have this car? And your license. You do have your license, right? Tell me you have that. My parents will officially ground me for the rest of my life if I'm riding in a car with someone without a license. I'll have to walk to UNC next fall."

"If you're riding with someone without a license *again*, right?" I can't keep a smile from kicking up one side of my mouth as the memory of us winning the race against Riley and then kissing in the housing development afterward comes to me. Not like I haven't thought about those moments a million times since El and I broke up, but it feels more real somehow. More possible now that El Blum is in my car.

"Again," El confirms, returning my smile with a look of her own that shows me how much of that race night she remembers.

I pull my wallet out of my bag and flip it open. My new driver's license picture, the one where I'm grinning like a kid who's just gotten the present they've been waiting for all year, stares back at us.

"Aww, you look nerdy, happy, and street legal," El says.

"That last one is the important part."

"I still can't believe your dad let you get your license. Did you get into any trouble at all?"

"Oh yeah, definitely." Quickly, I fill her in about what happened after Richmond, telling her a bit about the talk with my dad, my own set of consequences, us sending my F1 Academy application in, me getting my license, Grandma Jolene getting back from Italy and gifting me the Hornet, and me generally driving very, very carefully.

"So, it all worked out for you?" El says, carefully.

"Mostly. Or it's moving in the right direction, I guess. I don't know if I'll get into the academy, but at least I have the chance to try."

"That's important."

Silence falls again, and then El says softly, "I am sorry though, JoJo. I mean, I know I gave you an apology 1969 Dodge Charger key chain, but I want to say it. I'm sorry I was such an asshole in Richmond. I'm sorry for breaking us." She lets out a long, aching sigh, and then starts to run a hand through her hair, but stops when she remembers she has a bike helmet on. Hastily, she unbuckles it, scowling as she does so.

"I'm sorry, too," I say, laughing as she flings the helmet into the back seat. "I've been meaning to text you, but I just didn't know if you wanted to talk to me again."

"I didn't," El admits. "At least not at first. I was hurting and it was awful and I felt so stupid for not seeing what was happening with Max. Or with thinking everything would be better just because I showed up on her doorstep."

"Hope isn't stupid," I say.

El nods. "No, that's not what I mean. It's just that I talked to my mom, and I realize now that I didn't really understand what was happening. Like Max isn't who I thought she was, and my parents didn't throw her out because they hate her, or because she made a few mistakes. It's a long story, but the point is that it's complicated. And I didn't have the whole picture. Maybe I never will, but the point is, it's not something I can fix or force, and I shouldn't have tried to."

"You were dealing with a lot," I say gently, as I work the Dodge Charger onto my own key chain.

"I was," El agrees. "But I shouldn't have taken it out on you."

"You were grieving your sister. Grief makes us do and say things we might not have done ordinarily."

El rests a hand on my shoulder softly. "But, JoJo, you were grieving your mom. Not your irresponsible sister, who is still very much alive. Your loss is so much bigger than mine."

Tears fill my eyes, and I look at the pictures of Jamie Chadwick and Sara Christian on the dashboard. El's right, of course, but it's not that simple. I know that now.

"Grief is grief, El," I say, leaning my cheek on her hand for just a moment. "It's not a competitive sport. It's not a race. You can lose someone even when they're still alive, and you can still feel close to someone, even when they're gone."

El's finger lightly touches my cheek, a gesture so tender, it nearly undoes me.

"That's true," she says. "But I was still an asshole to you. I'm sorry."

"You weren't the only one. I was an asshole, too, and I'm sorry, too."

"Well, cheers to both of us being assholes," El says with a wobbly laugh. She moves her hand off my shoulder, and swipes at her eyes. "What would you say if I asked you to go get a milkshake with me?"

"I'd say yes, of course. But only if it's a date."

"Of course it's a date. What else would it be when we go to Shake Shack?"

I can't help the bright, joyful laugh that bursts out of me at that. Putting the key in the ignition, I rev the engine once, plop on my sunglasses, and peel away like Letty Ortiz.

Shake Shack is packed and we get our fries and shakes to go. Then, we drive to a scenic overlook just outside of town. The Appalachian Mountains spread out in front of us, rolling waves of green and bluish gray. There are no other cars at the overlook, and we're sitting in the Hornet with the windows down.

"You know this is where everyone in school goes to make out?" El says, dipping a fry in her shake.

"I had no idea," I replied, but of course I knew. Grandma Jolene had told me about this spot on the day we moved in, and I'd been generally avoiding it since. But today feels different. El and I are speaking again. We're on a date of sorts. It's a perfect place to drink milkshakes.

"Yep," El says. "My parents told me Max used to come here all the time with her friends, too. Lots of shady shit happens here late at night."

"Good thing it's not late at night."

El raises her milkshake cup up in a toast and I knock mine gently against hers. We slurp our shakes, as a warm breeze floats in through the window.

El's left hand is on the gearshift, and I reach out, putting my right on top of hers. She looks at me, her eyes intense.

"So, what's next?" I ask. "What happens if I get into the F1 Academy?"

El laces her fingers through mine and traces one of my knuckles with her pointer finger. "I don't know."

"Is that okay? The not knowing?"

El scoots a little close to me. "I think so. I'm trying to stay in the present more. To be here now and not hold on too tight."

"I think that's good, but it's scary to lose control." I think of a car smashing into a wall at Daytona and flames engulfing it. I think of waking up beside El and wanting so much to linger in the soft morning light that filtered in through the curtains of the It'll Do Motel, and then our fight later that day. I think of me getting into the F1 Academy and us being an ocean apart or breaking up all over again.

"It's terrifying," El admits. "But necessary. You can't be brave if you're trying to control everything."

"You've always been brave, El Blum. Even when you couldn't see it."

"You've always been worth being brave for, JoJo Emerson-Boyd."

Her words are whispers against my lips as she leans closer. I close my eyes and bridge the final sliver of space between us, pushing my lips gently against her. She kisses me back, softly at first, and then more insistent, brave indeed in a way that sends heat through my body.

I scoot closer, only to be stopped by the gearshift jutting into my hip.

El kisses me again, her hand tangling into my hair, and I remember for one wild ridiculous moment that my parents fell in love over a gearshift, too.

Because that's what I feel all at once, an unexpected, aching, furious love for this girl who smells like sunshine and nachos and who has hurt me and healed me and who makes me laugh and kisses me like I matter.

"We can be brave together," I say, pulling away from the kiss for just a moment, so I can put my shake down and stop being impaled by the gearshift. "We'll just take it one quarter mile at a time."

I want to throw out more *Fast & Furious* banter, but El stops my next sentence with another kiss, and all I can do is lean into it and see where this road takes us.

# *EPILOGUE*

## Seven Months Later

Postcard One:

*Hi, El!*

*Congratulations, future collegiate!!! Chapel Hill doesn't even know they're about to have a wild card among them. <3*

*Things are good here but I miss you. A lot. Like, yes, I'm always surrounded by people and living in England and traveling the F1 Academy circuit is exciting, but do you know how hard it is to get good chili cheese fries around here? IMPOSSIBLE. Also, I miss beating you at Mario Kart. And kissing you. And stealing cars with you. (Maybe I shouldn't put that into writing?? lol.)*

*Call me and can't wait to see you next month!*

*xoxo, JoJo*

Postcard Two:

Hey, Jo,

You know, I appreciated the immediate congrats by text and video call, but the congratulations postcard a week later? *Chef's kiss*

I'm so excited to come for spring break—I can't believe it's already next week!!! I'll slip some chili cheese fries in my carry-on; everyone knows they taste best after two days at room temperature. I'll be the one in the UNC–Chapel Hill cap, and the Team Emerson-Boyd T-shirt. Where you ride, I ride, etc. :)

Love, El

# *AUTHORS' NOTE*

Hi from Jamie and Rebecca. We hope you've had as much fun reading this book as we did writing it, and we wanted to take a moment to tell you the story of how this book came to be.

In August of 2021, Jamie and her partner were living through a parent's worst nightmare, and to bear it somehow, they were bingeing a lot of favorite movies and shows, including a full rewatch of the *Fast & Furious* franchise. Jamie had always liked the series, but in this particular time of personal tragedy, *F&F*'s gleefully over-the-top action, as well as the movies' emotional theme of family, hit differently. The movies provided an escape. In the back of Jamie's mind while watching *F9* one night, she thought, *I'd love to write a YA contemporary* F&F *homage someday* . . . .

Only a day or two after this idea struck Jamie, Rebecca's tweet about Michelle Rodriguez's motorcycle boots–wearing badass Letty Ortiz crossed Jamie's timeline, along with an MSWL (in literary agent language, a manuscript wish list item) for an "f/f car heist adventure-romance novel." Rebecca doesn't recall exactly what prompted them to tweet this; probably a pandemic-era comfort rewatch of the series, and remembering the first time they saw Letty Ortiz as a teen. Jamie and Rebecca only really knew each other and of each other's work through social media, but the tweet made Jamie bold. Like Letty Ortiz sliding a car under a semitruck, she slid into Rebecca's DMs that same night with this message: "OK. But seriously if you don't get this book in your inbox. When you have some time and if you want I will totally co-write this with you . . . ."

And so a friendship and the seeds of *Furious* were born. Through a flurry of DMs over the next few weeks—a flurry both fast and furious—they talked about their love of the movies, and of Michelle Rodriguez, about being bi girls, about parenting and heartache, and the pieces of this novel began to emerge. They kept writing through Jamie's and her family's great loss and unspeakable heartbreak. Beyond the act of drafting together, they spent months trading *F&F* jokes, playing D&D, and becoming dear friends as their story grew from a little idea into a book about racing, yes, but also about grief, love, and family; about running away from the past and facing the future; about two girls who found each other at the worst moment in their lives, but also, the moment when they needed each other most.

# ACKNOWLEDGMENTS

For every book that gets published, it takes a whole crew, not unlike those needed in a heist or a racing pit. *FURIOUS* was no different, and we're grateful to so many people for helping this book across finish line.

First, thank you to our wonderful agents, Kate Testerman and Eric Smith. We appreciate you loving this book from the beginning, seeing its potential, and helping it find a home, and are grateful for everything you do.

Thank you to our amazing editor, Lauren Knowles, for delighting us with your love of the *F&F* franchise, and for really understanding our vision from that first call. We couldn't imagine more capable hands for this book to be in!

Thank you to the team at Page Street: Cas Jones, Shannon Dolley, Lauren Cepero, and Meg Palmer.

Thanks to our wonderful cover designer, Katie Beasley, and to our cover artist, Babs, for a beautiful illustration that so perfectly captures the heart (and summertime, sapphic pining vibes) of this story.

Thank you to Michelle Rodriguez for gifting us with Letty Ortiz, and thanks also to the entire *F&F* franchise for getting us both through some dark times.

Thank you to the bookish pals and author friends who helped and supported us along the way: Megan England, Rosiee Thor, Tehlor Kay Mejia, Tess Sharpe, Jen Ferguson, Noelle Salazar, and Lizzy Mason.

Thank you, dear readers, for sticking with us both for so many books, both solo and co-written. We can't wait to journey to new places with you too! (hint, hint)

## From Jamie:

Thank you, Rebecca, for saying yes to this wild idea to write a book together based on a tweet and some shared love of furious girls in motorcycle boots. I'm so grateful to you for the endless messages, calls, brainstorming, stories, and good care. Much love to you, my friend.

And thank you to my dear family, Adam, Marcy, and Liam. I love you all so much. Where you all ride, I ride. Always.

## From Rebecca:

Thank you, Jamie, for the spontaneous DM that brought us from friendly to dear friends; you made this book much more than it was, and are the best partner in plotting I could have asked for! Lots of love to you.

Thank you, Tom, for answering every noontime text and 2:00 a.m. question along the lines of "hey, babe, what does motorcycle chain cleaner smell like?" of which there were many. As both a primary source of research and a life partner, you're invaluable.

And thank you to the beans, Asher and Anya, for being you.

# ABOUT THE AUTHORS

**Rebecca Podos** is the Lambda Literary Awards–winning author of YA novels, including *The Mystery of Hollow Places, Like Water, The Wise and the Wicked*, and *From Dust, a Flame*. She is co-editor of the YA romance anthology *Fools in Love*, and has a short story featured in the collection *At Midnight*. By day, she's an agent at the Rees Literary Agency in Boston, and can be found on her website, rebeccapodos.com.

**Jamie Pacton** is an award-winning author who grew up minutes away from the National Storytelling Center in the mountains of East Tennessee. She's never been to an F1 or Nascar race, and she only started watching F1 because of the Netflix show *Drive to Survive*, but somehow all those things found their way into this book. She does, however, know a lot about endless summers in the south, the *Fast & Furious* franchise, grief, and falling too fast for someone at exactly the right time. She has a MA in English Literature, and currently teaches English at the college level. Her YA contemporary books include *Furious, Lucky Girl*, and *The Life and (Medieval) Times of Kit Sweetly*. Her YA fantasy novels include *The Absinthe Underground* and *The Vermilion Emporium*. Currently, she lives in Wisconsin with her family. Find her at jamiepacton.com or @jamiepacton on Instagram, TikTok, and X.